rehoming breanna huxley

keli o'connor

Green Crow Publishing

To Phil

Imagine Winning a Modern Adirondack Cabin with the HHTV Dream Home Giveaway!

You could win a custom-built woodland retreat just outside Spokane, Washington, surrounded by breathtaking mountainside views!

Complete with state-of-the-art energy-saving appliances, a jacuzzi, and floorboard heating, this Dream Home offers everything needed for rest, relaxation, and rejuvenation.

If that wasn't enough, this year's fully-furnished prize package comes equipped with a brand-new Range Rover and $50,000.00 cash!

Enter to Win!

one

. . .

It wasn't every day that a patient pooped his pants at work, but every time it happened, I could almost guarantee that I'd be in the room. If I had the money, I'd make the wager and likely win every time. Not because it was hospice care or the geriatric ward of a hospital. No, it was just a general care medical practice. Everyone scheduled that day had been on the books for months. But, in the same way the octogenarians all seem to magically run out of oxygen as soon as they step foot in the door, the nonagenarians all seemed to wait until I brought them back into the exam room and started taking their vitals to poop themselves.

"It's okay, sir," I said as I guided him and his daughter—or maybe granddaughter—out of the exam chair. "The restroom is across the hall." I offered his young companion a stack of paper towels, which she accepted with a forced half-smile.

With hunched shoulders, she mouthed the words, "I'm so sorry," and took the reins of the wheelchair.

"It's fine, really," I silently replied. It wasn't *fine*, per se. Nobody was ever really "fine" in situations like that;

probably not him, and definitely not me. *Tolerable* would've been a better description. Or better, *typical*.

It was why hospitals and clinics always had laminate surfaces and smelled like bleach. And, like most older medical buildings, whoever designed our office made it easy to clean and perfectly mundane. Gray composite counters, gray linoleum flooring. Polished and non-porous. Sterile. Steel beam-piped walls throughout the chalky cinder block halls. Utilitarian, cold. The most expressive part of working at the Franklin Family Health Center was that we got to buy our own scrubs, but they also had to be gray. Since we didn't get reimbursed for the scrubs, all of us in the medical assistant pool always elected for the cheapest—and thus least flattering —option.

The worst part about the cheap gray scrubs was that they stained easily. And the worst thing about the patient in the exam room was that he had a complete blowout. And the worst part about cleaning his mess off the chair was that I got some on my shirt.

And a little bodily waste wasn't enough to warrant going home early. I found that out when I asked the office manager, Angela, and she instead produced a somehow cheaper and uglier scrub top than the one I had worn to work.

"Here, Breanna," she said, handing me the stiff, sandpaper-grade top. "Just make sure you return it as soon as you can. Otherwise, we'll have to dock it from your next pay."

Yes. Because that unisex extra-large that could fit two of me was exactly what I wanted occupying space in my dresser. There was barely enough room in there for the few clothes I had.

In the employee restroom, where it smelled like someone replaced the air freshener with a canister of Lysol, I changed my shirt and tried to wipe what excess I could from my top before the stain set for good. Satisfied with the slight progress I'd made, I folded the shirt into a plastic grocery bag I found under the sink and placed it beside the row of metal lockers where employees were supposed to stick their jackets and phones while working. A peek at my phone from my front scrub pocket revealed it was only nine. I mumbled a curse or two under my breath. Only seven hours left in the workday. At least I shared my shift with Kara.

"Another one? How does this keep happening to you?" she asked and snapped on a pair of lavender nitrile gloves. "Unreal."

She'd been my work wife the entire six years I worked at the health center. She was everything I always wanted to be: tall, charming, known for a perfect complexion. When we first started as freshmen, I'd created a narrative that she was otherworldly. Like, I pretended that she had horse hooves or an extra boob hidden under her collegiate hoodie to make me feel better about how perfect she was. It didn't take long for her to win me over, become my closest friend in and out of class, and eventually at work.

Like me, she thought of her move from a less-than-desirable home to the dorms more as an escape than the traditional teenage party dream, and—to say the least—it was something we bonded on from day one. We grew up too fast and learned that upsetting others was akin to hitting them with a car, so we defaulted to people-pleasing anyone and everyone. But we got each other. And we didn't need to walk on eggshells around one another. And, my God, did it feel nice to let my guard down for once. Sometimes, I felt like she was the only person on the planet who actually understood me.

However, her loveliness and our deep emotional connection

notwithstanding, I was still not entirely convinced she wasn't hiding hooves inside her rubber nursing clogs.

"My God, can we go one day without having to deal with poop everywhere? Is that too much to ask for?" Kara peeled her soiled gloves off, defeated.

I could have told her that bowel incontinence was relatively common in the elderly. That upwards of one in five people over sixty-five were afflicted, and the older the patient, the more likely they were to have issues. That many older adults left the earth the way they came in, under round-the-clock care, in diapers, being fed a liquid diet, and that the patients who came in to see us didn't mean to have these accidents—that it was often extremely embarrassing for them.

But if a lifetime of awkwardness had taught me anything, it was to keep my mouth shut when people were annoyed. Even if I knew the answer to the problem at hand. Scratch that—*especially* if I knew the answer to the problem at hand. Although I couldn't imagine Kara ever being upset with me, and knew she probably wouldn't snap at me for telling her a little info-dumping about the degradation of the human excretory system with age, I still figured it was better to not risk it.

"I cleaned what I could," she said with a huff. "We're just going to have to close the room down for the day. None of this is in my job description."

I wiped a bead of sweat off my forehead with my wrist. "Sure isn't."

Then again, nowhere in our employee handbook did it say to do a quarter of what we were expected to do. Each medical assistant knew we were doing the work of one and a half people so Angela wouldn't have to hire more workers. That cute trick made her and the office budget look stellar to her bosses but pure evil to her underlings, and there was nothing we could do about it. The one time we brought it up at our mandatory monthly Saturday morning meeting, Angela deflected it and kindly reminded all the staff that our employment was at-will and that at-will employment worked both ways.

"Speaking of human excrement," Kara joked, "have you heard from Vic lately?"

As a matter of fact, I had the evening prior. For the greater part of two years, Victor and I had been in an on-again-off-again relationship, and for the last year of it, he was staying with me in my way-too-small apartment. We seemed to live down each other's throats, bumping into each other and butting heads. He'd moved all his things out two months before, but admittedly, I still thought about him every day.

We exited the dirty exam room, and Kara taped an "Out of Order" sign to the door as I pulled my phone out to show her the two-hour message exchange. Angela barreled back around the corner, glistening with sweat, although it was a sunless October morning, and we'd only been open thirty minutes.

"How many times do I have to tell you two?" Angela asked, her hands and hair flying with her exaggerated gestures. "No cell phones on the floor. Go put them in your lockers. If I see them again, you're both getting write-ups." As if we weren't enjoying our jobs enough already.

She pointed indiscriminately at me, Kara, my phone, and the direction of the lockers as she rounded the hall, her rubber-soled flats slapping the floor. It bewildered me that we were adults trusted enough to work in patient care, administering medicine to the sick and elderly, but we were still not considered responsible enough to keep our phones on us.

Once she bounded down the hall, she turned on the television that hung in the upper corner of the patient waiting room. House & Home TV. Stealing glimpses of fixer-uppers between patients was probably the best part of the job. I caught about thirty seconds of a show with the cute Texan couple who flipped old farmhouses before a commercial for the upcoming annual dream special came on. The window-clad and warmly-lit modern mountain house sat cliffside on a sprawling four-acre lot outside charming Spokane, Washington, surrounded by evergreen forests and mountain views. Next up was an ad for the latest depression drug the FDA approved. The kind with a group of happy, laughing people who all nod at each other in slow motion. Sharing inside jokes that never existed. Wide smiles of Chiclet teeth, perfectly aligned and bright. I hated them. I hated that place.

With Angela safely out of sight, I pulled my phone back out. Kara and I sat in the nurse's touch-down station to wait for the next patient to check in while I brought up my text messages, but the computer had other plans for us, blinking that someone had checked in and was ready for their exam.

"I'll take this one if you get the next," Kara said as she stood up. "Hopefully, he went to the bathroom before he got here."

I looked at the screen and noticed Ms. Rowe, a sweet and eccentric older lady who always wore over-the-top glasses and showed me pictures of her rescue dogs, was next to check in for a shingles follow-up. "Deal." Kara gave me an affirmative nod, grabbed a plastic folder sleeve, slipped her patient's information print-out into it, and ducked around to the waiting room.

Alone at the nurse touch-down, phone in hand, with the quiet Texan twang on the TV around the corner, I peeled my eyes away from an old barn renovation and looked up the happy-people-in-slow-motion drug. Was I depressed? Probably.

Would I try that pill that reportedly may cause dementia-related psychosis or suicidal thoughts and behaviors?

Probably not.

Instead of closing the tab completely, I looked to see if HHTV had announced their Dream Home winner.

Nope.

According to their website, they would only announce it after the winner had been notified, and I certainly hadn't received any notification. Downtrodden, I flipped back to the psych drug; maybe I did want to laugh and nod at strangers at an outdoor bistro after all.

Buzz. A new text from Victor.

TODAY 9:27 AM

Hey

You still good for dinner?

Of course I said I was.

"What? Why?" Kara nearly shouted once she'd gotten all caught up.

After all we'd been through, I felt I deserved an apology. And dinner. That's what I told Kara, at least.

"Yes, you do, but he can apologize over the phone, and you can find literally anyone else to have dinner with. Look at yourself! Anyone and everyone should be fighting for a chance to take you out."

Kara obviously had a type, and that type was me. She had the deep umber skin of a goddess and the stature and poise of a Milan runway model. If the odds of having Barbie's proportions were one in two billion, she had to be one of those four gorgeous creatures currently walking the earth.

Seriously. She could pull anyone she pleased but had an affinity for short, chubby girls with golden-fawn skin and freckles who resembled me. It was a realization I made years too late; her past three exes all looked like they could have been my sisters. Hell, her current girlfriend, Liza, not only looked like me if I were an e-girl but also got her AuDHD diagnosis years after any sort of treatment options were no longer offered (because, according to many medical practitioners, adults with autism and/or attention deficit disorders magically outgrew the accommodations and therapies offered to children? Yeah, right.). I was sure that was why we became so close so quickly.

Sadly, I'd found that the only people who fancied girls like me were few and far between. If I happened upon someone who met my standards (explicitly expressed interest in me), I made it my life's work to ensure the relationship panned out. Even if that meant not asking if we were officially in a relationship.

Ultimately, I told Victor I would meet him after work on South Street, but Kara's disapproval started sending me down the rabbit hole of self-doubt.

TODAY 9:34 AM

Hey, look, I'm sorry things ended the way they did.

The air between our phones had been thick with smoke from our blowout. And even if it wasn't my fault, I felt obligated to apologize.

Nonono, I'm the sorry one. You did nothing wrong.

I just want to talk to you. Hang out, get some dinner.

I messed up, but I'd fix things if you let me.

A triple text. From the guy who told me he needed some space. He certainly didn't leave much space between those texts. Maybe he had a change of heart, and really, when I looked down at my scrubs and back up at Angela, who was charging back down the hall and catching me with my phone out again, I supposed I could have stood for a little change myself.

two

. . .

Timing never seemed to work out the way I hoped it would. I planned to go home to drop off my dirty scrub top and change into something a bit more fashionable, but the last patient of the day checked in a full fifty-six minutes after his scheduled appointment time and prevented that from happening. Instead, I caught an overcrowded bus and two successive trains to South Street, hustled down the few blocks to the restaurant, and found that I still had hours left. I wiped the sweat from my brow and cursed myself for not stopping home to see my dog, Hippo, before rushing for nothing. Luckily, and because she was the best friend a girl could ask for, Kara agreed to dart by my apartment and walk Hip—the only payment she asked was that it would be the last time I saw Victor. But really, she loved any excuse to hang out with dogs—especially since losing her brindle Staffy-mix last year —and it sounded like she was half-joking anyway, so I agreed.

Walking the same streets in the same city daily made it easy to lose sight of its charms. *The camera lens acts as a frame, singling out some of the minute details often overlooked when we rush from one part of our lives to the next.*

Before I grew up and got my health science degree, I dabbled in photography, earning an associate's that did nothing but bleed my bank account dry from student loan payments. I wish I could say that it was worth it to prove everyone wrong, that I got an art degree and made it doing something I loved doing, but the only thing I got from it was grief. My mom said I deserved to pay fifteen thousand for it because it was selfish of me to pursue a degree in a major that lists "barista" as a possible job in the career pathways portion of the college brochure. My boyfriend at the time told me I was childish to go to school for a hobby.

"With the rise of social media platforms like Creatr, anyone could be a photographer," he'd said. "Why would you want to pay to do what everyone else does for free?"

He was right, apparently.

But still, I liked my hobby, even if that's all it was. Philadelphia was full of vitality and spirit with its murals and street art at nearly every intersection, but South Street was where the city truly came to life. All the concrete and grime of the sidewalks and gutters waned, eclipsed by the enchanting mosaic murals of shards of mirror and broken glass. African and Indigenous influences woven into people's stories, a pair of all-seeing eyes overtop a diner, bay-window-clad rowhomes-turned-storefronts painted with anything to grab the attention of the street's many passersby (and to compete with their neighbors).

All I had was my phone and a screen full of editing apps since I had to sell my Canon DSLR after graduation, but I still managed to photograph seemingly every square foot of the street until I hit the pier at the end, then sat for a bit and killed some time on my phone while waiting for Victor.

❧ ❧ ❧

Scratch-offs are the rich-poor man's game. You have to lose money to win money. Sweepstakes, however, are free. At best, I'd enter my name and email address and get added to some list for weekly coupons at my local bakery. At worst, my information was stored and sold on the dark web. Neither was pleasant, but I could only imagine the egg on some hacker's face when they would get ahold of my debit card information and find there'd only be $0.14 in my bank account, or worse, a negative balance.

I'd only won a single contest in all the countless sweeps I'd entered. A couple of years back, the shelter I adopted Hippo from held its annual dog-walking event, and I won a decorative wreath with foam cut-out bones tied throughout it. Yards of amethyst tulle, bunched and gathered with purple and white gingham ribbon threaded throughout it. Someone spent a good afternoon making it, but it was the tackiest thing. I kept it hanging on the interior of my apartment door as a reminder that my luck wasn't all that bad, although it probably could be better.

Once my daily quota of sweeps had been met, I edited a few choice photos I'd captured during the stroll down. Satisfied with my selection of filters, I posted them onto my social feeds, then proceeded to scout more sweeps and fill in entry after entry for contests for various freebies, gift cards, and giveaways. I even entered one for a hand-painted SMEG Dolce&Gabbana stand mixer, which seemed wildly indulgent for me at its two-thousand-dollar-recommended retail cost. That single appliance was worth more than the culmination of my earthly belongings and bank accounts. It was pretty, with its contrasting reds and yellows, old-world flowers, and cross-hatched brushstrokes, but I'd be just as happy to win a t-shirt or free donut.

A notification dropped down from the top of my phone—a text message from Victor.

TODAY 6:57 PM

Here.

I looked up and around, scanning the faces of a spattering of walkers. When I saw him, my body tingled all over. Any memories of him ghosting me shrank until they were nearly invisible. I loved those warm hazel eyes and crooked smile. Without saying as much as a single word, he managed to make the drudgery of my crappy work melt away.

"Hey," he greeted me, his smile warm and genial. "You look great." It was our first face-to-face exchange in weeks, and it was a lie.

Vic, nonetheless, did look great. He always did. Dressed cap to patent boot in his rail conductor uniform, he could make polyester suiting look sharp. He'd still be a solid eight if he weren't six foot six, but his height easily brought him to a ten. He knew he looked good, and he knew I thought he looked good, and I was sure he wanted to hear me say it. Instead, I replied with a solitary, "Thanks," to not give him the satisfaction of the compliment in return and switched attention over to more pressing matters. "So, where should we go to eat?"

"Oh. Well, I looked online and saw that today's special is fifty-cent pierogis over at Tattooed Mom?" he suggested, but it came out more as a question.

I took a double-take. T-Mom's was my favorite restaurant, but he couldn't stand the place. For one, he hated its graffiti sticker wall coverings and bumper car seating. Two, he felt the Dum-Dums and plastic tops awaiting playful patrons at the table were too childish. Vic much preferred the ambiance of a Starbucks to the street-art flair eclecticism of the restaurant that housed one of Philadelphia's top ten most iconic bathrooms.

Something was up.

Maybe I was overanalyzing everything like usual, but perhaps it was intuition. A deep, sinking pit formed in my stomach; I couldn't rid myself of the idea that Vic had something up his sleeve. Our shallow conversation during the half-mile walk was barely more than chit-chat about the weather and a recap of how awful each of our workdays had been.

Hours seemed to pass in the twelve minutes it took to walk to the restaurant. A waiter came out from behind the bar where he'd been socializing with bartenders, greeted us, and seated us in the lower level at a camelback sofa, the sort of vintage velour and wood sofa with citrine and umber filigree upholstery that showed up in every grandmother's old photos. Every wall was painted the same shade of flat shamrock green and decorated with paintings and sculptures from local artists. Mismatched bistro sets and wing chairs facing coffee tables hosted a diverse crowd of patrons from the full array of Philly's illustrious underground music scenes.

We ordered our drinks and our meals, and we talked. Simple chit-chatting at first, as if breaking the ice for an exciting new date. Within moments, it felt as if we were never apart.

"Hey," Vic started, twisting a napkin in his hands, "I'm sorry for everything. Everything. I should never have said what I did. I never wanted to hurt you."

"It's okay, I shouldn't have—"

"No, seriously. You deserve better than I treated you. You didn't do anything wrong. I was stressed and lashed out at you even though it wasn't your fault. Nothing was." He looked down into his lap and raised his gaze to meet mine. "I love you."

And, just that fast, I was back in love. I guess I never fell out of love, but now I was more than ever. My eyes tinged and teared, my voice shrinking to just a whisper. "I love you too, Vic."

"Two pierogi," the waiter chirped as he placed our appetizers in front of us, snapping me out of my trance, "and two cheesesteaks, one vegan."

Our waiter came and went like a tide throughout the evening, a barometer of our enjoyment at the moment, and I shoved more food than I knew could fit into my mouth. I shoveled food in with abandon, hoping that words I'd regret wouldn't come out if I kept pushing them back with greasy carbs. Vic looked to be attempting the same, but much slower. He'd take a bite, look up, and nod at me as if to say, "I don't hate it," but remained quiet otherwise.

With our bellies full, Victor paid our tab, telling me he insisted, and we made our way up through Old City, past Independence Hall and the Liberty Bell—the scenery we'd learned to take advantage of—but it looked especially pretty when it was lit at night. We planned to get ice cream at the old-timey soda jerk dessert counter at the end of Market Street, but we were just blocks away when Vic paused to look at the old First Bank building. The columns shot high into the night sky, chiaroscuro lighting painting its white stucco face, casting haunting black shadows on the windows and old crevices like a Caravaggio painting.

"Beautiful," he said, almost in a whisper.

"It does look pretty cool at night," I conceded. Where I always casually enjoyed the bright colors and compositions of the murals and street art throughout the city, architecture had always been Victor's special interest. Without deviation. The neoclassical train station, the skyscrapers of center city. That brutalist-eyesore Roundhouse. Normally, we'd butt heads over whether art helped or hurt rowhomes and office buildings ("A perfectly-constructed building doesn't need paint to improve it," he'd said more than once), but there in that historical park, I had to admit that the stately gray portico of the First Bank was perfect without a giant Keith Haring decorating its north side.

"Breanna," Vic said and turned to face me, "tonight has been perfect. I shouldn't have messed things up like I did, but I can't live without you."

I stopped studying the open-air museum around us and turned to him. "I can't either."

Victor blinked back the mist in his eyes and grabbed my hand. "I love you so much." He brought my hand to his mouth and kissed it. "Please, take me back."

three

. . .

There was not a doubt in my mind that my mildewy basement apartment wasn't up to code. The cement walls weren't insulated, so there was barely any climate control save for my space heater in the winter and oscillating tower fan in the summer. Between the debt I'd accumulated over the past decade and how scantly Franklin Family paid, I guess I was lucky that there were places like that available on Craigslist. No credit checks, no problem. As long as you didn't mind the thousand-legged bugs and questionable mold patches growing throughout the ceilings.

My landlords, Artem and Masha, were an older Eastern European couple who refused to wear hearing aids. All day and all night, they maxed their television volume and yelled over the TV to hear each other talk. Most of the time, they spoke the language of their homeland, and I couldn't understand what was being said, but I could clearly hear the elevation of speech and frustration in each question.

"Хочаш гарбаты, дарагая?"

"Што?"

"Хочаце гарбаты??"

"Што??"

"Я спытаў, калі вы хочаце чаю!"

"ШТО?!"

When I first moved in, Masha was aggressively friendly, offering leftover fried potatoes and stewed vegetables after dinners and knocking down my door to ask me questions about where I was from or how my day at work was. Artem tended to leave me alone for the most part. The only time he pursued me was when the rent was due, but on the not-so-off chance I did not have the rent money on me when he asked, he would follow me to the bank to get it.

The apartment itself was small, which made sense considering the size of the house above. Philadelphia wasn't as crowded as New York, but property was scant with so many people vying for their own piece of the city. The houses in the city's Northeast section were slightly larger than their Center City counterparts, but not by much.

The only walls in the basement were the ones supporting the two stories above it, so I suppose calling it a studio would be technically correct, though a studio sounded like it would have been bigger. Everything in the room had multiple uses; the daybed couch, the dresser TV entertainment area, the mini-fridge kitchenette that my single-burner hotplate sat on —even the webs that spiders spun in the corners worked as nature-made fly traps. But one of the cruelest jokes about not having enough money to afford a place to prepare fresh meals from scratch was that you had to buy premade foods or order out, both of which cost substantially more than meal preparation.

At least I didn't have to pay for laundry.

Adjoining my living space was a small cove with a stacked washer and dryer. In my leasing contract, the owners stated that they would come into my apartment to access the laundry on Monday mornings while I was at work and that I could use them whenever I needed to. Masha explained that she wouldn't go through my belongings, but I had no actual way of knowing even if she did. At first, that clause, which felt very illegal, bugged me out, but I signed on the dotted line when I realized I had nothing worth snooping through. And who knows, perhaps my lack of anything interesting was why they gave me leftover stewed carrots. No matter. Pity food was still free food, and since all I could afford was to live in some Craigslist basement apartment, any free food was appreciated.

But was living there with my barely-minimum-wage paycheck ideal?

No. Not at all.

I spent six years working nights and weekends to put myself through school to ensure I wouldn't have to live like that. It turned out there weren't a lot of well-paying job opportunities in healthcare unless you had a nursing degree or a medical doctorate, which I did not. The biggest lesson I learned from my years of school was that I wasted time and money that I'd spend forever paying back and would remain below the poverty line while trying. The American Dream, as it would turn out, would've been much easier to obtain if I was neurotypical with two parents who slept comfortably nuzzled within the duvets of middle-classdom.

It wasn't really me or my upbringing, per se. I never knew my father; if my mom knew who he was, she never told me. The place where his name would have been on my birth certificate was left blank. My earliest memories in childhood were always of Mom and I moving around from one place to another with all our belongings in our backpacks, sleeping wherever we could. Couches, foyers. In elementary school, we settled in a single-room basement apartment for a few years where everything was covered in thick black mold and smelled like mildew and cat pee, though, much to my displeasure, we didn't have any pets.

The reason I had always been so good at being poor as an adult was because we had no money growing up; Mom had been on disability since she slipped some discs in her back in her early twenties following a car accident, which she swore wasn't her fault. And I guessed dealing with a strange kid on a fixed income wasn't hard enough for her, so she doubled down and dove deeper into her pain pills to liven things up a bit.

Growing up in poverty didn't make me like being poor as an adult any better. Seeing the hell Mom went through, if anything, made me realize how much I wanted my life to be different. It was a terrible thing to say that I used my own mother, the one constant I ever had throughout my life, as a goalpost for how not to live. But she did whatever she wanted to in life, and I saw where it got her. Alive but not living. A mother capable of abandoning her child to make her life easier. Her life, to me, had been a case study of why it was important to make significant sacrifices if you wanted to have any sort of chance of dreaming the American Dream.

So, where did I go wrong?

I made so many sacrifices, and I was still there, in that surely-illegal rental unit, with no money to my name, the weight of debt, and the world crushing my lungs and making it hard to draw a deep, steady breath.

🐾 🐾 🐾

I awoke just past two in the morning, and, to my surprise, Victor was no longer in my bed. I tiptoed to the ground-level window and stood on the balls of my feet trying to get a view of his car on the street, but it had also vanished. Dropping back to my heels, I slumped. My phone laid dormant on the floor beside my bed, and I picked it up to find a text from hours before.

YESTERDAY 11:43 PM

Sorry, I had to run. Busy day ahead.

If it weren't for the kissy face he'd sent right after, I probably would've felt a little hurt, but knowing Victor and how infrequently he used emojis, I smiled so deeply I felt it in my chest.

TODAY 2:05 AM

It's all good.

If I'd slept at all the rest of the night, it must had only been for minutes or maybe seconds. The remaining hours were spent with my eyes open, facing the dark ceiling, buzzing, picking at my leftovers, feeding the remainder to Hippo (who let most of it hit the floor before lapping it up), and staring back at the dark ceiling. Mentally tracing every step in life that guided me to that exact moment. Happy. Energized. Hopeful. All I ever wanted was a family who loved me. A husband, some kids, and a little home to call our own. Getting back together with Victor last night was the first step to seeing my wishes come true.

Come 5 a.m., my alarm on my phone sounded, and I hit the button to dismiss it. One eye closed, the other squinted, studied my home screen, and sifted through the notifications I'd accumulated overnight. It would appear, as if some crude joke, that I somehow fell into a deep sleep a mere hour before needing to rise for the day. In my message cache was one from Kara, who awoke a half hour prior and panicked about the prospect of facing another day of work.

TODAY 4:27 AM

I'm not sure how many more days of patient care I have in me. Like, I want to help people, but don't you feel like they're getting increasingly aggressive toward us?

Do you think we can retire?

I only have $12 to make it til next payday, so I don't think I can yet.

Crap. In all my glee from the previous night, I hadn't thought about having to go back to work the next day. It seemed cruel that I would be forced to work my pre-determined hours when all I wanted to do was make up for lost time with Victor and fill Kara in on the details of the date. *Maybe I should call out,* I thought. No, it was too late; I was already wide awake and had to pee. I'd just suck it up and go to work. Again.

Patient care was not for everyone, myself included. To make the job worse, Angela opened up the schedule to cram three or four patients into a single time slot, allowing her to bill three or four times more than before because she decided insurance payouts weren't enough to pad her budget anymore. That made patients quickly become bitter over how long they'd been waiting, and how we, the staff, should do something to change it, or how we, the staff, should at least buy them lunch if they had to wait that long. Every day, dozens of patients would verbally assault the medical assistants with their honey-do list of complaints because they wouldn't want to risk offending the doctor to whom they entrusted their care. No, better to throw a fit at the support staff who make slightly over minimum wage and have no ability to make substantial changes with the scheduling template.

Maybe, just maybe, I was burnt out.

So, like every other workday, I put on the same scrubs that I draped over the foot of the daybed after work the day before and went to work anyway. At least I could still fill Kara in on everything.

While walking to the bus, I tripped on an uneven patch of sidewalk, fell, and scraped my palms and left knee. The bus was pulling up as I picked myself up, but I managed to run and caught it before noticing the scuff in my pants and blood pooling underneath the fabric. I didn't have any tissues to stop the bleeding, so I instead fetched the office-loaned scrub top I had stuffed in my backpack to return to Angela to blot my knee. None of that reaffirmed my decision to get out of bed and go to work that morning.

At the next stop, a woman who didn't understand that cell phones could be used without the speakerphone feature, and the most wretched-smelling man, got on. The woman took a handicap seat in the front, and the stinky gentleman nestled up into the seat beside mine, although there were easily a dozen free seats throughout the bus. Then, I realized that I could hold my breath for about forty-five seconds on average, forty-seven at most. I also realized that my bus ride to work was eighteen minutes long and that there were worse things on earth than hell.

The bus pulled to my stop, and I hopped out directly into a puddle before walking the remaining block and a half to the office. Six steps behind was the speakerphone lady, who had not let anyone have their own thoughts in almost twenty minutes and was still carrying on her public-private conversation. I made my way to the back of the building to attempt to clean the blood from my pant knee before I set up for the morning and unlocked the front door, where the speakerphone lady was waiting for her 8 a.m. doctor's appointment.

Befitting the past twenty-four hours, I was the first one scheduled to work and had the privilege of taking her back for her annual checkup. She remained on the phone for the entire check-in process and the greater part of the time in the intake exam room while she stuck a finger up, mouthed the words "hold on" and continued talking on the phone until she was ready to end the call. "I told her that.... She never listens.... Some people can be so inconsiderate...." But fifteen minutes into her exam, my phone buzzed. I quickly checked it and saw an incoming call from a line within the office.

"Excuse me?" she snapped. "Don't you think it's rude to check your phone while I'm talking?"

If I had rolled my eyes any harder, I would have snapped my optic nerves. "Sorry," I started, "I had to make sure it wasn't your doctor paging me." That was not exactly the truth, but that didn't matter because she was already looking at her ringing phone, which she promptly answered.

"Okay. You take that, and I'll come back for you when you're ready," I said and quickly excused myself from the room before exploding. I had a new voicemail in my notifications, which was odd; if Angela needed me, she could have just texted me. I checked my texts and saw nothing new from Vic, which was disappointing, but I reasoned he was probably busy with a couch on the tracks or something.

I went back to the call list and voicemails, but my transcripts were unavailable. I held the phone to my ear to see what Angela had wanted to bark about, but instead, I heard an exasperated Kara on the other end.

"Bree.... You don't have much time to make sure your hair looks good, and your face is okay—"

Interesting. It was probably the most cryptic voicemail I'd ever received. And from the work phone, no less. For good measure, I flipped my camera phone toward me to use as a mirror to check myself in case Kara was up to something, and, as expected from my terrible morning, I looked ghastly. Like, would it have hurt to brush my hair that morning? Probably not, but it was too late now. Running my fingers through my rat's nest would have to do.

After I returned to the exam room and managed to ask most of the preliminary consultation questions, I sent the speakerphone lady out to the waiting room for the doctor. I decided to get a breakroom coffee to help lift my spirits and eyelids. When I opened the door, time slowed to a near stop. Inside, the faces were blurred; some, like Kara and Angela, were recognizable, but others were new. And others, like Victor's, I didn't even register. I couldn't—he had no reason to be in the breakroom. The lights were bright, much brighter than usual, and there were cameras, microphones, soft boxes, and a rainbow assortment of balloons. Balloons? Mylar balloons. And a novelty check.

"Breanna Huxley," one of the blurred faces, a man began, "you're the winner of the HHTV Dream Home!"

> *When blood pressure suddenly rises in sudden stress or anxiety, the blood pumping through the vessels in the ears can race so fast that it creates a sound that we perceive as ringing.*

I'm the what?

Victor reached out to hug me, and Kara jumped up and down, but I couldn't hear what they were saying over the bells tolling in my head. My vision tunneled. My blood pressure must have been stratospheric.

None of it could be real. Good things didn't happen to me. For example, not a full hour before, I fell and skinned my knee, ripping my work pants. Remembering that, I looked down at my state of dress and thought about how I looked in my phone's camera and how terrible I must have appeared.

"How long did you know about this?" I managed to ask Kara.

"I just found out about fifteen minutes ago," she replied, tears streaming down her face. "I can't believe it!"

"Congratulations!" Angela shouted, her cheeks ruddy and red. Even she looked excited. All of the doctors, too. My focus began to sharpen, and I started seeing the cameras and lights for what they were instead of abstract objects in time and space.

And that's when I realized that it was really happening.

four

. . .

The odds of winning a house from a television giveaway were less than one in 175 million. That said, only about two dozen people of the nearly 330 million Americans had even won one of the houses from the Dream Home contest. I knew this because I'd been entering the contest since my eighteenth birthday and always looked up the stats to justify why I never won.

But now I was somehow one of those lucky people.

Angela directed the doctors and staff back out to the floor after the initial surprise was filmed since it was still a workday and there were still patients to see. She arranged for me to have the rest of the day off to interview with the Dream Home people and likely get the camera crew away from the medical practice.

Outside, at the corner across from the practice, Victor and I spent the remainder of the morning hours shooting and reshooting interview footage. The happy folks at HHTV were used to dealing with jerks that made recording difficult, but I guess they weren't ready for Philly. Questions had to be re-asked dozens of times when a parade of cars drove by and shouted at us, or the rumble of their bass would mess with the boom mics. At one point, I heard the sound guy ask himself indignantly why there were chicken bones all over the sidewalk like he'd never seen such a sight.

The camera crew and sound team packed up their craft, clicking rods and caps into place and stuffing equipment into their van.

"Thank you for your time here," the interviewer began, "and sorry for all the retakes. I know you're probably excited to get packing and everything."

"Oh, no. I'm sorry for all the," I looked around my shoulders and gestured vaguely, "this. If you can get past all the noise and litter, it's not too bad around here, but I know it's a lot."

"Well, in a few months, you'll be enjoying your Dream Home in Spokane and won't have to deal with any of this anymore," he said with a chuckle and shook my hand a final time. "Congratulations."

A producer who'd been standing behind the lighting guy for the morning stepped forward as the last boxes and bags were being hauled away and ran through the next steps of the Dream Home process with me. "In the coming days, someone'll reach out to you to arrange flying out for the Winner's Weekend celebration," he said, and I tried to make mental notes. "However, in the meantime, you'll probably want to start looking into retaining an accountant. If you don't have one already, that is."

I chortled at his joke and then quickly realized that he was not, in fact, joking.

An accountant. Really? Me? I couldn't even afford the twenty-two-dollar biweekly dental insurance coverage that work offered me, and now I had to hire people?

"Oh, right. Got it," I said, as I tried to commit all the Winner's Weekend dates and details to memory. I needed to figure out where I could find a cheap accountant, and, maybe more importantly, I needed to figure out what an accountant did. Something with money, probably, but I never had more than a couple maxed-out credit cards and my single debit card. The thought that someone could have more money than they could handle by themselves was unfathomable. Then I realized the producer was still standing there, watching my thought-spiral. "Oh! Right. Really, thank you so much for everything. This has been very, very surreal."

We all shook hands, exchanged our final goodbyes, and the crew drove away, leaving me on the corner with my thousands of thoughts and Vic catching his breath. "Is this real life?"

"I legitimately have no idea." I tried gathering my thoughts, but it proved more difficult than herding puppies. "Like, this is all too good to be true, right? There's gotta be another crew waiting around a corner somewhere, ready to jump out and take it all back from me. Right?"

"It certainly feels that way," he said and stroked his jaw with his palm. "This has to be the wildest day of my life."

Still stunned and overstimulated by the whirlwind of cameras, I turned and focused from the middle of nowhere to his face. "You're telling me." For a good thirty seconds or so, we just stared at each other, exhausted, like we'd both just run a marathon or made up after a tumultuous, yet passionate breakup. "Now what?"

"I don't know about you, but my nerves are shot." Victor lifted a straight hand perpendicular to his chest, revealing an uncontrollable jitter. "I could probably use something to eat before anything."

I lifted my hand and saw the same quivers. *When was the last time I ate? Yesterday? This morning?* Too long ago. "Me too." I might not have had my prize package yet, but I had a few dollars left in my pocket to last me until payday, which was enough reason to collect my half-million-dollar thoughts and buy a six-dollar street cart falafel for us to split.

A half a million dollars. Anything above ten thousand sounded made up to me, so I couldn't begin to digest what that amount of money meant. The prize package included a fully-furnished, four-bedroom, four-and-a-half bath cliffside home in the mountains a few minutes outside of what the commercials referred to as "attractive" Spokane, Washington, with a brand-new luxury SUV and fifty thousand dollars cash for whatever else I could ever think to put into the house. In my apartment, I had approximately three belongings; that prize felt almost too good to be true.

At the cart, I ordered my falafel over rice (the pita cost extra), and we ate it against the exhaust-stained stone walls of a train overpass. With the rails rattling and roaring from above, I took my phone from my pocket and searched "accountants near me," but closed it before reading the results; I didn't have any of the prize money yet. Another tab and another search led me down a rabbit hole of the perils of lottery winnings and what one should do if one were to ever hit the jackpot. Rule Number One: hire a lawyer. *First, an accountant, and now a lawyer? What's next, a judge?* I was in way over my head.

To prevent another all-out panic attack, I scrolled over to the official Dream Home website to really study the pictures: the wrap-around wooden porch with the built-in hot tub, the open-concept living area, the en suites, and the walk-in closets. Accordion doors that let the outdoors in. My own personal library.

My personal library.

All mine.

Just as my breath began to steady, a wave of reality washed over me. Liquid streamed through my eyes and nose, down my neck, and onto my clothes. Instead of breathing, I heaved air and brayed like an old donkey. An ugly, ugly cry. Ugly cry squared. I can't say I was sad; in fact, I think I was happy, but I couldn't tell for sure what I was feeling at that moment. The anxiety of having to prepare so much, plus the guilt of winning, plus all the unknowns of how much my life would change from such a hefty windfall, sent me into a panic attack right there on the sidewalk.

My vision narrowed to complete darkness, except for the bright flashes of light from every direction. The ringing in my ears reached a deafening pitch, and my breath escaped me. In the dark, a hand grasped onto my shoulder. Victor. *Victor? What is he doing here? Or at work?* My heart and my thoughts raced.

He wrapped his arm around me and told me to calm down, which didn't work. It never did, but at least I wasn't alone.

When my eyesight eventually un-tunneled and my hearing returned, my thoughts became linear again. More linear, at least. I still had clusters of answerless questions floating around my brain, like, "Where do I go from here?" and "How did we get here?" and "Is this real?" but I was certainly glad I didn't have to brave it all alone. Only after I settled down a bit longer and my breathing became rhythmic again did Vic tell me he had to head to work. He apologized for not warning me beforehand and that his boss couldn't grant him more than the morning to be there for the reveal.

"That's fair," I told him and sniffed up an old tear. Spending the day with Victor would have been nice, but seeing him for a few hours that morning was good enough for me. "I'm surprised to see you here at all."

A wide smile graced his face, and he said, "I wouldn't have missed it for the world." With a kiss on my forehead and a squeeze of my shoulder, he climbed the wet stairs to the train platform overhead, and I used the leftover napkins from the falafel cart to wipe my cheeks and blow my nose. In a current, I felt my brain jump back into my body, which jumped back into the city around me. The streets and storefronts made sense to me again. I stood up, dusted off, and crossed the street to the bus stop to go home, and at that moment, I made up my mind. If I didn't have to work and couldn't make any real progress on the house business, I was going to enjoy my first weekday off in six years.

Retracing my steps from hours before, I walked the block and a half to the transit stop, caught a bus less dense with afternoon commuters, skipped off the step (careful to avoid any uneven pavement and tripping hazards), and entered my apartment for one of the last times. Hippo greeted me with dances and whole butt wags, as being home four hours early was a welcome change to her routine of loafing in the crumbs of dust mote and dog-hair-filled sunny spots scattered about the floor. I scooped her face into my hands and snuck kisses atop her head before her excitement bubbled over, and she kissed me back, her blubbery tongue slick with drool. It was a good thing she loved me so much because the sheer force of her licks knocked me right off my feet and onto her level. She could easily destroy me if she had any desire to. But I suppose the same could be said of any relationship.

"That's enough, that's enough!" I called out with a snort and gave her a hug. Heaps of dogs were doted on and squeezed as puppies and less as they aged, but it had been the opposite with Hippo. I rescued her back when Vic and I were on a break, and I needed someone to cuddle up to. She'd lost her entire litter of puppies eight days earlier, likely due to her youth (Hippo was only six months old at the time) and whatever else she'd endured during her short lifetime, and was justifiably more broken-hearted than I. Some of the scars along her face and body were still new, and she winced at touch in our first weeks together, but we quickly warmed up to each other. Back then, her skin stretched taut over her ribs and spine, but fur and fat filled the voids over the years, and she started living up to her name. When I'd pet her sides, they were pocked and pitted, but she'd still roll over and grant me access to her belly. She trusted me more than anyone on Earth, and the feeling was mutual. I could hug her for hours, and she would let me. It was all I ever wanted to do.

"Do you wanna go for walkies?" I asked. "Walkies" was one of Hippo's favorite words, but it was nothing compared to "harness," which she would only wear for longer, more adventurous walks. The scraps of her docked ears perked, and the nub of her tail wagged when I continued, "With a *harness*?" Hippo reared and bucked like a pent bronco. "Okay, okay," I said, calming her back down, easing the harness on, clipping the leash to her back, and heading to the park.

The sky appeared bluer and the air fresher than it had six hours before, or maybe I just hadn't noticed it. The sun had warmed the city enough to where only a light jacket was warranted, but autumn meant the sun set early. Beams of late afternoon sun gleamed through the voids on tree branches and brightened the remaining honey and marmalade leaves. Hippo and I walked along a sidewalk under the falling leaves and broke from the prescribed path when I caught sight of a creek that split the sea of grass on either side of us. Minnows swam at the surface like unseasoned synchronized swimmers until Hippo clunked into the water and scared them under rocks and weeds.

It was the best day of my life. So far.

Hippo shook off beads of excess water, and we returned to the trail, the early evening sun shining citrine through tall blades of grass. Any birds who had stayed that late in the season had packed away for the night, their songs replaced by those of children in the distance who'd gotten out of school for the day. We had less energy in our steps as we forged our way out of the park, but I was somehow more receptive to the sights and scents, absorbing all that was around me. Hippo turned toward the sun and sniffed at the sky. We were both simply living in the moment.

Aside from taking some landscape shots on my camera, I hadn't even thought to look at my phone in the two hours we'd been exploring that hidden pocket of nature in the city. No social media, texts, email, or stress about work. Completely untethered from the worries of the days and months and years prior.

Once we crossed the final street and I put the key in the rear basement door to my apartment, I let Hippo off her leash and checked my messages. Kara had texted me, but so had Angela and my mom. I wish Mom reaching out to me had been a surprise. Since moving out on my own at seventeen, I typically only received word from her when she needed something, but she always had a funny way of smelling out money in people.

TODAY 12:15 PM

CALL ME

Kara, accompanied by four missed calls.

TODAY 12:32 PM

BREANNA!!! I SAW YOU ON TV!!!

CALL ME

HOW COULD YOU NOT THINK TO LET ME KNOW ABOUT THIS

> HOW LONG HAVE YOU BEEN HIDING
> THIS?

> I'M THE LAST TO KNOW, AS USUAL

Mom.

Last was a message from Angela, who was less than enthusiastic about my winnings.

> TODAY 1:01 PM
>
> Hello, Breanna. Will you be coming into work tomorrow? Congrats again.

I called Kara, not ready for a guilt trip from Mom or Angela.

"I can't believe all this," Kara whispered. "This sort of thing happens to people with *good* luck, not people like us."

"I know," I assured her.

Ray Charles could have easily written "If It Wasn't for Bad Luck" based on my life. Kara's, too. We were the sort of people who'd learned through experience that hard work helped keep your head above water and that the bootstrap story was actually a fable.

"Apparently, I have to go out to Spokane to record some sort of reveal special before I can get the keys. It also comes with a car and a cash prize, but I have the option to just take the money instead. I don't know. My brain has sort of shut down from the overload."

"Spokane is a long way away," said Kara. "I don't know what I'll do without you here."

"Honestly, I don't know what I'd do without you, either."

35

After an hour and a half on the phone and a full day's worth of emotional exhaustion, I texted Angela with a simple "no" and told Mom I'd call her the next day. All I wanted to do was curl into a cozy cocoon with Hippo and sleep until all of the TV specials and paperwork blew over, and I could emerge a beautiful butterfly with a new house in the woods.

five

. . .

The alarm on my phone sang me a song, and I was up, agitated. I once read that abrasive alerts set a harsh tone for the rest of the day, so it was best to use whimsical wake-up tunes to ease yourself out of slumber. Still, I quickly associated the peaceful ringtone with the queasiness of not wanting to face another day of work, and now, whenever I heard it, a deep uneasiness churned inside me. Even if it was midday and on someone else's phone when they received a call. I'd be at the mall, smelling the bath bombs from Lush that I couldn't afford, when a phone call in the distance would twist my belly into knots, and my breath would run away from me.

I awoke with the same jitters as I did every other time I heard those sweet chimes and bells, but that time, I could tell myself that I didn't have to go back to the office. Maybe I wouldn't ever have to work again. Still, that disquiet of the alarm wasn't easy to rid, and when it did finally subside, it settled back in when I realized I was still lost about getting my new house. Worse still, I had to call Mom back.

I showered, ate breakfast, made a grocery list, and did all I could to delay calling her, but during my second walk with Hippo, she took the initiative and called me.

"Breanna!"

"Hey, Mom, how are you?"

"Alright, I guess, but more importantly, how are you? Amazing?"

Honestly, no, I wasn't amazing, but I couldn't just tell her that. She'd interrogate me about why, or how maybe I should give her money, so I just agreed.

"Yeah, you could say—"

"Seattle! I've never even been to the West Coast!"

"Spokane—"

"I saw the house on TV, and it looks great. And I saw Victor was there with you! Are you two back together? I always liked him. Aiden and Jaiden did, too. They were so sad when you broke up but would love it out there in Washington!"

Aiden and Jaiden? Typical mom, using her non-accidental children as a bargaining chip to guilt my assistance. Mom married their dad when I was fifteen, had the twins when I turned sixteen, and was divorced by the time I moved out. They'd always been cute with fair blonde hair and ocean blue eyes, a stark contrast to Mom's least favorite child. Mom and her parents doted on them since they were born (until Grandpa passed and Grandma moved out to Daytona Beach with the remaining retirement money) and thrust how perfect and gorgeous they were whenever she called to hit me up for some cash until her paycheck cleared. Usually, she'd throw how her life could have been so different if not for me in my face for good measure, as if my birth and her financial woes were somehow my fault. But in that call, her harsh criticisms were noticeably missing.

"Yeah, we're back together, but I don't know about Aiden and Jaiden. They hate going outside when it's cold or wet, and that's all there is out there. Rain and snow, often frigid. I don't even know if they have summer out there."

"But there's a hot tub, and the rooms are huge."

I knew what she wanted, but I wasn't about to give her the satisfaction.

"Yeah, they probably would like it when you come by to *visit*."

Good. Squash that idea before she—

"Actually, that's something I wanted to talk to you about. How many bedrooms does that house have? Four? Five? That's an awful lot of house for two people."

"It's the perfect amount for us and Hippo. And who knows, maybe we'll give you grandchildren one day," I hinted with a smile she could likely hear.

"What? No, that's way too big for you guys and a dog. And if you have any kids, I'll need to be there to see them. Besides, I think it'd be a nice change of pace for all of us to move out west."

There was no way in hell I was going to let that happen.

"No way in hell."

Here I thought Mom was going to hound me for money. In reality, she wanted free room and board *and* money. I hadn't even claimed my prize yet, and she was already deciding how I should use it.

"Why not?" she barked back at me as if she was entitled to everything with my name on it, just like she had for the past three decades.

"Do you want all of my prize money too? And the new car while you're at it?"

"Breanna Marie! You aren't—"

"Don't 'Breanna Marie' me!" I yelled before hanging up.

I hated how we could barely have a conversation anymore that didn't end up that way, but in the moment, it always felt good to be the one who hung up first. Usually, she'd be the one to abruptly end the call, but she wanted something from me. A lot more than usual.

When Mom tried to call back, I didn't answer. Instead, I texted her that I needed to think about everything and that I'd call her back later, and then texted Victor to gripe.

TODAY 10:45 AM

Mom wants to move in with us in the new house.

With the kids.

Did you tell her that's not happening??

> Yeah, but she is convinced otherwise.

Well, maybe you shouldn't take the house then.

> What?

> I just won a house! I'm not gonna just hand it back to HHTV!

No, that's not what I mean.

I looked it up online, and apparently, when you win a lavish prize like this, the winner has to pay outrageous taxes on it.

You're better off taking the cash payout for the whole thing.

Victor texted me a link, and I checked it out with a high degree of skepticism.

TODAY 10:57 AM

> This blog doesn't even look legit.

> Besides, Spokane looked so nice.

> And secluded.

It did, but I don't think it's feasible. Like, if you get that house, how are you gonna afford to live there? The west coast is notoriously expensive.

How dare he, I thought. Back together for less than twenty-four hours, and already he didn't want me to live in the free house I'd won. Granted, it did feel like we never were apart since making up. Victor always had that way of captivating me.

Anyway, what he said about the high cost of living in Washington might have been true, but that shouldn't have been enough reason to squash my Dream Home dream like that. Besides, the East Coast wasn't exactly cheap. Maybe that gargantuan life-changing opportunity stressed him out beyond words, and he didn't want to send me into another panic attack, especially after just having one on the side of the road under the train station, but that was no reason to throw a whole house away.

> Well, I don't think anyone should be making any decisions before we actually see the house.

I hit "send" even though I'd already made up my mind.

six

. . .

It was already early afternoon when I realized I'd never called Mom back. I'd spent the better part of the day playing tug-o-war with Hippo indoors since it was especially cold and gray, and I didn't want to risk getting stuck in a stray rain shower.

But even though we were cramped inside, I didn't care. The small space full of mold spores I'd been confined to for the past several years wouldn't do me any more harm at that moment; besides, I only had what I'd imagined to be weeks left there anyway. With a tuckered-out and panting dog resting her planet-sized head in my lap, my worries about money and houses and Mom seemed to evaporate.

Once my head cleared a bit and my pulse lowered enough, I collected my thoughts and pulled my phone off the charger to call Mom back. She picked up after only one ring.

"Breanna!"

She sang my name into the microphone. Mom was not traditionally excited to hear from me, but considering the circumstances, she laid her enthusiasm on thick for me.

"How's my baby girl?"

Perhaps a bit *too* thick.

"I'm okay, Mom. Look, I thought about it and—"

"Hold on, now, before you make any big choices here, I think it's important to think about how much me and the kids love and care about you."

Thinking back on all the thirty-four years of my life, I didn't think I'd ever heard Mom say she loved me. I'd heard her tell Aiden and Jaiden, but I never received as much as a single "I love you" from Mom. Not as a kid, not as an adult. I guessed I never thought too deeply about it; it was just how we were. I supposed we knew we loved each other in some sense, and we never needed to say it out loud. Hearing Mom tell me over the phone at that most convenient time made my stomach knot. She had the capability to tell me she loved me for years, but she only chose to say it to me while trying to barter better living arrangements.

"I know, but—"

I choked it out, unsure if I *actually* knew. But what? How could I tell the woman who raised and then depended on me that I was cutting her off? That she couldn't mooch off me and needed to stand on her own for once? That I was tired of being *her* mother? Panicked, I blurted out the first thing that came to mind.

"I talked it over with Victor, and we might not take the house."

"What? Why? What are you talking about?"

Her voice raised an octave, and I knew she was moments, maybe even seconds away from shrieking at me. We may have been separated by cell phones, but I still knew better than to anger her.

"We might take a cash payout instead of the house."

I lied, trying to smooth things over. I had no plans of taking the money and running, but I needed an out, and I never knew what to say under pressure.

"Well, that's fine. We can all buy a big house together."

⚉ ⚉ ⚉

TODAY 3:12 PM

No way.

Victor replied after I texted him Mom's counterattack.

We are not letting that woman stay with us.

Did you tell her she's an adult and can live by herself?

Ouch. She was a bit dramatic and often problematic, but Victor didn't have to talk about her so harshly. That was my job, but I only earned that right from being her daughter, and besides, Mom adored him. Still, I felt the same way.

I told her I'm not sure what we're doing yet, but not to get her hopes up.

If you need me to talk to her, I will.

Having Victor talk to my mom about that was the last thing I wanted. Mom loved him so much and would be crushed if he told her she couldn't have her way. And, though it felt like years already, we'd only been back together for less than a day. Maybe that wasn't the best circumstance for them to reunite.

> No, it's fine. I'll talk to her.

I put my phone in my pocket and rose to make a cup of noodle soup when my phone buzzed again. Kara. I'd only talked to her once since the ambush.

TODAY 3:20 PM

Hey!!! How are you doing???

> OMG, this has been such a crazy week! And it's not even over.

After sending that text, I realized that it was, in fact, Friday.

I bet!

But I have soooo many questions. One- have you officially quit yet? Angela has been PACING at work.

Two- when do you move??? I don't want you to leave!

And three- WHAT WAS VICTOR DOING AT THE REVEAL??? Are you back together? Lol.

> There is so much to unpack here.

I hadn't quit yet, but I was sure Angela's pacing was less about her grief over losing me as an employee and more about the worry of having to work a Saturday for once in her life. I told her I didn't want to leave her either, which was the truth, and that I didn't know when I'd be leaving for either the home viewing or for good. Victor was a bit harder to explain.

> YOU'RE WHAT?

>> Back together. We made up on our date after loads of apologies. I was gonna tell you at work yesterday, but then everything else happened.

> Bree, I support you whatever you do, but don't jump into things too fast. Get past this house thing first before you start thinking about Victor.

> I mean, Hippo doesn't even like him.

I was taken aback. No congratulations? No, "I'm so happy for you"?

>> Hippo doesn't like any men.

As long as I'd known her, she'd cower at the sight of any guy she'd come across. Besides, her distrust of Victor because of his gender didn't mean she hated him.

> I don't know... She's usually a pretty good judge of character...

>> Look, I know you and Vic haven't always been the best of friends, but he makes me really happy.

Send.

Kara didn't say anything more, and I proceeded to eat my soup, dangling noodles over Hippo's mouth for her to catch.

"*You're* happy for me, aren't you, baby?" I asked her in my goo-gooiest tone. She swallowed the noodles without chewing and licked my hand of residual broth. "Yeah, you are." Even in my loneliest times, when no one else seemed to get me, Hippo did.

With lunch eaten and a few hours left in the working day, I packed up the laundered scrub top Angela let me borrow and headed over to work.

According to a research article from some scholarly journal one of the docs once left in the employee bathroom, unhappy workers were more likely to suffer from stroke, heart attack, and a slew of mental health disorders than the fortunate folk who liked their jobs. That meant that, for many, the reward for sucking it up, clocking into that job they couldn't stand to make ends meet, and restraining themselves to not say what they would really want to say to that one manager (Angela) was a poor health practice. Top all that off with the fact that over half of Americans were unhappy with their jobs—not indifferent, *unhappy*—and most were there because they didn't feel like they had any other choice.

That was the camp I fell into.

Not anymore, I thought as I took my bus over to Franklin Family. The trip over to the office wasn't bad. Honestly, I could probably say it was good. Triumphant. Almost as if the fates decided that I no longer needed to suffer for whatever abominable thing I must've done in a past life. Or maybe they just took pity on me. Whichever, I made it from my soon-to-be-former apartment to my soon-to-be-former job without so much as a scratch.

It felt strange walking in with street clothes on, as if my body was rejecting me being in that place. More so than usual. I marched up to the front desk and asked if Angela was around, knowing full well that she would be (and available). After an overhead beckoning, she emerged from her front office and ushered me to a seat across from her laminated faux-birch desk. She flipped into her well-worn office chair and began to lightly chit-chat as if we were old friends out for coffee. A few days before, she threatened to fire me for using my phone, and there she was, cozy and gabbing, giggling and reminiscing.

"Right," I drawled, bringing our conversation back to the present. "Well, I brought in that top you let me borrow. I've washed it and everything, so it's good to go."

"Oh, that?" Angela asked, tossing a hand in the air. "I'm not worried about that; we have plenty."

A few days ago, she threatened to dock my pay if I didn't return it.

"Gotcha. Well, I brought it, so...." I said and handed her the shirt. "I don't really need it anymore." She grabbed it and tossed it to the floor under her desk.

"When do you move to Washington? Have you made any big plans yet?"

"I have no idea. I haven't even started packing yet," I said before realizing I could probably pack all my belongings into a single box. "Someone from the contest should be contacting me soon to set up everything, I guess."

"Well, that's still exciting, right?" I felt a tinge of secondhand embarrassment from her level of forced enthusiasm. "I supposed you'll have some time to kill while you figure everything out, huh? I mean, who knows how long it'll take before you receive any of your prize money. If you want to work here a few hours here and there, I can add you back on the schedule. You know. Temporarily."

Really? "I—"

"Besides, you haven't officially given your two weeks. You wouldn't want to burn a bridge with your longest employer since you'll eventually need to find a job out in Spokane. You're bound to need at least some sort of professional reference."

I rapidly ran the numbers in my head. If I got the house and the money along with it, would I still have to work, or could I live off of it out west? Was fifty thousand dollars enough to coast on? It seemed like a lot, especially if I didn't have to pay rent, but it was probably not enough to retire on.

"Lemme think about it over the weekend, and I'll get back to you by Monday," I eventually replied, slowly.

"That's fine; if you want, I can add you on for the week, and you can call me if you decide not to come in," Angela said, smiling. I hated that smile.

She saw me out of her office, and I made my way back to the bus stop. A buzz on my phone had me feeling hopeful, but when I glanced down, it lit up with an email from my bank. My account was overdrawn.

I texted Angela.

TODAY 5:34 PM

I thought about it, and Monday works for me.

Even though it didn't.

seven

. . .

Hey! Did you come by work today?

Hi! I did.

I was so dumbstruck by Angela asking me to pick up shifts that I forgot to find Kara and say hi.

I had to give Angela that scrub top I borrowed. But I'll be back to work Monday!

Oh.

Got it.

Nononono! Angela asked me if I'd work next week, and it caught me so off guard I panicked and bolted out! What are you doing after work?

Silence. No disappearing bubbles, no anything. I boarded my bus and rode home, getting off at my normal stop. As the bus

51

pulled off, the back tires clipped a puddle along the corner and drenched me head to toe with a swell of opaque gray sludge water. My white parka was coated in muck and silt. *At least I'll be able to afford one once my prize check has cleared*, I thought. Fifty grand richer, I could afford as many coats as I wanted.

At home, Hippo greeted me; even if it felt like the rest of the world was against me, I could guarantee she'd be right there with me, by and on my side. She got some head scratches before I tossed my jacket and jeans in the wash and leaned my black and white Chuck Taylors against my space heater to dry. Still no word from Kara. Or Victor, for that matter. I pulled on some clean sweatpants and a pullover hoodie from my alma mater and cuddled up close to Hippo. With her head in my lap, I called Victor.

No answer.

I started to text him, but he was faster.

TODAY 6:18 PM

Everything okay?

Yeah, I just haven't heard from you today.

I watched the antsy text bubbles bounce around.

Sorry. I've been super busy at work.

How's everything over there?

It was easy to forget that other people still had to work and carry on with the mundane aspects of their lives while I was off, probably because I only had off on Sundays and federal holidays. Staying home with nothing to do certainly felt better than being at work, but after doing nothing but see patients day in and day out for what seemed like an eternity, I felt bad for not doing anything. Bored. Lonely, even. At least I had a dog to nuzzle up to.

> Everything is great over here; I'm just hanging out at home. What are your plans after work?

I dunno. I may end up working a double. Try to get the most out of this last paycheck.

Last paycheck? Maybe he mulled it over, thought better of it, and decided moving out west would work.

> Are you quitting? So we can move out to Spokane?

I really think Washington is a bad idea, babe.

We'll talk about it later.

He had to go back from his break but asked me to think about what I truly wanted. The screen turned dark, and I sat on the bed, holding the phone in both hands in the quiet. I could've called my mom, but I wasn't that desperate for conversation. Besides, I had a perfectly good Hippo to whom I could devote all of my attention.

"Hey, good baby," I cooed and scratched behind her ear nubs, thumbing the marbled edges from the ruins of her ears. She closed her eyes, leaned into my hand, and stretched her sturdy legs across my lap. Hippo wasn't fat, but she had a layer of insulation over her muscle, which looked impressive when stretched and flexed in certain lighting. Her stomach wasn't tight, the vestiges of the litter she carried when she herself was still a baby. Still, she loved belly rubs like any other dog, and I would do anything to make her happy, especially after the life I imagined she lived before I came into the picture. "Do you want a treat, girl?"

Her ears perked up, and her soft, black teddy bear eyes widened. "Do you want," I said and paused just long enough that she started tapping her paws in anticipation, but not before she could let out a whimper or cry, "peanut butter?" Hippo danced around the bed and hopped to the floor, leading the way across the apartment to the family-sized jar of peanut butter that we shared. We played "peanut butter pitbull," a game where I asked her if she was a peanut butter pitbull, and she yelped to confirm that she, in fact, was, and I dropped a heaping spoonful down to her to catch and gobble down. Admittedly, she used to be better at catching the gobs, but she did a great job cleaning it all off the floors if she missed it. Watching her lap up the mess from the unsealed cement basement, I ate a slightly smaller blob off the spoon and looked around, gauging my surroundings. There wasn't too much there, nothing of much use anyway, but then it was just as good a time as any to begin organizing my life. I gathered the piles of books around the room and stacked them together at the head of my bed, inspected a ratty pair of sneakers that I had hidden under the foot of the bed (I determined they could be thrown out), and systematically assessed every article of clothing I had. Trash, keep, donate. Same for the small knick-knacks and tchotchkes I'd collected over time. Once I threw out the garbage, I emptied and organized the backpack I wore to work, filled it up with things to donate, and set it beside the door for my next outing. By the time I finished, it was past seven.

Kara should be about done working, I figured, so I texted her again.

TODAY 7:02 PM

Hey. How was work?

Six minutes later, a reply back.

TODAY 7:08 PM

Good.

A few more seconds and another message.

Heading out for dinner with Liza. You?

I had no clue. How was I doing? What was I doing? Tonight? In general? I couldn't begin to answer any of those questions. My whole world jumbled over the past three days, yet I was lost in the same maze I'd lived in my whole life. Stuck in between lives.

Dunno.

I dropped my phone on the bed, flopped beside it, and rested my head against the wall. One more day until payday.

🐾 🐾 🐾

Maybe it was from growing up with a mother I had to walk on eggshells around, or maybe it was the years of screwing up and upsetting others, but I'd never been one for confrontation. I got enough of it naturally; no need to stir the pot and bring more trouble on myself. Whenever I heard a conversation accelerating and sensed the tension rising, I deescalated it the only way I knew—by changing the subject or pretending the other never happened. As communication drifted further away from in-person or over the phone and more toward the typed variety, I could always swipe the conversation away. Let it cool off and pick it back up after mindlessly scrolling the internet or liking photos of strangers' dogs on social media. Some would call that avoidance, and they'd be right.

As I continued to pretend that there wasn't something building up between me and Kara, I messed around on Creatr, filtering and editing pictures to post of Hippo. Around 7:30, my screen lit up gray, and Victor's name scrolled across the top like a marquee. I must have forgotten to save an image of his contact on my phone again.

"I'm just getting home from work," he said, "and think I'm going to take a quick nap before figuring out what I'm doing here for dinner. I just wanted to call and say hello, that's all."

My heart skipped a beat.

He quickly debriefed me on his day, and I drank it in, his deep, silky voice pouring through my ear and massaging the pleasure receptors of my brain. He sounded so warm, even when he talked about something as mundane as his workday; I would have been nuts to end that moment.

I guess I was always a bit nuts, though.

"So," I began after he rounded up his commute home, "I've been thinking more about it, and I still think it's best to move out west. Start over completely."

"I dunno, Bree. Is this what you *really* want? You wanna move however many *thousands* of miles away from everyone you know and care about? For what? What does that house give you that the cash and Philly wouldn't?"

My dream. Freedom. *Life.* A chance to start over and do things right. To do whatever I wanted without caring what everyone else thought of me or what I did and how I did it wrong. I was done with living under the spell of my mom. I deserved better. I deserved that. Something that big happened less than once in a lifetime for 99.9 percent of people; it'd be irresponsible *not* to take advantage of that opportunity.

"What would stop you from doing all of that here? Cut off who you don't like, keep who you do, and live it up in the city. On the plus side, you wouldn't have to move far from Kara while your other coworkers are forced to see you thriving. Sounds like a done deal to me."

I told him it wasn't his deal to make, but he made some valid points.

"I know I'm right. You do, too. This whole thing is unbelievable and exciting, but I know you. I know how big a deal changes are for you, and this is an enormous change."

All of that was true, I conceded.

"I don't want to see you overwhelmed, Bree. I love you too much for that."

My face and heart rushed with warmth. Victor really did know me better than I knew myself in some ways. Perhaps he was right about that. The scales were beginning to tip.

"I'm gonna go and take that nap. Think about everything and what you really want. I'll talk to you later."

Later. Everything always got put off until later. I sighed and exchanged my love and goodbyes with him before hanging up.

Back in the silence of my apartment, where it was just Hippo and I, with the faint whirring of the heater system and the televised applause from some game show quietly roaring overhead, I slumped my shoulders and turned to the dog.

"What should we do for dinner, girl?" I asked her, knowing full well that she'd be eating dog food. However, I had no food left in the house and no money left to buy anything. "Peanut butter it is," I told her, dropping her another spoonful before eating a few scoops myself.

One more day until payday.

eight

. . .

My alarms woke me up at my normal time again. Desperately, I flipped my screen from the clock to my bank app and checked my account. Payday.

I could breathe with my whole chest for the first time in a long time. My landlords agreed to let me use my security deposit as my rent until the New Year, and I already paid my phone bill for the month, so the money in my account was mine and mine alone. And it was burning a hole straight through my pocket.

After a shower and a breakfast of more peanut butter, I got dressed in my dingy parka, still stained with street scum after two runs through the wash, and put a teeny puffer jacket on Hippo to start out our day of errands. The carnation pink coat made her look like the sweet little baby I knew her to be, but the fabric that bunched around her armpits and stretched taut around her back stiffened her steps and accentuated her bully gait. I picked it up from the Children's Department of Goodwill when I first adopted her—when she was still just slightly more than a skeleton—and the jacket hung loose.

Steady meals and lots of love had her filling it out like a sausage casing.

With her leash clipped and my backpack slung around my right shoulder, we locked up and headed to the donation center, where I dropped off my former belongings and peered through the window for anything that stuck out as especially useful. At the front of the store was a table full of colorful bakeware and stately serving dishes that I debated over until I remembered that I was there to get rid of things—and that I couldn't cook. *Maybe that's something I can learn to do one day when I have a kitchen.* I daydreamed about baking, roasting, or whatever else people did with ovens, pulling out dinner rolls and casseroles. Wearing aprons and oven mitts and using the good dishes (because I would have two sets of dishes, clearly) pulled from the special hutch in the dining room with the windows to display said dishes. Hippo tugged at her lead, and I blinked back to reality, focusing my sight from the middle distance to the storefront and back to my current financial situation. I still only had a single hot plate and a half-cubic-foot microwave atop my dresser.

Hippo and I continued down the line of strip mall shops, me window shopping and she sniffing dried splotches of God knows what along the heavily-worn cement sidewalks. We stopped at the pet store to buy some treats and at the breakfast nook across the street for a sesame seed bagel, carefree and enjoying our morning together.

Once our bellies were full, we stopped through Hip's favorite park again, but that time, there were significantly more leaves on the ground from the prior day's wind and rain. A blanket of fiery foliage crunched under our feet as we strayed from our path along the split rail fence and onto a hill overlooking the creek. She found a four-foot-long stick to call her own and paraded it with pride, crunching on leaves and cracking open their fresh tea scent as she danced with all her heart. I took a long, deep breath of the woods around me, intoxicated by the fresh air and fall crispness. It was hard to believe it was merely blocks away from the exhaust and waste (possibly hominal) along the city sidewalk.

"Why don't you ever stop to smell the *pretty* smells?" I asked her as if she'd understand me. She did, however, pause, look at me, and tilt her head as if to attempt to digest my words, but she quickly gave up and turned her undivided attention back to her new stick. I grabbed one end, and we played a bout of tug-o-war, but she only let me win once before deciding she wanted the thing to herself. Funny how she would decrease her strength and resistance as she played when she could easily rip the thing from me whenever she wanted. Then again, I could physically cast her away like the person before me did, but emotionally, I knew I couldn't. Maybe that was her biggest fear.

Growing up, I always gravitated toward animals. I was always the weird, lonely kid who talked to stray cats and the neighbors' dogs because I felt like they got me more than my classmates did. Sometimes, I still felt like animals understood me better than any person ever could. But I remembered being in first grade, going to the school library, pulling out the encyclopedia, and copying passages about every dog breed— word for word— into a notebook. While every other kid was collecting all the trivia they could about the members of their favorite boy bands, I was researching the reason why Hungarian Pulis had fur dreaded into cords (to protect them from weather and wolves) or why Mexican Xolos had no fur at all (a genetic mutation that also caused them to not have premolar teeth).

I never had any baby dolls as a kid, and I never really minded; I had my generic plush doggy, who I pretended was a real puppy, and I was happy with that. Niki, I called her. Her ears were ragged, and her once-white and black spotted pelt turned a filthy taupe, but I loved that dog more than anything in the world. At least until I adopted Hippo. And the thought of doing anything to hurt her—physically or emotionally—made me sick.

Hippo played and played until she grew bored of her stick. She cast it aside and found a succession of three more—varying from thin twigs to what I would've considered a small log—and eventually grew tired of those before abandoning them where she stood. When sticks no longer satisfied her, she trotted alongside me with the meatiest of smiles. "You're such a pretty girl," I told her, petting her head and cheeks. As much as I loved taking photos of landscapes and details of the city, Hippo was always my favorite subject to lens. My muse. "Here, baby, sit here."

Hippo sat along the hillside, tongue out and panting, and I pulled my phone out to take her portrait. I knelt, stood, circled, and crouched, getting her best likeness from every angle. Satisfied with some, we returned to the leaf-dappled trail and took a few more. Grabbing a random yet enticing stick, I coaxed her over close and let her play, snagging some candids in the process. Before I knew it, my stomach growled loud enough to give Hippo a head-cocking pause, and I realized it was already nearly lunchtime. I could have spent the entire day there with her. Perhaps our entire lives. Alas, my stomach began to pang, so I decided to put a pin in playing for the day for our next meal, promising Hippo that we'd come back soon. We wound our way back to the main drag and walked home, collecting an order of ginger mock duck and coconut curry from the corner Thai restaurant on the way. Lunch and dinner done. In between bites, I posted a series of photos of her online with a fair amount of success—two hundred fifty likes and twelve new followers—and relaxed with her nestled in my arms.

The weekend dribbled and flooded past me—time worked in mysterious and aggravating ways when you had nothing and everything to do simultaneously. With my paycheck bleeding dry from my wallet, I bought myself a new laptop and spent a significant amount of time doing things I'd never remember. Creatr, silly animal videos, web browsing. I searched high and low, likely confusing anyone who would ever review my search history, but eventually landed on an ad for a DNA kit from a family history site. All my life, I'd only known my mom, her parents, and the twins. Kara always joked that Liza was my long-lost sister and tried to convince me to take a test. Liza even emailed me a coupon code to a DNA site she found. As much as I laughed it off, I always secretly hoped that maybe we shared some paternal blood, even if it was a mere drop, so I figured I'd give it a shot. Open Pandora's box. Ninety-nine dollars later (after the discount), I received a tracking number for my familial past. And, because I didn't want Hippo to feel left out, I ordered her a breed and genetic trait identifier, too.

Somehow, I managed to make it to work on Monday without any physical trauma, but the stress of facing another week at the office afforded me very little sleep.

Alarm sings.

Grey scrubs on.

Stained coat fastened.

Speakerphone bus patrons talking too loud.

At the office, everyone wanted to buddy up to me to ask about my plans and make less-than-funny jokes about me not forgetting about them when I got my winnings, as if the time they all made my life miserable could be wiped away by thirty seconds of flattery and chit-chat. The one person noticeably absent from the parade of well-wishers was the only person I ever cared to talk to while on the clock.

Kara busied herself the entire shift, seeing patients, wiping counters, and taking out trash. I approached her throughout the day, and she greeted me cheerfully but not sincerely. She worked straight through lunch, which was normal when we were busy and short-staffed, and the office was always both those things. I only decided to take it because I no longer cared about that place; in a week or so, I'd be gone. When she rushed out at the end of the day without saying goodbye, I grew concerned and, honestly, a bit offended. If I was being more honest, I'd say that I was more offended than concerned, but still concerned nonetheless.

TODAY 5:17 PM

Hey

Is everything okay?

Yeah, sorry, just in a rush to get home.

Hate it there.

Dude, same.

At least you get to leave and never come back.

Was that what all of that was about? If Kara felt left out, she could've just said so—honestly, the thought of leaving her on the East Coast and heading west broke my heart, and I thought of asking her to come fly out with me once I settled into the new house. *Or maybe...,* I thought, *maybe she's jealous.* I mean, I got it—I would be, too. Everyone else at work was, to my amusement (why else would they practically ask me for pity money so blatantly?), but I never wanted to upset Kara in any way. Really, she deserved a break like that just as much, if not more, than me. I shot her back another text to say that I would fly her out, too, then slipped my phone back into my pocket.

❧ ❧ ❧

When it comes to things like autism, ADHD, and a host of other disorders, the benchmark for medical research has historically been male. What does this look like in young boys? What does this look like in adolescent guys? What does this look like in men? Researching women's bodies has always been behind the curve, even with things like period symptoms that were once chalked up to being in our heads, and menopause, which we still don't know too much about. And women have been having and ending their cycles since the dawn of time.

Neuroscience and psychology, as we know them today, are relatively new fields in medicine. Whereas even early humans performed things like amputations and people from millennia past performed bloodletting and applied herbs to wounds for care, the science of the brain is ever-evolving. Lobotomies — which used to be performed on women with psych disorders, mental illness, and even postpartum depression — were only outlawed less than fifty years ago. I knew this because Mom's mom just missed the cutoff. Historically, the thought of women acting differently was scary, and it took years for scientists (read: men) to realize that people born female just present differently than those born male.

Kara understood that, and she understood me. Just like Liza understood me. And I always thought I understood them, too.

I tried not to think about Kara too much on my way home. When I got there, I filled Hippo's water bowl, opened the fridge for something that wasn't there, repeated that charade about half a dozen times, and finally broke down and rang Kara. Between checking my mini fridge for the sixth and seventh times (still empty), I realized that asking someone to move three time zones away via text message probably wasn't the best call. These things were better communicated in-person with full stomachs and sound minds, but on the phone after a hectic work day was the next best thing.

I danced around the kitchen during the first ring to pour out dog kibble. During the second, I fetched my water bottle and spun to sit on the bed. The third cut off abruptly. Weird. I called back, and that time, the first ring didn't even complete. She really hit the F-U button on me.

My thumbs slapped my phone, and I punched out a message as fast as possible.

TODAY 6:01 PM

Um, you good?

Yeah. I'm busy.

Like I said earlier.

She couldn't have meant that to come off so curtly.

Okay, fine. Can you call me later when you get a chance?

No response.

Kara, what has gotten into you?

What's got into ME? What do you think?

> You're off in your own head worrying about how things will be after you move, and I'm stuck in my dead-end job with my shitty apartment and shitty life.

Shitty? Here, I thought Kara had it all—an awesome girlfriend, an apartment on the nicer side of town, even if it was a tad on the small side—I would have sold a kidney to have what she had.

> Plus, you got back with Victor! After you swore you wouldn't! Now it's like nothing ever happened! You might forgive him for everything, but it's not so easy for me.

> Dude, I was totally gonna help you out when I got my check; I just wanted it to be a surprise. Also, I love Vic. I know you aren't his biggest fan, but can you at least try to be happy for me?

> Happy for you? Really? Because you're leaving for the other side of the country with this guy who doesn't even deserve you? All those nights I stayed up consoling you after he left, and you ran right back to him.

> Yeah, Bree. I'm SO HAPPY for you. THRILLED.

> You know what? Keep your money. I don't need your pity.

> Have a good life out there, Bree.

When I closed my eyes, I could still see the words on the screen. *Have a good life.* Four years of undergrad, a decade of Franklin Family, and endless rock bottoms, and that was how it was ending? My heart banged against my ribcage, demanding I fight back. Fight her, fight to keep her friendship, fight for something. But I couldn't. Not for lack of trying. I couldn't think to see straight, and once I did, the tears blotted out my sight. I tossed my phone to the bed beside me and tried to scream into my pillow, but only let out a whimper. Like Kara, my voice had given up on me.

Fourteen years of thoughts swirled around my head until they all came to a crashing halt in the present. I got up from my elbows and sat on my bed, then picked my phone up to respond.

I must've typed out what I wanted to say six times before deleting every word. She'd never told me she didn't like Victor, not so explicitly, but now she made him her line in the sand. She may have stayed up with me as I cried my eyes and my heart out over him, but he wasn't the only guy I'd ever cried over. Plus, I'd done the same for her with her exes, too. It was what friends did. Or that's what I thought, at least. But then again, I thought I understood her. Now it looked like I was out the one shoulder I had to cry on.

I finally texted her.

TODAY 7:40 PM

I will.

I deleted the conversation and ended our location sharing, then cried again, that time into Hippo's side. She licked my face and soothed my wounds, as she had done countless times. My rock. I wiped my face with my shirt collar, then collapsed backward onto my mattress and went to bed without dinner.

nine

. . .

If I slept, I didn't realize it. Ending my friendship with Kara somehow felt worse than when I broke up with Vic a few months before, like the one person I could go to with anything had been ripped from me. What was worse was that with her, she took Liza—the closest thing to a sister I had. I was never really good at making friends in the first place and tended to let friendships dissolve faster than I could make them, but now I had none except for my dog.

Hippo roused early and woke me well before my alarms had a chance to. Eating peanut butter from the jar and pacing the floor was better than sleeping anyway, I figured. My face was dry with tears and residual dog licks when my phone sang to me. Outside, the sun was asleep, just as it had been when I got home the evening prior. I hated that time of year. I missed the sun. I missed Kara.

Part of me wanted to call out of work. Maybe three-quarters of me. And just when I thought that place couldn't get any worse, the one thing I liked about it was gone. No—worse. She'd still be there in the same building as me, working in the same nursing stations and eating in the same breakroom, but our friendship as we knew it was gone.

"At least I still have you, girl," I said to Hippo, kissing the velvety wrinkles between her ears. I had Vic, too, and couldn't be happier about it, but Hippo had been the only one who never left me since I first met her, and even that was likely because she had no choice. "Is that why you love me, girl? Because you have to?"

Hippo plopped her head onto my hand, and I scratched underneath her jaw. "If that was the sole reason why, I guess you certainly have a funny way of showing it." I smiled for a fraction of a moment but quickly sunk into myself again. "Maybe *I'm* the problem," I whispered as she stretched as long as the bed. "Maybe it would be better for everyone if we moved out west, after all."

Hip whipped her head around when I stopped petting her and tried to nudge my arm with her nose. I petted her one more time before getting changed back into my scrubs, daydreaming about starting over from scratch. Moving cross-country was the perfect reason to not have friends, so it wasn't like I'd have to explain why I didn't know anyone out there. Assuming that I'd find anyone out there who would want to talk to me. And Vic got it. He was the same way. *He'd probably love living in the woods by ourselves, come to think of it.* One final pat on the head for Hip, and I sulked out the door.

Another fall and skinned knee later, I returned to work. To my surprise and relief, Kara called out sick; at least there'd be no awkward exchanges while I was stuck there, but it still had me worried. All I wanted to do was text her to make sure she was okay, but I couldn't. Not after the night before.

Around noon, my phone buzzed in my pocket. The number was blocked, but I didn't have a patient at the time, and, if the past week taught me anything, answering the phone every once in a while could prove beneficial. I scurried into an exam room, closed the door for privacy, checked my hair in the reflection of a framed painting of a sailboat (just in case I was about to get ambushed again), and answered the phone.

"Hello?" I asked, doing a terrible job concealing my skepticism.

Good thing I actually answered—on the other end was a representative from HHTV who was ready to help me and Vic book our flights and hotel for the big reveal special. Together, we briefly reviewed the timetable of my trip (including the fun activities the network planned for us to record for bonus footage), the full filming schedule (which would put a reality TV star to shame), and what to expect along the way (lots of overstimulation). And the mini-bombshell: although I'd be at my new house, it wasn't officially mine yet. Papers had to be signed, and taxes had to be paid. I wouldn't get the keys to the house for quite some time, apparently. Months, even, and that was if we were lucky.

"After filming," the perky assistant explained on the phone, "you'll have a meeting with legal for the logistics of the prize package—the boring stuff," she said.

She collected Victor's information for the hotel reservation and airfare. I made sure she sent us both an email with the details so I wouldn't forget anything, as I tended to do. When the call ended, I was able to catch glimpses of the world around me again, as if the storm clouds overhead were finally starting to break. For the first time in a long time, I could breathe without reminding myself to. If only I could figure out how friendship worked, I'd be set.

We hung up, and I immediately called Victor.

"Hey baby, what's up?"

"Hey, stranger," I answered back.

We texted every day, but I realized I hadn't actually seen him since dinner the week before.

"I just got off the phone with the house people. Looks like we're flying out to Washington."

"Wait, I thought we were leaning towards the payout," Victor said with concern in his throat. "We can't just up and move to the other side of the country like that."

"No, I know. They're flying us both out for the TV special. While we're out there, we'll talk to someone about everything. Apparently, the whole process can take several months or more."

"I see," Vic said, his voice calmer. "When do we fly out?"

"Next week." I paused to look at the calendar on my phone. "I guess we'll have to take off a few days." My voice got quieter as I realized I may have to keep working until all the paperwork was finalized. "But, hey," I chirped, trying to lighten my own mood, "what are you getting into tonight? Wanna come over for dinner? I was thinking about getting some Hakka noodles and samosas—"

"I'd love to, but I already told my parents I'd eat with them tonight."

For a moment, we both hung on the line without a word. I never got along with his parents; it's not like they were especially mean, but they only pretended to like me for

Victor's sake. If I tried to chime in on a conversation with his family members, they'd drawl out a long "okay" and roll their eyes, or quickly change subjects, or, worse still, ignore me.

"I'm sorry, baby—"

"It's okay, seriously," I said, pretending it was. "Maybe tomorrow."

"Let me check my work schedule, and I'll let you know for sure, okay? I gotta get back to the train, though—love you."

My cue; the call was nearing its end.

"Love you, too."

Too drained for another call, I texted Mom and made arrangements for her to watch Hippo while I was gone. We hadn't been apart more than a day since I adopted her, and the thought of leaving her behind was almost too much to bear; texting granted me enough space to not have to think too heavily about it. Still, I became emotional. Just as my breathing started to trip on itself, there was a knock at the door. Angela poked her head in and looked around before she found me. "There you are—the waiting room's overflowing out here."

"Sorry, HHTV called me," I said, which was true, even if they weren't the only people I spent the entire forty-five minutes talking to. "I'm gonna need time off next week, but I can come back the week after."

Angela looked like she wanted to be upset, but the news of an extra body to help out around the office seemed to balance her scales. "Alright, I'll look at the schedule and see what I can do for you." All I needed for her to treat me as a human being was half a million dollars over my head. I wish I'd known that when I started working that godforsaken job; maybe I could've pretended to be a real estate heiress the whole time.

❧ ❧ ❧

Upon returning home, I collected my mail and was shocked to see my DNA kits had arrived so quickly. Excited as I was to explore my ancestry, I needed love more, so I tossed the box and my bills to the side and laid next to Hippo. Acting as her big spoon, I gave her as many cuddles and kisses as she'd allow (about two and a half minutes' worth) before begging me to take her for a walk.

The Indochinese I ordered arrived as we were rounding back around the block, and I tore into it before the door to the apartment could close behind us. I shoveled the noodles into my mouth, apologizing repeatedly to Hippo that dogs can't have spicy foods, and read the instructions for the DNA kit. "'Register your kit online.' Sounds easy enough," I told Hippo. "'Fill the vile to the line with saliva'—can do—oh wait. It says I have to wait at least thirty minutes after eating or drinking to spit." I eyed my food, my fork, and the box, and thought, *screw it.* I threw the kit aside and polished off the remainder of my noodles.

With dinner out of the way, I opened up Hippo's DNA kit and used the specialty cotton swab inside to swipe the inside of her rubbery lips before pouring out her nightly bowl full of kibble. Once she polished off her dinner, we took our nightly walk, where we dropped her drool off in the mail, and I snapped some photos of her under the dramatic lighting of a streetlamp, which I posted online with a cheesy caption: "Let the streetlights guide you home." An instant hit (for my account), with about five hundred likes in the first hour. Back at our moldy apartment, I filled my time by triple-checking my itinerary online, refreshing my Creatr feed for new likes, and cramming my empty backpack to the zipper with clothes and necessities for my upcoming flight. Anything to prevent myself from having to be alone with my thoughts for too long.

❀ ❀ ❀

The workweek felt torturous. Kara returned mid-week, and I spent the remainder of my shifts ducking behind walls and into empty exam rooms to avoid eye contact with her. Vic came over for a couple hours Thursday, but because he'd been busy with doubles to make up hours for the trip to Washington, we mostly only spoke to each other through text exchanges the rest of the week. At least we'd be together for five and a half days straight in Spokane.

My alarm blasted me awake on Sunday. Normally, Sundays were the only time I could sleep in, so I'd only set the alarm the night before and must've forgotten to change it from the doomsday siren it defaulted to. I was panicked, but I was up. Being up and anxious was probably not a bad thing since my flight was scheduled for the afternoon, and I had no sense of how much time I needed to get through security. And, after only remembering to spit in the stupid vial while eating for almost a week, I finally did it that morning before breakfast. With the label adhered and the bottle tucked into the provided biohazard bag, I sealed the package back up and placed it beside my overstuffed backpack.

Hippo sat on the bathmat beside me as I showered, as she always did. She had no way of knowing that I'd be leaving her for the worst part of the week, and it broke my heart that I couldn't communicate that to her. Mom would be over soon to take her to her house in the suburbs, and I packed her a goodie bag full of treats and her favorite toys. Most of me wanted her to not get too sad that I was gone, but the smallest part of me was selfish and hoped she'd miss me like I'd be missing her. The last thing I wanted or needed was my dog deciding that she liked it better at her grandma's than she did with me. When I got out of the shower, I let Hippo lick the excess water off my shins as I toweled off and choked up. I didn't want to go without her.

But I had to. Mom came by with the twins in tow, who both squealed with delight over a doggy sleepover since Mom would never let them get a dog of their own, and my heart swelled. *She may not be a permanent member of their household, but at least they'll get to experience life with a dog for a week,* I thought. That's more than I ever got as a kid. That, however, didn't make slipping Hippo's lime-green, doggy-sized backpack over her shoulders and walking her out to the car any easier. Hip and I exchanged goodbyes much longer than my combined hellos and farewells to my blood relatives, but she was gone before I knew it. Before I could finish turning around to get back inside, my eyes stung with tears, and before I could close the door behind me, I was weeping. That time, there'd be no one to share peanut butter with.

Moments after Mom pulled off, Vic arrived. Sniffing back my tears, I threw my bag over my shoulder and locked up behind us.

"Babe, it's fine," Vic assured me. "You'll be back home with her sooner than you think."

"I know, but I just love her so much," I bawled.

"It's okay. Besides, we'll have a week of uninterrupted

together time out there. We haven't had that in a long time. Just me, you, and the mountains."

He was right about the alone time—it had probably been years since we'd had that much time together without one of us having to go to work or some unexpected emergency popping up—but I wasn't sure it was okay without my dog. She'd love the mountains. She'd probably appreciate them more than Victor or I could. I felt an ache in my chest and mustered up an, "Okay."

"It'll be alright, I promise," he said and summoned an Uber from his phone.

I leaned my arm into his side and sat in silence while we waited for our chariot—a newish model Jeep Cherokee—and continued the non-conversation once it arrived.

ten

. . .

I knew the airport would be big, but I had no idea it would be an entire-city-big. Knotted roads spiraled toward the terminal, intermingled and mangled amongst each other. Lanes merged and multiplied while cars beeped and screeched. It appeared as if everyone was desperate to leave town. Our driver was no different.

Oswald, as the app on Vic's phone called him, reeked of cigarettes and whatever dollar-store caliber body spray he used in an attempt to cover his smoky smell. He mumbled curses under his breath as his Jeep jerked and braked. A vein nearly burst through his neck when he mashed his palm into his horn to express his displeasure with the silvery Kia Soul in front of us, and he sweat beads even though he blasted his air conditioner in the late fall cool, but he got us to the airport in time and alive, which was all I could have hoped for. Five stars. I prayed the plane would do the same.

Inside, we presented our documents, took our shoes off for clearance, and explored the mall that was the airport's self-touted "first-class" shopping experience. Vic had flown on a handful of flights before, but I'd never had the chance. For me, jet-setting was something only the affluent did. If I didn't count the trip to the Nursing Assistance Conference in Baltimore two years back and that one weekend Kara and I took to New York City to meet her ex from MatchUp, the trip out to Washington would probably be considered the first real vacation I'd ever been on.

We wandered and window-shopped, wasting time until boredom set in. By the third coffee and convenience storefront, we'd figured we'd seen enough. One last pass at a book and travel pillow joint, and I splurged on a newly-released rom-com with a dog on the cover for the flight.

Man, did I miss Hippo.

A scratchy intercom overhead announced the boarding of our plane, urging flyers to stand in line by boarding pass groups. We joined the line, but only after every other letter. *Group F,* I thought. *How appropriate.* The plane's cabin seemed much smaller and cozier than I imagined, like someone stretched out a sedan. Still, as we bobbed our way down the aisle toward our back seats, the novelty started to wane. We placed our bags under the seats in front of us and fastened our belts when it all set in. I drew a long, full breath through my nose and slowly, steadily blew out through my pursed lips. *I'm going* home. *My home.* Our *home.* It just didn't feel that way without my dog.

Heavy-chested, I gulped the air again and sighed, looking out the window to the traffic controllers on the ground as they waved their stubby lights and directed the pilots to the runway. Vic touched my knee and said, "No need to be nervous," but my nerves were gone. I just missed my puppy. I nodded to him, took out my new book, and read about a girl and a guy with their meet cute and how his big shaggy dog kept getting slobber and fur and mud on her dresses at the worst times. By the time she learned to love the guy and his dog, we were already halfway to the West Coast.

Our flight landed at eight in the evening. Victor and I managed to cram everything we needed into our respective backpacks, so there was no need to wait around for baggage claims. We meandered off the plane, got lost in the airport trying to find the exit, and hopped into another Uber. For a day full of sitting down while strangers chauffeured me around, I sure was exhausted.

As soon as my face hit the hotel bed, I was out. The room was clean and bright, which was fancy for me, but Vic said it was pretty standard. It wasn't until the next morning that I realized the exterior was built like a castle, spindle and all. However, our ride to my new house had been dispatched early, so I didn't have much time to ogle the building.

Instead, I had plenty of time to *ooh* and *ahh* at the frosted pines and icy lake views. A blanket of fresh snow must've been laid overnight because the ground was definitely a lot greener when I went to bed the night prior.

"It really is beautiful," I whispered to Vic, who looked lost in the shades of white out his window.

"Yeah, but it's a bit too cold for my liking," he said, rapidly bouncing his leg up and down.

I checked the weather app on my phone and saw the current temperature: twenty-eight degrees. "I guess it is *a little* chilly."

We rounded winding roads and reached our destination: a sprawling, newly-built, mid-century-modern-inspired house with floor-to-ceiling windows and round, organic walls tucked cozily into the woods. The TV crew must've arrived much earlier to shovel and salt the driveway because it looked like a red carpet entry sans carpet. The view from every angle took my breath away. Before I could steady my breathing or find any words worthy enough, the guy who surprised me at work approached with an outstretched hand.

"Hey, Breanna. Thomas Harmon with HHTV. How've you been?"

"I—I'm okay," I managed to relay back to him. "This place is incredible."

"I'm glad you think so," he said as the camera crew connected poles, lights, and drones around us. He gave me an outline of the shoot and what would be expected of me. He told me that the snow had made for some exquisite exterior shots, so our portion of the interior walkthrough had to be pushed back a bit. A woman who introduced herself as a producer ushered Victor and I to a trailer with breakfast foods and coffee to hold us over while the drone crew finished their aerial shots. I took a bagel and a banana and sat next to Vic with his breakfast sandwich where we both ate, waited, ate seconds, then waited even longer before taking thirds.

When the time came for us to leave the trailer to begin filming, I was easily twelve pounds heavier. Probably not the best feeling to have with cameras pointed directly toward my face.

The house was beautiful on TV, but it was downright ethereal in person. Ashen hardwood floors, expansive open-concept living-dining-kitchen, crystal-white walls and gleaming granite countertops. And three toilets—three! I remembered the days when my single toilet didn't work, and I'd had to dump a bucket of water from the tub into it to flush. Three seemed a bit excessive.

The cameras caught our reactions as Vic and I turned every corner and opened every door. Wide eyes and gaping mouths. On the ride over, I told myself I'd do the socially responsible thing and cover my mouth. Still, all that went out the window and down the mountainside as soon as I entered. Even Victor was at a loss for words when we walked past the window wall revealing the backyard, and he saw the jacuzzi overlooking the snow-capped forest canopy. The house was a work of art. Better yet, it was *my* work of art.

We continued filming and gasping, retaking shots as needed when the camera missed certain reactions or wasn't satisfied with the natural ones we'd given. The stimulation was all too much for my brain to process, and it promptly shut down, causing me to not say much other than "wow" and "oh my God" at every turn. Producers had to coach me on new things I could say because I simply couldn't speak otherwise. I couldn't imagine my fed responses sounded genuine toward the end of shooting. Victor was much better at that than me; maybe he secretly wanted to keep the house more than he let on. Or maybe he was just really good at masking.

With every room discovered and discovered again for additional footage, the producers took me aside for some interview shots, and Victor stepped outside for a breath of fresh air. Hair and makeup gave me a quick sprucing up where I stood, and one of the producers spun me to the exact angle he needed for the best shot. I answered questions about how much I loved the house and which features were my favorite. How lucky I felt to have won. After forty minutes of questions and retakes later, my mouth ached from smiling. But, to my luck, when I thought the muscles in my face would blow out from forcing smiles, the interview concluded. *Thank God that's over*, the crew probably thought. I knew I did. Host Tom ushered me back through the house to the back deck, where I was met with more lights and more cameras. And Victor.

I walked out to him, standing in the middle of the backyard, and he took my hand in his. In an instant, all the grief I'd given him in my head for telling me I shouldn't keep the house evaporated into the sky. "Bree, you have been my best friend and rock since we met," he began. My ears began ringing, drowning out all the sounds around me. Victor reached into his jeans pocket and dropped to his left knee. "Breanna Marie Huxley, will you—"

In an instant, I was transported back to second grade, when the popular girls at school cornered me before the final bell. "Trash," they called me. Asked me if they had bathtubs at the homeless shelter. "Dirty." I ran to my bunk from the bus and clutched my Niki dog so hard I thought I could have ripped her.

Mom wasn't there. She rarely was. "One day," I whispered to my stuffed dog, "we won't have to live here. And we'll have a family that loves us."

And there, in front of the cameras and production team at HHTV, my dreams came true.

"Yes," I said and nodded. I wiped the mist from my eyes and let a smile overtake my face. "Yes, yes, yes!"

Victor slid a silvery ring onto my left hand and rose to embrace me. It was real—not some childhood fantasy I'd played out in my head a million times—and it was broadcast for all of America to see.

The production team clapped and congratulated us while cameras rolled and others snapped photos of us. I wiped the tears from my eyes and gave Victor one last hug before he took my hand and ushered me down the sidewalk for the last of the HHTV footage, something he told me the crew planned for the special.

When filming was finished for the day, the crew packed up their equipment, allowing Vic and I time to explore the expansive views outdoors.

We took dozens of selfies together, and I captured a picture of my ring-adorned hand spread out with the snowcapped trees and mountainside in the distance. Before I realized what I was doing, I sent the photo to Kara and watched the ellipses bubble appear, disappear, and reappear like the butterflies in my stomach. Then nothing.

"Hippo would love it here," I told him to distract myself as we marched through the snow to the end of the property. I fought to catch my breath.

"She'd probably like it better where it was above freezing and she wasn't at risk of getting eaten by a bear," he joked back.

"True. But this place is so beautiful," I said, never wanting to leave.

"It is, but the nearest grocery store or restaurant is miles away. We'd have to completely change our lives around."

"Sounds like you're playing with the idea a bit," I said, elbowing his side. "Besides, they're giving us a car to get to the town. It's not like we'd have to walk anywhere."

"Yeah," he said with a shrug and retreated inside his head, as he always did when I said the wrong thing or overstepped my bounds. *We were having such a good time*, I thought. *I didn't mean to go and ruin it.*

We wandered on for another half an hour, pointing out things to look at and taking pictures of said things, then using said things as the backdrop for my newly-adorned hand. When the snow resumed, and we got too cold and wet, we got back in our ride and back to the hotel. The day ran past us, and we had to find dinner before the snowfall made the roads impassible.

eleven

. . .

By the time we returned to the hotel, it was apparent we missed any outdoor dining opportunity. Yes, we probably could have gotten a ride into town; yes, my ratty Chuck Taylors and messy parka could have protected me from the elements enough, but I was exhausted anyway. We decided—together—that we could put the cold aside for another day and ordered dinner from room service. Victor ordered some monstrous burger piled high with every condiment the kitchen could offer, and I elected for the garden salad and, because our room was all-inclusive, an extra order of fries. It was the right call for sure because I mistakenly thought hotel food would be as appealing as the rooms and the decor. That was not the case.

Vic's burger was humongous and smelled like meat and grease and cheese and various tomato-based sauces. My nose and stomach could barely tolerate it. Conversely, my food was a bed of wilted iceberg lettuce with scant vegetable marbling throughout it and a single pouch of "lite" Italian dressing. The fries were baked instead of fried and only slightly better than unsalted, but at least they were something.

As I laid on the bed and nibbled on them, my eyes grew heavier, and I eventually fell asleep. I awoke to my phone song at my usual 5 a.m. and found Victor still sound asleep beside me, the profile of his face outlined in moonlight. On my other side, the plate with the remainder of my french fries sat on the bed next to my pillow. Then I realized I still had a fry in my hand. The fries weren't terribly palatable, but I promptly stuffed the one I fell asleep clutching and the others into my mouth and rose to meet the day.

The warm-hearted producers of the Dream Home Special were kind enough to pay for a few outings that Vic and I could enjoy—the catch, however, was that they'd film the entire thing for b-roll footage they could later splice into the program. The idea of being watched while I attempted to have fun was less than appealing. Still, I realized I'd most likely never have the chance to do anything like that again, so I reluctantly agreed.

Up first was a tubing adventure down the side of Mount Spokane. We knew it'd be cold, but not ten degrees cold. Our measly puffer coats and two layers of pants were hardly a bargaining chip against the weather (and here I thought my jacket and Chuck Taylors would help me). Luckily for us, though, the ski lodge carried walls of laser yellow and hot pink snowsuits at less-than-reasonable prices. Victor graciously fronted me the money (as long as I could pay his credit card bill when I got my payout), and I walked away with a neon Japanese sunset jacket and construction work orange pants. He, with his intensity and seriousness, picked the subtle electric blue with lime green stripes matching set.

At the base of the mountain, we picked up our oversized tubes and stomped through feet of snow to the cable car, where we were lifted what seemed like miles above the forest floor to our destination. The camera crew rode in the lift before us and watched our every move, listening to our every word as if I wasn't already nervous and painfully awkward as it was. The conversation felt forced between us, and we acted as much like a cute couple as we'd want to be seen as on TV as possible, but we must've appeared as robotic as we felt. Finally, after what seemed like hours, we made it to the top of the hill and proceeded to let loose.

We hopped off our car and met our tube guide, Eric, for a hopefully crash-free crash course on the mountain. Most of Eric's face was covered by lemon-yellow metallic ski goggles, but the areas exposed had grown pink and chapped in the blustery chill. Wisps of platinum blond hair crept from the back of his head to the front of his hood, and his teeth shone whiter than the snow around him. He was a total eighties ski-hunk stereotype.

Eric taught us the proper way to tube versus the improper way, which seemed funner, and I zipped down the side of the hill both ways in repetition for hours. Vic had his fill on the first two goes, and though he would never admit it, I think he felt a smidge self-conscious around Eric. He'd only look at him with a side eye when he thought no one else was looking, then puff out his puffer suit-clad chest and attempt to have a more macho air about him. He sat the rest of the trip out in the warmth of the lodge, but I wasn't about to waste my chance at a good time.

It was only after I bumped a tad too hard into a neighboring small child's tube (barely my fault) that I decided it was best to pull in for the day. I met Vic at the top of the hill, and we caught another cable car to the foot where we changed into dry clothes and caught a ride back to the hotel. After lunch, it was time to explore the Manitoba Park and Botanical Gardens.

According to the photos online, the gardens grew lush and vibrant in warmer months but became a crystal wonderland in the snow. Icicles dripped from branches, and pops of red berries dotted the perimeter. The midday sun started melting the snow, and water beads rained to the ground, creating a mushy ground covering.

"This place kinda sucks," Victor said in a hushed tone, as if not to look like a total grump on camera, as he wearily mapped each step. "Like, the mountain was okay, but this place is flat-out awful."

"Really?" I asked, shocked. "Look at the trees and the fountain. It's so romantic here."

"It's wet and cold, and the fountain isn't even working. Hardly romantic."

I couldn't help but roll my eyes and nudge his side with my elbow. "Come on, let's see what's over here," I said, guiding him down a snowy path.

It immediately became clear that Vic wasn't enjoying the outing as much as I did. His body tensed, and he nervously tapped his hands to his sides, chewing his bottom lip. He stuck it out as long as he could, which was about seven minutes, but eventually wandered back to the gift shop where his work boots and pants would stay dry. Which was for the better. It granted me the time to explore every pathway and cove in the gardens, where I collected images to post online for a couple hundred likes without the gnawing feeling that I was wasting his time. All around me, my surroundings awed me, from the glistening diamond flecks on the snow's surface to the meticulously manicured bushes and shrubs, but being alone amongst the trees made me homesick. Not necessarily for my apartment, or even Philly, but for Hippo. For Kara. For normalcy.

When my heartbreak set in, I looked around and remembered the camera crew all around me. "I think I'm ready to go back," I told them. After a few more questions and answers about how much I enjoyed the views and the snow and the contrast to life on the East Coast, we doubled back to the gift shop. There, I found a startled Victor poking away at his phone.

"I didn't realize you'd be back so soon," he said, swiping some screens away.

"Yeah, I guess I'm just tired, is all. Ready to head on out of here?"

"I thought you'd never ask," he said, pocketing his phone. "Let's blow this popsicle stand."

🐾 🐾 🐾

The roads on the way back to our room were wet and shiny at all angles from the melting snow. The temperature rose throughout the day and was unseasonably warm, according to our driver, who whirled us down the backroads to our hotel. It was quite a change of pace to have a relaxing ride, but all I wanted was a hot meal and bed. "Why so bummed?" asked Victor as I quietly stared out the window and past the trees rushing by. "You haven't said anything since the garden."

"I miss Hippo," I told him, never breaking my gaze. She'd never make me feel guilty for wanting to explore a garden or anywhere else, for that matter. "I just wanna go home."

Victor squeezed my knee, and I turned toward him. "Same."

"Really?"

"This is all just a lot. Like, I'm going to all these events with a camera in my face, and I barely get a second to myself. I am way out of my comfort zone here. So yeah, home sounds pretty good right about now." Victor rested his head against his window with a thud and sighed.

Guilt overtook me. Here I was, experiencing a once-in-a-lifetime prize and getting so wrapped up in the future that I had forgotten about Victor in the now. The whole trip had been overstimulating for both of us at various times, but he didn't bounce back as quickly as I did. The past few days had probably been torture for him. "I'm sorry," I said and touched his hand. "Are you okay? Is there anything I can do? We only have one more day until we meet with the lawyers about everything, and then we get to fly back."

Victor gave a small nod and contorted his mouth to what I thought was supposed to be a smile, then did hardly more than stare out the window for the rest of the ride. I mirrored him, watching the mountains zoom past and daydreaming about bringing Hippo back to the gardens for walkies.

twelve

. . .

Victor perked up the next morning, renewed. Perhaps a good night's sleep was what he needed to feel better; it was a big week for me, but it was equally as big for him. He proposed to me in front of all of HHTV, a feat that would shake even the most extroverted neurotypical person. Plus, there was a camera in his face for a couple of days on a divergent schedule in a strange new place. And then there was the different foods situation. Over a breakfast of less-than-stellar bagels, we made some small talk about how the bagels back east are far superior and how at least it's not hot and humid out west, and how people outside of Philly wouldn't eat at any national chain of sandwich shops if they knew what a real sandwich tasted like. Anything to skate around the elephant in the room: how I made the day before so awkward.

"Hey, I'm sorry about yesterday," I cut in after braying over a stupid foot-long joke tapered down. "You feelin' better today?"

"It's okay. And yeah, I'm fine, but I might sit some of today out if that's okay with you."

Victor had always needed more time to bounce back when he became overstimulated; sometimes, a little bit of alone time was what he needed to compose himself enough to recharge his batteries. Honestly, though, after days of back-to-back filming and bright lights and non-stop interviews, a little bit of time by myself sounded good to me, too. "Are you sure?"

"Yeah, I just don't think I can handle another day of snow right now, but you go. Don't let me ruin your fun," he said with a wink.

The producers hadn't lined anything up for us that day; in all fairness, it was a generous break before we had to meet with the lawyers about the property, which would probably be stressful and require a full day of mental preparation. *You know what*, I thought and pulled up my phone's map app, *I should have a me day; I deserve it.* Looking up small shops and eateries in downtown Spokane, I mentally plotted out a miniature self-care adventure that I could whisk myself into.

The ride to the town felt significantly shorter than the ride back the day before, likely from the absence of gravity pulling from beside me. Without Victor, I could let loose for a few hours without worrying about whether or not I was taking too long or exhausting him. Still, the absence of everything else—Hippo, Kara, the Northeast, a decent vegan cheesesteak—weighed heavily.

I pushed all that to the side, though, determined to have a good day. The warmth and sun from the day before and the temperature never dipping below freezing last night turned the snow into a slushy mush that lined the streets and sidewalks. The roads had collected charcoal globs of icy chunks that sprayed up with each passing car. I carefully navigated away from traffic to avoid an unwelcome shower and ducked into a natural pet boutique.

Inside, natural cotton rope collars and leads with polished brass clips lined a stately hunter-green wall. Baskets of toys and bones laid out a pathway along the floor that was sure to grab the attention of any four-legged customers and the wallets of the people attached to them. Somewhere toward the back of the store, the hum of clippers and the yapping of a small dog competed with New Age music.

I wandered the length of the shop, touching textures and testing durability, eventually deciding on a squeaky duck with recycled seatbelt tendrils, an extra-large pink faux-pearl collar, and a pink dip-dyed leash with rose-tinted hardware. The total came out to over sixty-five dollars, which felt like a sucker punch when the cashier asked for payment, but Hippo was worth it. Besides, I still had a few dollars to get me by until HHTV cut me a check. The cashier wrapped all my presents in paw-printed tissue paper and delicately placed them into a branded gift bag, and I was off to the next stop—a coffee shop.

Spokane had coffee shops like Philadelphia had falafel trucks. It seemed as if I only needed to take three steps before accidentally walking into one. The one I stepped into felt smaller than my apartment back home and had no tables to sit at, but it smelled of the warmest, friendliest dark roasts and buttery croissants. I ordered a hot chai with frothy oat milk and a loaf of fresh-baked pretzel bread (I couldn't say no) and left the shop to wander down the street. The doorbell tinkled behind me as I breathed in the cinnamon of my tea. I looked to either side, with the whole world ahead of me, and tried to figure out where to go and what to do next. As an introvert, I found the walk alone to be nothing short of a dream, but it wasn't the same as walking beside my best friend in the world. So, with the twenty-ounce chai in my right hand and both a bag full of dog gifts and the bakery bag full of pretzel bread on my left, I broke down and did the one thing I dreaded since leaving for Washington. I FaceTimed my mom.

"Hey, Bree," my mom greeted me with a chipper smile. "How's it going out there?"

"It's okay. The house is much prettier than I thought it'd be. But it's weird; all the buildings here are tans and greys or brick, and I haven't seen a single mural on any of them."

I looked around and thought that Vic would drool for the buildings surrounding me. For a second, I felt a pang in my chest.

"Hey—is Hippo around?"

To be fair, I did want to say "hi" to Mom and tell her I was safe, but my true reason for calling was really to see my baby.

"Yeah, let me just—" she sighed as she stood up, rocking the camera back and forth. "She's the most misbehavin'est dog I ever saw. The first thing she did when she got here was chew that rope toy you gave me into shreds. And she wouldn't let it go when Aiden tried to grab it and play fetch with her. She's a pitbull, after all. Makes me kinda afraid to keep her around the boys, really."

Like I hadn't heard that before. Every time I posted a picture of Hippo online, some random jerk always felt compelled to comment something stupid, like, "Only a matter of time until you get bit," or, "Hope your dog doesn't eat your children." I didn't even have kids.

"You know, Chihuahuas are more likely to bite people than pitbulls, right? Cocker Spaniels, too," I told Mom, angry but trying not to let her get to me. "And she'll do that with rope toys. Usually, they're reduced to scraps within the hour. She probably thought Aiden wanted to play tug-o-war with her. It's one of her favorite games."

"Well, she's a bit too aggressive for my liking." When she flipped back down to her couch, she toggled the camera to a very sad-looking Hippo. "Look, girl, it's your mama."

"Hi, baby!" I squealed when she came into view. Her head perked up a bit from the ball she'd tucked herself into, but her ears remained tucked back, defensive. "Who's a good girl?"

Hippo tucked her neck back into herself, almost as if she were cowering, and darted her eyes back and forth around the room, watching her surroundings.

"What's the matter, girl?"

"She's been like that, moping in the corner. Probably better off that way anyway. Less destructive, for sure. Honestly, this is probably the happiest she's been since you left."

I fought back tears and told Hip that I missed her. Only a couple more days and we'd be back home together.

"Thank God," Mom said, then weaseled her way back into my Dream Home. "So, how is it out there? What's the house like? Is it big enough for the whole lot of us?"

Not this again. Could it really be so hard, I thought, *for her to pretend that there were reasons other than this house or money or bills worth talking to me about?* But, unhealthy as it was, that was Mom—and the only familial dynamic we'd ever known. And, equally unhealthily, the only way I knew to respond was not to confront her head-on but instead act like the phone signal was breaking up during my response.

"It… a lot… mayb—… when I get home."

"What? I think your phone is cutting out or something. Maybe it's my phone—I can't leave the front window without it losing reception."

"Oh… I…. back later then," I said and quickly hung up.

I texted her that I'd give her all the details when I came back to Philly—it was my vacation, after all, and I wasn't about to let her suck me down any more than I already was.

Shops and bars faded past me as I meandered down one block after another. I'd catch a whiff of warm fried foods or the sounds of chatter and cutlery clinking to dinnerware behind me, but I could hardly focus on any of it. As soon as a scent or sound hit me, I'd push past it before it could hit my brain, where all of my thoughts churned an endless loop of Hippo looking so sad and Mom neglecting her, or worse. *No*, I told myself; Mom might have been a lot of things, but she was no animal abuser. But still. Maybe I shouldn't have wished she'd miss me. I should have instead wished that she and Mom would get along while I was away. Like other grandmoms and grand-dogs do. I shouldn't have been so selfish.

The stores and cafes around me all looked the same. Or, more likely, maybe I'd already seen them, and I'd been too distracted to notice. I circled the streets once more and found myself back at the same coffee shop, or maybe a doppelganger to the one I visited before, and realized that in all my pacing and attempts to run away from Mom, I hadn't once thought to check in on Victor. With a tinge of guilt pressing on my chest, I texted him to see how the morning and afternoon treated him and conjured an Uber back to the hotel. Hopefully he got his fill of alone time in my absence and could keep my mind off Hippo for a while.

When I entered the room, I heard Vic in the shower and placed my things on the kitchenette counter. The digital clock on the microwave read 3:12 p.m., too early for dinner but the perfect time to munch on some pretzel loaf. The soft pattering of shower water cut abruptly, and Victor opened the door to find me popping a hunk of bread into my mouth, which, in retrospect, probably wasn't the sexiest of looks. For a split second, his eyes widened, and he startled back. Then, he regained composure when he realized it was only me.

"I didn't realize you were here yet," he managed, and I offered him a knot, but he refused with a dismissive hand wave. "I just need to get my bearings, that's all."

"That's fine," I said and snuggled in close to his towel-wrapped hips. "But—chalk it up to my keen observation skills—I've noticed you don't have any clothes on."

Victor parried my hand. "Babe—no—I *just* got out of the shower." I must have pulled a wounded face without realizing it, though, because he quickly doubled back and said, "And I think I hurt my back when we went tubing. It's sore all along my spine."

Oh. Weird. A sore back hadn't really stopped him before, but maybe my come-hither pretzel stare was less attractive than I imagined. "Gotcha," I said, trying to ignore the sting of his rejection. "So, what do you say we take it easy then? Perhaps go into town for dinner tonight?" I asked as I studied my bread to take attention off his towel. "Take your mind off the pain. We've ordered in every night we've been here, and it'd be nice to see the city at night."

"It's going to be cold and wet out," he started but stopped when he saw me deflate a full size smaller. It beat a physical rejection, but still. I must've looked especially pitiful, however, because after a short pause and a look of contemplation, he said, "But we can go if that's what you want to do."

"That is what I want to do," I said in defense of my feelings. "Go out and have a nice date night to celebrate our engagement. Without cameras in our faces. Besides, it'll get you outta this room for a bit."

Victor smiled with tight lips and gave me an affirmative nod. "Sounds good." He snuggled his face against mine and gave me a kiss on the temple, and I warmed to my core. He might not have been the most affectionate person, but that only made moments like that feel more special. Maybe that was what bothered Kara about him so much; she just didn't understand Victor like I did.

thirteen

. . .

As the late fall sun began to set, we summoned another car—a generic, pearlescent charcoal sedan with poor heating—and rode back into town. Headlights bounced back and forth between the wet pavement and other cars, and the strings of clear lights the township had hung for the upcoming holiday season slowly warmed me from the inside. I reached for Vic's hand, and he rubbed his thumb along my knuckles as I held it. The driver's phone GPS pinged, telling us we'd arrived at the restaurant, and we hopped out onto the wet sidewalk, careful to not land in any gray snow mounds.

Past the aged stained-glass windows and evergreen flower boxes, warm yellow mood lighting showered happy, hungry patrons on what I imagined was also their date nights or maybe after-work meetups. The hostess seated us at the remaining two-top table directly beside the window front, affording us both the opportunity to people-watch as we waited for our meals: his pan-seared Alaskan halibut and my spicy ginger peanut noodles. I hadn't eaten anything with eyes (except the occasional potato) since college, and the thought of a full-bodied fried fish across the table from me had my stomach in knots, but I was determined not to let my perturbation ruin our night out. Vic smoothed his pant legs under the table and unfolded his napkin while I peered out at a middle-aged woman with cropped hair walking a sweater-clad greyhound. "I'm nervous," his leash proclaimed. "Needs space."

Me too, little guy, me too.

Back at his side of the table, Vic was playing on his phone, clicking, zooming, swiping. I tried to look at the reflection of his screen from the window but couldn't tell what he was doing. "Whatcha looking at?" I asked him, pretending to look down my nose with a raised brow.

"This workout bench and weight system," he said, showing me his phone. "Says it's on sale for two grand. Normally three," he turned his phone back and studied it again. "Seems like a good deal."

"You don't lift weights," I reminded him. In all the time we'd been together, the only time he'd ever held anything above twenty pounds was when he lugged his backpack onto the plane.

"Yeah, but that's only because I couldn't afford something like this before. I think I might start, though," he said, absorbed in his phone's glow. I cocked my head and looked off through the restraint walls. Sure, I would buy him anything to make him happy, but I hadn't even started making plans with the prize money, and I was the one who'd won it. Like, I hadn't even decided whether I wanted to keep the house. What good was a home gym without a home to put it in? And we had a wedding we had to begin planning! Caterers and venues and dresses. Not to mention all of the debt we had between us. There were countless ways we could spend the prize money, but workout gear?

I opened my mouth to ask about what sort of wedding he'd like to have when the waiter brought our drinks and first plates: chickpea fritters with curry drizzle and crispy herbed risotto balls. It snapped me out of my wedding thought spiral and caused me to contort my mouth into awkward, toothy, and closed-mouth smiles to the waiter. Victor didn't notice—I didn't think—since he hadn't taken his eyes off his phone, but he eventually pocketed it and dove into our appetizers. Had it been long enough to bring up wedding planning, or was I overthinking things again? "I don't think you need to work out or anything; you look great the way you are," I finally said after what I thought was too steady a silence and forked my food. "Like, if you want to get healthy, that's one thing, but don't think you need to get buff or anything to impress me." I smiled and looked up at him. "I think you're perfect just the way you are."

"Well, thank you. I appreciate it, but I think I'd like to put some weight on. Thicken out a bit," he said with a smile between bites. *Has he always been this self-conscious?* I asked myself. Victor always seemed so confident, or maybe he only appeared that way because of his height.

Another dog, a Border Collie, treaded the sidewalk beside us, and I nearly broke my neck following it with my eyes.

"Then again, it would be nice to have you look at me the way you look at dogs. Maybe getting ripped would help."

"Hey—" I said, pretending to be offended. "Well, if you were a dog, I probably *would* pay more attention to you." I gave him a smirk, and he rolled his eyes at me. "But I think you're plenty cute."

"Gee, thanks," he said with a lofty hint of sarcasm into his lager as he took a sip. The waiter waltzed around the restaurant floor, greeting hungry guests and delivering meals. He escorted our discarded plates away and replaced them with our main dishes of noodles and an entire fish. My golden noodles were nutty with a perfect amount of zing and heat, but it was hard to enjoy over the smell of the fish opposite me. I grimaced without intending to, and Victor forked his fish, saying, "You wouldn't have a problem with me eating fish if I was a dog."

"Dogs don't eat fish like that. You're thinking of cats," I told him, pretending not to be upset by the sight of his dinner's sunken-in eyes.

"Close enough." He must have seen how uneasy his meal made me because as soon as he finished his food, he called the waiter to take it off the table and out of my sight, to both my extreme embarrassment and relief. The waiter didn't seem offended, as a food service worker acted when they wanted to save face for a tip, but I didn't point that out to Vic. *Besides*, I comforted myself, *we'll tip the guy beyond the customary twenty percent*. Still, I apologized to the server when he brought my food back to the kitchen while Vic was in the restroom. To make sure he knew I meant it, I hid an extra ten-dollar tip under my plate and got up before Victor could get close enough to the table to see it.

"Sorry if I've been a bit grouchy this week," Vic said, breaking the quiet as we strolled aimlessly through the town. "I know I'm not the easiest person to put up with."

Truth be told, I wasn't, either. That was just life, I guessed, but it was also why Vic and I kept running back to one another. We always just *got* each other.

"This is all just a lot to take in. Flying out here, the prize, the televised engagement. It's all great, but it's a bit overwhelming."

My face turned hot, and my stomach hit my feet. I thought everything was going well, so much better than the last time we tried to work things out. "Do—do you not want to marry me?" I mustered out with tears filling my eyes.

"No! I mean, yes—of course I want to marry you." He took my hand in his and smoothed my hair behind my ear with his other. "I love you with all my heart and couldn't live without you again. It's just that the excitement from that plus everything else is eating at me." We walked a few more steps over a melting snow mound with flecks of wrappers in it and stopped at the crosswalk when he finished his thought with, "I'm sorry."

Victor lowered his head and looked away from me. He'd always been that way. When pressure built up or his day was interrupted, Vic shut down and closed everyone in his life out until he felt ready to move on. Sometimes, that took minutes, and sometimes, it took hours or more. It was something he always wanted to work on but never knew how. But recognizing that he was feeling that way was a major improvement on his behalf; if he could continue progressing, then I could stand by him in sickness and in health.

I squeezed his hand and told him it was okay. That we just needed to communicate more. That we could get through anything if we tried. Victor squeezed my hand back, then brought it to his face and pressed his lips to my palm, and we decided to head back in for an early night. Not wanting to risk yet another rejection, I showered as soon as I got in and slipped into my pajamas, then under the covers for bed, where I found Vic already fast asleep and faintly snoring.

At 2:32 in the morning, my phone chimed. High-strung and never able to fully relax, I woke up immediately from it while a peaceful Victor snoozed undisturbed. I flicked my notification and fully wakened my phone to a text message from Kara.

TODAY 2:32 AM

We need to talk.

Inside the human eye, the retina, or the inner lining, contains roughly six million cones for daytime vision and one hundred twenty million rods for night vision. With a one-to-twenty ratio, you'd think that our eyes would adjust to the dark faster than to the light, but those cones are quick. In fact, it can take up to a half hour to fully adapt to the dark and only five minutes to readapt to the light. Even the smallest amount of light from a cell phone screen can trigger our cones and wake our brains from a deep state of rest.

And that was why I couldn't get back to sleep. That and anxiety.

I'd be lying if I said I didn't think of Kara during my trip. She was probably the thing I thought the most about after Hippo while I was out there, more than the Dream Home or the adventures I was having. As much as I tried, I couldn't rid her from my head.

And as much as I wanted to be the bigger person and shoot her a text to tell her I was thinking of her, I couldn't. Not yet.

I texted her with one eye still closed.

Hey, what's up?

Can I call you?

It's 2 in the morning here.

Oh.

Sorry.

Can I call you, though?

If Kara could only be one thing, she'd be headstrong.

Fine.

I opened the sliding glass door to the hotel balcony, joining the bumpy textured glass coffee table bistro set. I didn't want to wake Victor with my call, but I certainly didn't want to risk getting my butt wet on the black wire chairs, so I stood and leaned against the balcony rail. As quickly as the message switched from pending to delivered, my phone rang, and I answered it as fast.

In a single breath, Kara unloaded.

"Listen, Bree, I talked to Liza and really thought about everything, and I don't want anything to get in between us, like, you're my best friend, and I miss you, and I shouldn't have blown up how I did, and I am miserable here without you, and I'd rather be across the country and talking than you not be in my life altogether."

My eyes stung from the cold and the emotions building up in them and I choked out, "I miss you, too." Before I could finish, both of us were sobbing on our respective ends.

"I'm sorry I got upset at you about Victor, but I want you to know it's because I've seen you hurt before, and I don't want you to ever feel like that again," Kara said, sniffling. "I'll try to trust him if you really want to marry him, but just know that I'll make his life a living hell if he does anything to you again."

I dried my eyes with my sleeve and laughed. "I don't think he will, but deal."

Over the next three hours, we smoothed out the wrinkles in our friendship as she got ready for work and took her bus in. She kept me posted on the water cooler gossip (apparently, they'd already hired and fired my replacement, and Angela got an appropriate Karen-style haircut), and I told her about my adventures around town. Kara clocked into work and promised that she'd call me as soon as she got off, and I made my way down to the lobby for the complimentary breakfast, which I snuck back in to surprise Vic with. It was going to be an important day, and I would need food in my belly to concentrate as much as possible.

fourteen

. . .

After showering and changing into the most professional clothes I packed—a thrifted, black jersey wrap dress that I used to wear out for date nights, and the well-worn pair of hot pink ballet flats I originally bought for high school graduation. I covered it all with my bulky, dirty winter coat before heading out to my chariot: a brand new, matte black-on-black Range Rover (not unlike the one from the prize package). *Soon enough, I'll be driving one of these things*, I thought to myself as I nestled into the heated seats and breathed in the fresh, new car scent. *Soon.*

Victor decided to stay back at the hotel and pack our things while I dealt with the HHTV legal team. By law, we weren't quite married (yet), and he technically didn't need to be there, which I supposed was fair. Still, I was all nerves and could have used the emotional support.

You know who's good at that? Hippo.

The hired help at HHTV dropped me off at a different hotel— one considerably less charming than the one I stayed in, at least on the outside. An attendant at the desk ushered me into a private meeting room with a garish burgundy and gold carpet and four standard-sized tables pressed together to loosely resemble a single long one. It was ugly but still prettier than anywhere I'd ever lived.

As I waited for the meeting to begin, I tapped the holey soles of my flats against the low-pile floor and looked around at everyone seated around me. A pale, heavy-set, middle-aged man in a suit; a skinnier and spray-tanned man in a suit; a lady dressed in a fine-gauge sweater over a button-down shirt as if she modeled for an old Brooks Brothers catalogue. Everyone except the lone woman in the room had a gold watch—she'd conservatively donned pearls. Self-conscious about my lack of accessories and feeling underdressed, I pulled my frayed jacket sleeves over my balled hands and shrunk as small as I could. There was Hollywood money and privilege surrounding me, judging me. I wondered how many people in the room got to where they were based on their fathers or their last names. I could never know how it felt to be born into a good family, into money, to have it easy my whole life, but I felt I was about to find out. I could nearly taste it, and it tasted like a chocolate mousse, or whatever the wealthy ate. *By the end of this meeting, I'll be rich, too*, I thought and smirked. Rich by my standards, anyway.

Twenty-eight minutes after my scheduled appointment time, the last, most flashy woman of all entered the room. Diana Attenbury—sorry, *Mrs.* Attenbury, as she instructed me to call her—was a petite woman several inches shorter than me and no more than ninety pounds, by my guess. But she was deliberate. Her suit was immaculate, a white silk with a silkier teal camisole underneath. Her raven black hair was perfectly coiffed and sharply contrasted against her fair, liver-spotted skin. The ring on her left hand looked to weigh more than she did, but her necklace and stud earrings were as dainty as herself. Her voice was soft, but her words were methodical. In the courtroom, she was probably more of a pitbull than Hippo.

After the formal greetings, Mrs. Attenbury got straight to business, prying open the gaping holes of my bank accounts and asking about my stocks, properties, and retirement accounts. None of which I had. She tapped her pen to the table for a moment, staring into my soul, and gave me the broadest terms of my winnings.

"Okay, so there are two options on the table for you. The first option is you take the house, the car, the money—but pay the taxes on it. Considering the value of the total package, you're looking at roughly 125,000 in federal taxes alone. Tack on a few more thousand for Pennsylvania and Washington state taxes, and you're out maybe a few more. Nothing to break the bank."

My heart stopped. *125,000* dollars? I couldn't afford to eat dinner some nights, and they wanted me to pay over a hundred grand? I began to feel the stinging pain of the tears starting to well in my eyes and weakly asked, "How am I supposed to collect my prize if I don't have the money?" In my head, with a full-bodied voice, I cursed Victor for leaving me in that room full of money-sucking vampires when I needed him the most. He probably couldn't have done much more than hold my hand, but at least I wouldn't have been all alone.

"Well, to collect the *house*, you need to pay that money, but you have options. Now, judging by your current financial situation, you're likely unable to pay that amount upfront, correct?" Mrs. Attenbury looked over her reading glasses toward me, and I nodded in agreement. "Didn't think so. But you can use the fifty thousand dollars in accompanying prize money to put toward it. The house is yours as long as you can come up with the remaining seventy-five by tax time next year. Or, you can take option two: a partial-sum cash out."

The more rotund-suited gentleman chimed in. "We would give you the market value of the house, the car, and the money, but pay the taxes first, leaving you to pocket about 250,000, plus or minus."

My ears rang. Two-fifty was *significantly* less than I thought, but probably still more than me, my mom and her parents had earned in our collective lifetimes.

"Now, you don't have to decide immediately," Mrs. Attenbury added. "Take your time, think things through, talk it out with your family. I imagine this is quite a difficult decision."

Quite. Potentially the biggest of my entire life, definitely the biggest up to that point. I could pack up my life and start over with Victor across the country in the quiet of the woods and maybe have the family I'd dreamt of and fought for all my life, or I could take the money and run back to the bustle of Philly, where I had Kara and Mom and murals and job security. And what if Liza really was my sister? Could I really leave the only person I knew from that side of the family on the other side of the country?

Fortunately, I could sleep on it.

The orange, fake-tanned man pushed his glasses up the bridge of his nose and began tapping at his laptop. "Typically, we expect you to have an answer for us within the month, but seeing as the holidays are right around the bend, we can extend either offer to you until January." He lifted his glasses up and pulled back from his screen, then dropped them back down his nose. "Let's say the fifteenth. Three months away from Tax Day. It'll give us all time to get back to work from vacations and let you get your financial ducks in a row." The remaining suits around the table mumbled amongst each other and nodded in agreement.

I nodded, too, but secretly, I couldn't stop thinking about how they all could afford to take vacations until the middle of January.

Everyone rose and shook hands at the meeting's close, so I eagerly leaped to my feet and did the same. I walked out feeling excited but lost—well, confused more than anything— and hopped in the hired car that pulled off the lot and back toward my hotel.

The ride and subsequent walk into the hotel lobby were both a blur. I performed mental gymnastics in my head, trying to figure out the money I didn't have and how I would spend it. I must have pressed the button to take the elevator up because the door opened before me, snapping me out of the billions of possibilities bouncing around in my head.

A quarter-million dollars to do whatever I wanted with was tempting. Still, a house of my own, especially with those mountain views, was unheard of for someone like me. And it was fully furnished—with a hot tub!—but did I want to leave Kara and Liza thousands of miles away? And what about Mom? We'd been trying to reconcile things; maybe it wasn't the best time to move away. But if I didn't take the house, where would I go? I certainly didn't want to stay in Artem's basement forever, and couldn't even if I wanted to. Before I could even finish telling him about winning the house, he listed the apartment back on Craigslist. Maybe I could gussy up my resume and apply for some jobs on the West Coast when I got back home. Or—or—maybe I could land a cushy hospital gig. *Maybe Vic and I can stay in Philadelphia and buy a duplex next to Kara! She would be so excited. But what debt should*

I pay off first? And should I buy a car? Wait a minute—how much do weddings cost? What if we just have a private ceremony in the backyard of the Dream Home? Would HHTV want to record that, too?

My mind was flooded with hundreds of questions I couldn't answer yet but hopefully would be able to soon. At least with a house, I wouldn't have to figure out where I was going. Spokane was nice, but I didn't know if it felt like home. Maybe Philly wasn't home, either. But maybe it was.

Before I knew it, I was stepping off the elevator and bumping head-on into a pretty-yet-wholly-disorganized blonde woman who appeared to be in too much of a rush to check out.

"Sorry," we said in unison as she caught the elevator down. *Watch where you're going,* I thought and rolled my eyes at no one. On the floor beside my shoe, I caught a shimmer of light. I picked up the silver hook earring with a massive, dangly, diamond-encrusted emerald and studied it, briefly debating on pocketing it. She must have dropped it, the klutz (but then again, who was I to talk?). In the end, I decided to err on the side of karma and took the next lift downstairs to the front desk, where I handed it over for the lost and found. In a few short weeks, I'd be able to buy my own gaudy jewelry.

When the elevator door opened to my floor again, I was careful not to run directly into anyone and safely got into my room collision-free. Victor greeted me with a kiss on the cheek and asked how the meeting went, and I did my best to recount all that was said.

"250,000?" Victor balked after I told him the payout option. "That is nowhere *near* a million."

"Yeah," I said in my softest, most timid voice, trying to de-escalate the situation, "but that way, we could pay any additional money come tax time next year. It may be slightly less than we thought, but—"

"Slightly less? It's a quarter of what they promised you! What can you do with two-fifty? Seriously? That can't even buy a house in the suburbs. This is ridiculous."

Normally, that was where I'd tell Victor he was right and believe it, but in that instance, it was a stretch at best. Yeah, a quarter of a million dollars was less than we expected, and yes, it'd be hard to find a house in Philly for that budget, but that was still a lot of money. Nonetheless, I knew better than to point any of that out.

"You're right."

I finished going through relaying every single detail about all my options (including the enthralling tax systems that I didn't quite understand but that helped Victor zone out and away from being angry), and before we realized, it was nearly noon and an hour past our designated check-out time. It would have been nice if the HHTV people booked us a room with a later check-out time, knowing that I'd be meeting with their legal team for the entire morning, but I guess I overstayed my welcome when I no longer had a camera crew capturing content for their channel. To my luck, though, I drew a rock to Victor's scissors, and though he was shocked and appalled by how little the payout would be comparatively, he still politely called down to the front desk people, explaining our situation with the house meeting. Graciously, they bumped our check-out time until four, but that meant we only had a few hours to make it to the airport for our red-eye back to the East Coast. Harried, we shoved all of our clothes back into our bags (and packed in a few hotel bars of soap for good measure) and managed to bid the front desk clerks farewell by two. We agreed that we would be better off arriving at the airport hours early than seconds too late. And besides, I liked the novelty of the airport. There was something about being able to get a hot tea, a good book, and a warm meal, all within inches of each other, that I couldn't do in my neighborhood.

The grass was muted and chalky, like a plastic lawn chair that had spent too many summers under the sun. Corpses of weeds grew tawny and brittle, camouflaged against dead and dying trees along chain-linked fences. The air was cold, but the smell of pollution and sewage cut straight through. Deep breath in, deep breath out. It might not have been a remote mountain town, but I was home.

Home for now, at least. I walked the remaining feet from the bus back to the stoop of my apartment just as Mom pulled up with my most precious cargo: my best friend. My Hippo. Hip missed her step when she jumped out of the car and hit the ground with a thud, but it didn't stop her from barreling into my arms. I crouched down to her level, but she still knocked me to my butt with her brute force and excitement. She wailed, and I cried, and we hugged outside on my stoop for an eternity, but it wasn't long enough. When I tried to stand, she whimpered and Velcroed to the front of my legs, dousing me in slobber and preventing me from going anywhere, especially leaving her again. I would never think to.

"Bad dog!" my mom shouted from the window of her van. "She has been nothing but trouble, that thing." Hippo skittered behind me and cowered at the back of my calves at the sound of Mom's shouting.

"It's okay, girl," I cooed and soothed her head. "Why is she acting so scared?"

"She just does that," Mom called back as if she had become some sort of Hippo expert in the week she cared for her. In all my time living with her, Hippo only ever did that in the beginning, right after I brought her home for the first time.

"Did someone hit her or something?" I asked back, my blood heating to a simmer.

"Only when she deserved it."

"She *what*? Deserved it? *Deserved it?!* How? She's a dog. *A dog!*" And a very good one at that. The best dog. And Mom thought she *deserved* to be hit? I flew into a rage—I couldn't see, couldn't hear—only lash out. Shout, curse. I picked up a loose piece of concrete from the sidewalk under me and hurled it toward her back window; I missed, but it did leave a mean dent above the gas tank. In all the thirty-four years I'd lived on the planet, Mom had managed to find a way to hurt me at every opportunity, in every possible way, but that was inexcusable. Dogs were innocent. Dogs were pure. And Hippo had nothing but joy and kindness in her heart to offer.

I had reached my breaking point with Mom. With her selfishness, with her abuse.

Sure, I could have caused her and her hoopty more physical damage, but I knew that wouldn't bring me any peace. Charges, maybe, but not peace. Instead, I told her what I should have years before, but never had the heart to.

"You need to go. Now."

"Excuse me?"

"Go," I told her. "Don't come back. I want you out of my life."

"Breanna—"

"No. I'm dead serious. I'm done being your bank account,

done being your scapegoat, done being your mistake. *I. Am. Done.*"

"You can't just go and cut me off like that. Do you know how many times I could've dropped you off with Grandma and ran away? But I didn't. I'm all you have, Breanna. Like it or not, you're stuck with me."

All I wanted to do was yell and sob, to tell her I wish she would've left me—maybe then my life would have been better—but I couldn't get any of the words out. When I tried, sounds spilled out of me like a drainage ditch. *She's not worth it,* I finally managed to tell myself and closed my eyes, drawing a long breath in through my nose and a longer breath out of my mouth. I'd stopped babbling, but Mom continued until I abruptly cut her off. "If you don't leave right this second, I'm calling the cops and reporting you for animal abuse. And it looks like you're expired," I said, pointing to the license plate on the back of her car. "That's a ticket right there. And how about your license? Did you ever get it back after that last DUI?"

"You know what, Bree?" Mom asked and turned the key to fire up her engine. "Don't you call me ever again. Or the boys. And don't even think about visiting them. You're dead to us. All of us." She peeled off, and her tires cried an ugly screech, but I could barely hear it over the thrumming in my ears.

But with that, she was gone. Forever.

My heart broke. I loved the twins, as bratty as they could be, and Mom had been my only constant all my life. For as long as I could remember, it was always my mom and I against the world. Somewhere along the lines, though, it became Mom against the world, and I was merely her means of having a fighting chance. I knew that, but I never wanted to admit it because that would mean losing the only semblance of family

I'd ever known. But that was not how family was supposed to be. And now I was nothing to her.

The war drums beating in my ears slowly quieted, and the tunnel around my vision expanded past the periphery. The events of the last minutes, hours, and days had all been so much, and suddenly, I felt like I was back at the beginning, navigating the world alone. But I had my dog—my true family—back, and for that, I was on top of the world.

fifteen

. . .

It was already afternoon by the time I settled into the apartment. With Hippo on my lap and a belly full of peanut butter, she had calmed down, letting her tensed muscles relax. I thought to call Victor to tell him all about Hippo and how she'd been treated while we were away, but he had always liked Mom, and the last thing I wanted to hear was him making excuses for her. So I did what I always did when I couldn't turn to him and texted Kara instead, letting her know that I both got home safely and was cutting Mom out of my life. Again. For good that time.

TODAY 1:19 PM

OMG, is Hippo okay? Do you want me to slash her tires for you?

No, she'd probably suspect it was me anyway.

Although I thought the last thing I needed was a lecture from Victor about Mom, the *truly* last thing I needed was for the police to show up on my doorstep.

In between unpacking and daydreaming, we exchanged more messages about how I wouldn't be leaving Philly, not immediately, anyway, and about how much work sucked. In just a few short weeks, I'd either have a house she and Liza could crash at, or I would have enough money in my account to no longer have to worry about bills and still wouldn't mind helping her with hers.

> It might be less money than I thought I'd get, but more than I have now. It's still a lot of money.

> With all your loans and stuff paid off, you can probably quit Franklin Family forever.

> If you decide to stay here, that is.

> Maybe you can get back into photography or something. Make your own studio and do wedding pictures around the city. I'm sure Liza would build a website for you.

Kara's message gave me pause. Could I do that? Like, was making a living on pictures something I could actually do? With no one stopping me?

> Who was stopping you before?

> I couldn't afford to.

> Why not? Because you didn't think you could do it, so you played it safe and got a job? How did that turn out?

No one asked Kara to philosophize with me so hard, but she brought her A-game to the chat. I knew she wasn't attacking me, but I couldn't help but feel wounded. I suppose there was some truth in what she said. After the moment it took for me to process that wake-up call, I responded back.

What's been stopping you?

A text message Uno Reverse card.

It was her turn to stop and think about it. I finished emptying out my backpack and turned on my hot plate to boil water for tea. With a cup in my hand, I opened Creatr and overhauled my feed to curate only my best photography. *Edit, archive, delete.* A notification from Kara dropped from the top of my phone.

TODAY 1:54 PM

I guess it's just me.

Before I could respond, my email app notified me of the news: Hippo's DNA screening was completed. I clicked through the login info and found the genetic secrets of my baby girl—one hundred percent American Pit bull Terrier, which explained her signs of early breeding. I scrolled through lists of potential relatives, and how inbred she was (a lot, apparently), and something called a "wolfiness factor" and found the breed-relevant health conditions results. At first glance, Hippo looked like the picture of pitbull health. Still, a closer inspection revealed a lone genetic mutation amongst the pack. *PRA-crd1.* I clicked the link to learn more, and my heart sank. Because her parents were likely closely related, she'd inherited two copies of a broken gene, the *crd1*, or the mutation that caused progressive retinal atrophy. Those cones in the eye? The ones that provided our central vision and helped us see in the daylight? Hers were degenerating at a rapid rate. According to the website, dogs with that diagnosis would likely be completely blind by age two. I looked down at my dog and back to the phone. All the bumping into walls, her inability to catch the food I dropped her, her giant, dilated teddy-bear eyes.

Hippo was going blind.

No.

No, no, no, no, no.

I refreshed the page over and over to see if it was some kind of mistake. A glitch in the website's coding. Maybe I'd logged into some other dog's account by accident. The results never changed. Then I triple-checked vet websites to see what I could do to help her and how to save her sight, and got the same outcome: there was no known cure for that form of blindness. Nor was there anything available to slow its progression. When I couldn't take that as an answer, I checked her results page again, but the mutation never budged. There was nothing I could do to help her.

She didn't know why I began sobbing—she couldn't have—but that never mattered. As she always would, Hippo walked over, brought her head close to mine, and bathed my face with kisses while sitting in my lap like the lap dog that she was. I held her tight, apologized like she would understand, and told her that I would never give up on her, but she couldn't care less. She was just happy in my arms.

I called Kara, apologized for leaving her hanging, and told her the news. Hippo was her fur-niece, and she loved that dog as if she were her own, but still had enough space to look at the situation rationally.

"I know it's not news anyone would want to hear about their dog," she began, "but think about how lucky she is to have someone like you to take care of her. Plus, this seems like all the more reason to start your own photography biz. You can be your own boss, and no one can tell you that you can't bring Hippo to work. Plus, you can do that here, there, anywhere."

"You're right," I said, sniffing up tears. "Yeah. It's not like she's dying or anything, but I hate that she has to go through this. It's not fair."

I looked down into my lap at Hip's big, meaty face and scratched the rolls of skin around her jaw.

"She's already had to go through so much."

"Then it's settled. Start building up a photography portfolio and getting your name out there." Kara paused, drew an "uh" a second longer than comfortable, and found her words. "All this talking about you and Victor getting married has got me thinking about weddings, and I was thinking of proposing to Liza. I'd love it if you would, maybe, take the proposal sh—"

"Oh my God, of course I would!" I squealed into my phone and sniffed the remaining tears away. "It's about time, if I may add. You guys are perfect for each other. God, Kara, I'm so happy for you two!"

And I was. Sincerely. Part of me felt even happier for her engagement than mine, in a weird way. Aside from that bit of friction we held between us before I left for Washington, we'd never gone a single day without some form of communication since we met on campus. Kara and Liza deserved to be happy together. Plus, with both of us engaged, we could help plan each other's weddings, scope out venues together, and schedule tandem tastings. Be each other's maids of honor.

"Thanks, and I'll pay you—"

"No, you certainly won't," I cut her off. "First of all, I'm rich now; second, I *want* to do this for you guys. Besides, I know how much money you make at Franklin—you couldn't afford me," I joked. "But speaking of, do you think you're gonna stay there? Do you see yourself checking vitals and cleaning up after people forever?"

"I truly think I want to stay in health care," Kara said after mulling it over. "I want to help people, but I don't think I can keep doing what I'm doing. Not if the office doesn't make some drastic changes."

"Good luck with that," I said, rolling my eyes as if Kara would be able to see it through the phone.

One of the things I loved most about her, aside from how our conversations could jump from thought to disorganized thought in a matter of seconds, was how optimistic she could be, even in the most dire of situations. Me, not as much.

"Unless you can get the doctors on board, I don't see any changes in the foreseeable future."

It didn't used to be so bad at Franklin Family. We started out hopeful and full of compassion. After we graduated, all Kara and I wanted to do was help people. Have some sort of meaningful impact on people's lives. It was hard to pinpoint exactly where it all went wrong—when we stopped loving what we did—but I knew it happened sometime after a change in management began whittling down the office budget and replacing medical assistants when staff quit.

Kara paused a moment and thoughtfully whispered, "You're right," before rushing off the phone to make some calls.

I looked at the clock on my phone and realized it was nearly time for dinner, so I called Victor to ask him out. When his voicemail message began, I hung up and decided that ramen and peanut butter at home with Hippo was better than any fancy dinner anywhere else anyway.

sixteen

. . .

After a full night's rest and a hearty breakfast of the remaining steel-cut Irish oats I'd had sitting in a tin on a shelf for at least a year, I reluctantly called Angela to ask for some hours over the coming weeks.

"I'm not sure yet how long I'll still be in the city," I told her and fidgeted with the loose strands of hair that escaped my messy bun, "but it'll be until mid-January, at the very least."

"Oh, Breanna, I'm sorry," she said, her voice nasal and condescending. "I thought you would reach out to me last week about this. When I didn't hear from you, I thought that meant you were moving on from the practice. I've already filed all the paperwork and—"

My back stiffened straight. "Wait, wait, wait. Angela, I was in Washington filming for the Dream Home Special all last week. I told you this. You can't just fire me out of nowhere. I didn't do anything."

"You didn't, and that's the point. I was expecting to hear from you and waited all week for a response. I'm sorry."

My heart raced, swerving out of control, trying to avoid crashing into a wall. "Well, can't I just get my old job back? Do you want me to submit a new application somewhere?"

"No, I'm afraid we aren't hiring right now, unfortunately. Maybe check back in after the New Year, but the office is slow for the winter. You know how it gets around here."

Of course I knew. I'd faithfully worked there for over seven years.

If Angela punched me directly in the gut, it would have hurt less. For the greater part of a decade, my life revolved around Franklin Family. Overtime, no holidays off, no vacations, no sick days off. I kept a perfect attendance, and that was how the office repaid me. I sighed into the microphone.

"Will I at least get my sick and vacation bank paid out?"

"First of all," Liza told me through our video call, "you spelled your name wrong."

"Again?" I asked and looked at the heading of the document. "Sometimes, when I type too fast, I skip the second 'n.' There."

I added the letter back into my first name where it belonged and let Liza read some more.

"I do it all the time, too," she said, deep in thought. "I cannot tell you how embarrassing it is to e-sign a document as 'Lia.' Like, that can't leave a good first impression on an employer."

When she wasn't designing websites for local businesses and fellow freelancers, she helped desperate people in desperate need curate their resumes for a desperate fee. As a low person in lower places, I was the perfect client for her, and, out of the goodness of her heart, she agreed to help me for free (not that I didn't offer to pay her at least something).

Half an hour had passed since I began sharing my screen with her, pruning my excess words and feats when we got to what I felt was my greatest pain point: my useless degree.

"Do you think I should keep my associate's in there? Like, do you think it's necessary?"

"If you're applying for a position that could carry over those skills, I'd say yeah, keep it."

I thought for a moment. "I guess I'll keep it. In case a medical photographer position opens somewhere."

"Sounds good to me." Her eyes shifted side to side on my laptop screen as if carefully inspecting an intricate painting. "You misspelled 'bachelor's,' second line from the bottom, but aside from that, I think it's good."

"I bet. I always spell that word wrong."

She leaned back into her chair with a laugh. "Same."

After we combed through the entirety of my work history, adding here and subtracting there, I made up a half-dozen employee accounts on various job boards, all reflecting the same info I painstakingly wrote out with Liza (why make me enter it if you were just going to ask for my resume anyway?) and proceeded to apply for every medical assistant position available in or around Spokane. Even if I didn't have a chance. Medical photographer, cushy university hospital job, medical photographer at a cushy university hospital. I left no applicable stone unturned.

The following day, my last paycheck, which included a healthy payout from the months and months of accumulated paid time off that I'd never found myself able to use, hit my bank account, and it couldn't have come any sooner. My reserve from the check before dwindled in Spokane, and all the talking with Kara and Liza about photography had my brain hyper-fixating on everything cameras: a professional-grade Canon, reflectors, filters, bags, straps, backdrops. All the equipment needed to make an at-home photography studio. I compiled a master shopping list online and let it sit in my cart; if I awoke the next day and still wanted everything, I told myself it was meant to be. That money needed to last until I could find a new source of income, which, with Liza's help, would hopefully come sooner rather than later. But, after a measly half hour of combing wedding vendors and dropping a couple grand on flower and catering deposits, I convinced myself that an investment in a camera was an investment in myself and, potentially, in my career (what if any future employer wanted to see my work?). So, I bought it all.

Now, I just needed a home to put a studio in.

I spent days and weeks scouting real estate websites for hours at a time, clicking through short-term rental after short-term rental in the city within my non-existent budget, and made the shocking realization that my limited funds and underemployment weren't compatible with any self-respecting landlords in the city. That is unless I didn't mind living beside some turn-of-the-century factory producing terrible-smelling carcinogens or next to a crack den. At least I had a wealth of boxes to open and distract myself with.

"Wait, wait, wait," Victor said, jumping up from leaning on my dresser, thumb and forefinger rubbing his brows. "Back it up. Did you just say you got your final paycheck and spent all your potential rent money on photo equipment?"

"I mean, not all of it," I said, sitting cross-legged on the floor with all my new gear and the cardboard packaging they arrived in fanned around me in a semi-circle, "but I got a great deal off for Cyber Monday."

"That's all well and good, but how are we supposed to live until we get a house? You don't have a job right now. Like, I just reduced my hours at work, and you're spending money you don't even have on, what, *cameras*? I'm going to have to go back full time, and I'm never going to leave that hellhole, and I—"

"No-no-no, it's okay. Maybe I can set up my photo stuff and start getting my name out there online for—"

"And where are you going to set it all up?" He threw his arms into the air in frustration. "We don't have a place to live yet, Bree. Unless you're thinking about living out of all these boxes, which is practically all we'll be able to afford unless we pack up and move across the other side of the freaking country." Victor crossed his arms tight as if hugging himself. "My old roommate already got another renter lined up after I took my stuff to my parents'. Am I going to have to stay with them forever now?"

I knew his question was rhetorical, and I could have pointed out that we would have a place to live if I accepted the house in Washington, but I instead rubbed my hand on his calf and told him, "It won't be for long, it's just a hiccup. We'll get through this, I promise."

He held his head up and met my gaze. "Where are you going to go, then?"

I knew that his parents weren't the fondest of me and that they'd never let me move in with Victor in their house, not until we'd officially tied the knot, but that didn't dull the sting any. And I didn't have an answer. My security deposit only paid my rent until the end of the year, and if the last few weeks of December were anything like the past two months, the thirty-first would catch me fast. My landlords reminded me almost daily that New Year's Eve was quickly approaching, that I had to get my affairs in order and clean the floors before I left, and that they had a new tenant lined up to move in immediately after I left. *Are they moving the guy on New Year's Day or something?* I thought, but I never asked. They only cared about getting their rent money; God forbid they skip a month. Besides, it didn't change the fact that they were giving me no wiggle room in the matter.

"I don't know, but I'll think of something."

He huffed and puffed, but eventually, and after suggesting maybe I could stay with Kara, who he knew hated him, Victor left my apartment without blowing it down. I mean, I understood his frustration; if I could, I would've up and left that place, too. But since I had nowhere else to go, I'd have to stay in that moldy, musty basement with all of my new toys until I could devise another plan. And then I got an email.

Good morning, Ms. Huxley.

I saw your application and would like to set up a call to

talk to you a little more about the medical photographer position.

"Holy crap," I said to Hippo. "I think I scored a job interview for Spokane." I scrolled down to the end of the email and saw the company. The cushy university I coveted.

"This calls for a celebration, girl." She didn't pay me any mind and continued lying across my lap but stirred when I shimmied out from under her. With her leash in hand that I'd plucked from the doorknob, I hooked Hippo up to her harness and texted Kara.

TODAY 11:32 AM

Good news. Meet me at Front Street?

I sent the text as I slid my arm into my hoodie, first catching on the hood, then forcing my way into the sleeve. I tied the laces of my Chuck Taylors, and my phone binged.

Oh, totally.

🐾 🐾 🐾

It was an unseasonably warm late-autumn day. Spring-like, even. My phone said it was a mild sixty-eight degrees, and the vibrant blue sky was completely cloudless. We sat on the restaurant's outdoor patio, Hippo sprawled out at our feet. The waitress rounded with our drinks and our shared plate of buffalo cauliflower bites, which Hip was all too keen on trying to exploit from us.

"I got an email from a university hospital. They want to interview me over the phone for a medical photographer job."

"What? That's great!" Kara said, squealing and clapping her hands in excitement. "When is the interview?"

"Tomorrow. Later in the day, though, because of the time difference. Which sucks because I won't want to do anything before the call to make sure I don't miss it." I sighed.

"That's fair. Oh! Before I forget, Ms. Rowe came back for a follow-up yesterday," Kara said, unfurling her cutlery from a black cotton napkin. "She told me to say 'hi' to you."

"Oop—that's a HIPAA violation," I joshed and let Hippo lick a dollop of dressing off my finger, "but I won't tell on you."

"Gee, thanks. Appreciate that," Kara said as she sipped her Cinnamon Dolce Frappuccino. "Oh, and I thought about what you said about getting the doctors on board, and I talked to the docs at work. Turns out they aren't really happy with how things are either. Dr. Nguyen said she'll bring people in to conduct an audit to see if we could stand to hire some new MA's."

I dunked the bag of Earl Grey into my cup of hot water and blew the steam off the top. "Really? Why couldn't anything cool like that happen when I was still there?"

"If it's any consolation, I think it took you going for everyone to really crack. They still never filled your old position—it's crazier there than ever."

"She told me you guys weren't hiring anymore." I sat back in my chair and chewed on the thought. "You know, I called her and begged for my job back. She said the office was slow, and I wasn't needed anymore." *Why would she tell me they weren't hiring if the practice desperately needed the help?* I asked myself. Maybe Angela didn't want to replace me because she thought I'd grown lazy. But that didn't make any sense. She abused me for so long *because* I was such a hard worker. Aside from the doctors, Kara and I were the only people who showed up because we cared about patients. Everyone else who clocked in only did so for a paycheck and maybe a reason to get away from their less-than-glamorous home lives that they incessantly complained about in the breakroom. I mean, my home life wasn't glamorous, but—

"Bree. You're zoning out," Kara said, pressing her face into my vision. "Hello, Breanna. Did you hear what I just said?" I looked Kara in the face, then followed her neck and arm down to her hand and then toward the direction her finger was pointing.

seventeen

. . .

"Hey!" I shouted from my tippy-toes at the edge of the patio, and in my best (yet still terrible) cowboy western voice added, "Whatcha doin' 'round these parts?"

Victor had just begun crossing over to my side of the street when I caught his attention and, from what I could tell, I'd also caught him off guard. He looked as if he'd showered and shaved since I last saw him, and he was as handsome as I remembered him from when we first met. Tall, bronzed, perfect posture. Dressed in a button-up with the sleeves rolled up past the elbow, a look that always got me to purr. "I was just going across the street to meet up with some guys from work. What are *you* doing here?" he asked with a tip of his head to the bar at the intersection, then turned back to flash the most charming smile at me.

"Just having brunch with Kara." I leaned back to let him see her waving. Hippo jumped up at the chest-height fencing, resting her paws on the wrought iron railing, and let out a resounding *boof*. "And Hippo."

"Hey, girl." Victor gave Hippo a faint wave and Kara a two-finger salute off the side of his temple. "Well, I have to run, but I'll text you later. Promise." He gave me a peck on the cheek, and the woody spice from whatever cologne he'd sprayed himself with left me in a stupor.

> *Of all the key senses—sight, sound, taste, touch, and smell*
> *—it is the last that is closest linked to the memories we hold.*
> *The ear, nose, and throat physician who'd host a clinic on*
> *Tuesdays once told me that this was because the olfactory*
> *signals travel to the limbic system the quickest. That's why the*
> *smell of a vinyl decoration at the dollar store can instantly*
> *transport you to being four years old and swimming at the*
> *public pool on an inflatable tube.*

That's why, when I inhaled that cloud of Victor, my brain took me back to the night we walked around Old City in the dark, pointing out all the pieces of history that we lived around and took for granted. The Betsy Ross House. Independence Hall. The Liberty Bell. The night when he asked if I'd officially be his girlfriend. If I could forever live in that scent, and in that moment, I would.

I held my eyes closed, breathing him in, but when I opened them again, he'd already jogged across the way to meet with his buddies at the taphouse, and I floated back to my seat across from Kara.

"Did you tell him you were coming here?" Kara asked me as she finished her drink and dried the corners of her mouth with a napkin. I didn't, confirming it by combing through my texts after second-guessing myself. "Hmph. Weird." Maybe for some, but it seemed pretty on par for us. We were just aligned like that.

"So," Kara said without direct eye contact, "you want to come ring shopping with me? My weather app calls for this warm stretch to last until this weekend, but the cold and rain return Monday." We sorted loose bills from our wallets and pockets to settle our check, then, after straightening the cash into an orderly pile, she said, "I think I want to ask Liza on Saturday."

"That's so exciting!" I said and readied Hippo for our ride back to the apartment. "Let me take Hip home, and then we can go." We packed Hippo into the backseat of Kara's school bus, a yellow Subaru Outback, and Kara hopped in the front beside me. She looked around to make sure it was safe to pull out, lingering a second longer for a few cars to pass, which let me scan the street for any signs of Victor, but he had already gone inside. I thumbed the band of the rectangular, gray spinel solitaire on my left hand and asked, "What kind of ring do you have in mind?"

"I dunno. Liza isn't super fancy, but I want her to know I really put some thought into it." She chewed on her bottom lip and picked at her nail bed. "Nothing too big or crazy, and not a diamond. Something more personal, like something that no one else would have. And colorful. It should be pretty and joyful, like her."

I slid my hand in between my thighs to hide my gray solitaire from view. "We should go to one of those places on Jeweler's Row that sells old estate jewelry then. Maybe find some with some history or character. She'd probably love that."

"Oh, my God, Bree. That's perfect," Kara clapped and perked up to the wheel so quickly that it startled Hippo from her nap in the back. She settled back into a ball, but by the time she got to snoring again, we were pulling up to the apartment to drop her off. I told her we wouldn't be too long and to be a good girl, and then I rode with Kara to Center City in search of baubles.

We weaved in and out of shops, skirting the higher-end stores —the ones with the smarmy radio ads that *someone* must find amusing (otherwise, they wouldn't have made them, right?)

—and dipped into the smaller, more charming shops with boxes of estate costume jewelry or mechanical watches bursting from every wall and counter. Every piece had a life and a story, any one of them fit for a queen. Liza wore a six-and-a-half, which, as an act of fate, happened to be the same size as me, making the shopping experience that much easier for us. I removed my engagement band and pocketed it, then modeled ring after ring for Kara; they all looked magnificent on my finger, jubilant and gleaming, but nothing seemed good enough to her.

Nothing, until we saw *it*.

Kara was studying a case of brightly-colored gems when she spotted it. A slender yellow gold band adorned with three enameled daisies, each with yellow stamens and ombre petals. Carnation pink, lavender, and aqua. Light twirled around the ring, bouncing off each surface, making it hard to believe that it contained exactly zero stones. The man behind the counter handed it to Kara, who turned and slipped it onto my finger, and clasped her hands to her mouth. "I'll take it."

The jeweler pressed the ring into a midnight purple velvet box and placed the box into a small vellum bag with sheer ribbon handles. Kara vibrated as she handed over her cash in exchange for the only ring she saw fit for the woman of her dreams, and for an instant, I felt my skin and throat and chest tighten. Then, a flood of guilt washed over me. Kara had always sparked twinges of jealousy in me during the time I'd known her—her beauty, her level-headedness, her ease of talking to people—but those were also the reasons I loved her. At that moment, however, Kara stirred a jealousy in me that I couldn't explain, and I felt wrong for it.

I blinked away a wink of sadness and forced a smile for her. Kara was happy, and I was happy for her. And Liza. And their new life together. Kara took the bag by the handles and looked at me with her brows raised and toothy smile. "I'm actually doing this."

"You are," I said and squeezed her arm.

Bag in hand, I pushed my feelings down to my stomach, and we walked back to the car—it was Kara's time, and I had no right to sully the mood. She turned the ignition, and I turned my attention back to Kara, asking, "Do you know where you'll propose to her?"

"I was thinking about the Magic Gardens on South Street. It's where she took me on our first date, and it's super pretty and bright and probably great for photos."

"Aw, cute." I wiggled my butt into the front seat to get comfortable as she drove past Old City and asked me where Victor had taken me for our first date. *Was it that diner in New Jersey? Or was that our second date?* I couldn't remember, but it certainly wasn't the Gardens. "I've only seen that place from the sidewalk. What's it like inside?"

"You've never been inside? Oh my God, dude, it's so beautiful, especially when the sun shines. All the glass and mirror mosaics sparkle and cast rainbows everywhere, and it feels like you're in a fairy world."

"It sounds like it," I said and shrank down inside.

We drove through the 6th Street Bridge Underpass, my first time doing so since it'd been changed from a tower of bleak gray cement walls to an electric mural with neon lights that bounced light off the painted facades. The lime greens and hot pinks made my chest flutter, and I realized that there was so much of the city that I'd never even seen.

"Maybe I'll check it out with Victor sometime," I said, hopeful, although he probably wouldn't enjoy it as much as I would. He never liked South Street much. *I could probably convince him to go,* I thought, *if we make a day of it and check out the Christ Church Burial Grounds on 5th Street.* Toss some pennies at Ben Franklin's grave; he loved doing that.

Kara gave me a tight squeeze and dropped me off out front of the apartment as the sun made its final goodbye under the horizon. I took Hippo out for a walk under the streetlights, but cut it short. My head throbbed from thinking too much about everything, and I just wanted some dinner.

We rounded back home, past the glow of the falafel truck's flashing marquee light board and past the overhead halogen lamps of the twenty-four-hour gas station with the pothole-riddled sidewalks, and Hip and I settled into our jug of peanut butter. I nestled into my bed and texted Victor about my adventures in ring shopping, then the dream list of date ideas that I thought about during my commute home.

TODAY 7:31 PM

All of this sounds expensive. Like, all of it.

Yeah. I guess you're right.

eighteen

. . .

Victor forgot to text me after he got home but remembered the next morning.

TODAY 9:13 AM

I crashed in bed as soon as I got in. But I have a bit of good news.

Apparently, he got to talking with his coworkers about needing to work again, and they offered him more hours at his old job on the train.

In the meantime, some of the boys lined up various odd jobs here and there for me.

That's great!

Yeah, but unfortunately, my schedule is crammed. I probably won't be very available for anything until the weekend. But maybe we can plan something for Saturday?

Yeah. For sure.

But that was fine. Seriously. I had an interview to get ready for, anyway.

I spent the next several hours alternating between preening and pacing. After I'd walk the distance between the washer and my bed a few dozen times, I'd step into my cramped bathroom and tweeze out stray eyebrow hairs, then walk Hippo around the block and return to plucking my upper lip, then back to marching the apartment floor. Around 1:30, I decided to shower and dress into something presentable, even though my interview was over the phone, and sat on my bed beside my charging cell until my call at 3:30.

Even though I did nothing but prepare for the call all day, the ring of my phone sent me into a tailspin. *Should I have studied or something? What if I come off as weird or, worse, annoying and weird?* I let the phone ring a second longer, breathed in deep, exhaled deeper, and then answered the call as if I hadn't just avoided a panic attack and was a carefree, normal individual.

"Hello? Oh, hi! This is she."

Luckily, the manager, Dee, and I hit it off immediately. We both loved photography and dogs and a good falafel. We spent more time talking about ourselves than the job at hand, it seemed, and when it came to my credentials, Dee told me I was more than qualified for the position, even without necessarily working with her equipment.

"We typically train employees on-site, but it sounds like you already have a pretty good idea of how to work the camera."

"That's great," I said, delving into my imaging history before my recent camera purchase. "And whatever I don't know, I'd be willing to learn."

"That is exactly what we want to hear here." She paused and giggled at her rhyme. "Hear-here. I was a poet and didn't even know it."

I could already imagine the difference between Dee's office and Angela's, and I liked it. A lot.

"Sorry, we're all a bit silly here. Anyway, we've had a few photographers in the past who refused to adopt new technology, which we simply can't do in this day and age. There's some software that I wouldn't expect you to have any experience with, but it's point, shoot, upload, and send to patients' charts. If you can work a DSLR, you already know at least half of the role. Really, your background as a medical assistant is more of a bonus at this point."

Inside, I wanted to squeal. Excitedly, I bounced around on my bed, wiggling my butt into its seat. That almost didn't feel real. Until, that was, she asked the most important question.

"So, when would you be available to start?"

My heart dropped to my stomach. As much as I wanted the job, it never felt attainable, yet here Dee was, asking when I could begin training.

"Oh, well—that's the thing. I don't think I'll be able to start for a couple months." Although I was telling her about my predicament, everything came out more as an unsure question. "As crazy as it sounds, I actually won a house close to the hospital, but I think I won't be able to claim it and move in until... mid-January?"

After a brief silence on the line, I quickly backpedaled and tried to keep the job offer.

"But maybe I can try to find a place to live in the meantime, you know, before I can get the house permanently—"

"Did—did you just say you won a house?"

"Yeah," I said nervously, "the big, annual HHTV Dream Home contest. I can show you all the emails if you want. I swear I'm not making this up."

After the words left my mouth, I wondered if saying that explicitly made me seem like I was actually making things up.

"Let me put you on hold for a moment," Dee said and clicked me over to peaceful Muzak.

I waited with my phone pressed between my ear and shoulder, picking at my nails. Peeling, chewing, peeling, chewing. After about thirty seconds or so, Dee returned to the line with a boisterous laugh.

"Oh, my God. Breanna. I just looked up an article about the contest, and your name is all over it—that is out of this world!" she nearly yelled.

"Yeah, it's been crazy, to say the least." I nervously chuckled at her excitement. "So, does this mean I can still join you guys come in a couple months?"

The job wasn't mine—not yet—but I wasn't out of the running, either. Dee needed a photographer for the very near future and had a few more people to interview, but said that I could still get a call in the coming weeks. Either way, I was pumped. I could feel a big change coming. Now, all I had to do was play the waiting game, which would surely be a drag. At least, I thought it would. And, for the first afternoon there while I waited, it appeared as if I thought right.

Since I'd packed all my belongings into a few sad-looking cardboard boxes that lined the wall where my books used to rest, it felt less homey than ever. The trip out west and my subsequent spending spree tore through days on my calendar, and before I could catch up, I found myself nearly broke and mere days away from the solstice. I only had a couple weeks to finalize my decision, and without a car to drive around the city, locating a new apartment for my short stay before transitioning was more difficult than I cared to admit. It wasn't exactly like I could ride the train and pull over when I saw a "For Rent" sign. My best bet was to turn back to the internet for sketchy places with subpar living conditions, but I couldn't think of anything I'd wanted to do less. Instead, I did what I did best: ignored my problem and hoped it would clear up on its own.

And it worked, sort of. I flipped on Creatr to post an artsy-looking picture of Hippo resting in a sunny spot, dust motes dancing around her head. I stayed online to scroll endlessly until I saw it: mixed between photos of my friends from college and a few influencers who always made me feel worse about myself (and life choices) than usual popped a video of a guy and his brown brindle pitbull in front of a gorgeous ocean sunset. "Home is where the dog is," the caption read. At first, I blew it off as meaningless social media drivel, some influencer thinking he was a deep philosopher, passing himself off as a mystic. Still, after scrolling down a few more photos, I flipped back to it and clicked on his profile. Maybe it was the cute dog, maybe it was the pink and blue hues over the turquoise ocean, but I needed to see more. On his page were photos of the duo living their best lives at countless locations. Big cities, small towns, lake views, mountainsides. A video several rows down gave viewers a glimpse of the inside of his Chevy Tahoe, which he made into a traveling home. When he opened the hatch to let his dog hop into the back, he incidentally revealed his hot plate on a piece of plywood. I looked to the corner of my apartment, where all my possessions sat, then back to the video, then back to the corner with my hotplate right on top, as if it were asking me, "Are you thinking what I'm thinking?" I looked back at the video, then to Hippo, with her dinner plate eyes, which would soon lose the remaining glint of their vision.

"I sure am, hotplate."

I flipped off the internet and called Vic to tell him my plan—with the money I had left, I would buy a cheap car, pack our lives up, and take Hippo on a road trip. In our travels, I'd give her the adventure of a lifetime while she could still see and decide where exactly I would like to call home. I wouldn't have much money left in my account, but I figured I'd have enough to gas up for a few weeks and see a few sights.

"Babe, I know you get impulsive, and I think that's great—it's one of the things I love about you—but you should probably think this one through more. I'm returning to work next week, so I can't even go. And what happens if you run out of money while on the road? Then where will you go? Do you just live in your car forever off the side of the freeway? You don't even have a car yet, and you already think you'd be okay living out of it?" He stopped briefly, only to draw a big, authoritative breath. "It's definitely not the responsible thing to do, that's for sure."

I sighed into the phone. It did sound like a silly idea when he spelled it all out like that, but it didn't make me deflate any less. And now, I *definitely* didn't want to tell him about the job interview I scored for Spokane.

"Look, I'm sorry. Like, I thought we had the whole money and house thing figured out, and now we don't have either, and we're up against a wall. The whole thing is really stressing me out."

Maybe that was what had been bothering me, too. After the whirlwind month of dating, winning, proposals, decision-making, and changing careers, I suppose I got myself into a bit of a funk. No stability, no calm, no clear answers on anything when I should've had it all figured out. No wonder the steady trajectory of Kara's life made me a tad jealous.

"It's okay," I told him. "I know exactly what you mean."

"Hey, maybe we *should* go out this next weekend. Maybe not a whole weekend on the road, but get out and explore the Center City like you want. Take our minds off the money for a bit and try to restore some normalcy."

"Yeah," I said and smiled. *Maybe Vic and I can have what Kara and Liza have after all.* "That sounds wonderful. I'll work it out with Kara, too. Maybe after I finish with her proposal pics, I can meet up with you for an early dinner or something."

"That sounds great," Victor replied, and I could hear him smiling, too. "We can always go back to T-Mom's, then maybe check out the pier and get some ice cream."

Sometimes, the man just knew what words I needed to hear.

❄ ❄ ❄

Hippo and I spent the remaining portion of the week enjoying the warm front while it lasted, taking our daily walks and scoping out houses with rental signs. I certainly felt like leaning toward Washington, but I couldn't dream of leaving Victor out in Philly and moving there if he didn't want to. So, I looked for his sake. But by Saturday, I had covered every street in the neighborhood and the surrounding neighborhoods and then some more. The only home that didn't look like a complete gut job was several times over the amount of rent I could afford. *At least I tried*, I told myself. And I got to explore the city a bit more than I ever had time to previously, taking photos and building up my personal portfolio. A win in my book.

Moments before noon on Sunday, I caught a series of buses and trains down to South Street to meet with Kara and Liza. The rides were filled with their usual cast of characters: the woman assembling a hoagie on her lap from a plastic grocery bag of loose deli meat, the dozens of speakerphone people speaking loud enough to hear over the passengers next to them, a man hiding a raccoon in his jacket who made eye contact with me and raised a finger to his pursed lips as if to say, "Let's keep this little secret between us."

That's it, I told myself, Monday morning, I'd march down to the used car lot on the corner and throw a chunk of cash on a set of cheap wheels.

When I got to the Gardens, I pointed out to Liza that I brought my camera along to build up my portfolio so she wouldn't be too suspicious, which, if it were me and my thought spirals, probably would have raised my suspicions higher. "I'm trying to get back into photography," I backpedaled. "As a job." *Smooth.*

"Right. But didn't you already get that job in Spokane?"

"Not yet. I just had my phone interview. It could go either way," I said and held up my camera. "Besides, I figure having a backup plan wouldn't hurt."

With my hair in a ponytail and hers pulled back into a low bun at the nape of her neck, she really did look a lot like me. It almost made me feel like I wasn't third-wheeling it on their date, although I totally was. As we walked along, the gleaming reflections of broken glass and mirror cemented into mosaics along the exterior walls of the garden, Kara and Liza held hands and whispered intimate whispers to one another. I captured these candid moments on my camera along with the bicycle spokes and empty beer bottles that some artists transformed from trash to breathtaking beauty. The cerulean tiled walls led us down to an archway and back down a flight of twinkling stairs. There, under the found art sculptures and potted plants that had decided to begin a premature, warm-weather bloom in the winter, Kara dropped down to one knee and professed her love to her bride-to-be.

I'd been so enamored with the tiles that I didn't catch any of the soliloquy that Kara wrote, memorized, and recited for Liza. I hoped she treasured the moment and remembered it forever because I missed the entire thing. Luckily, I got the camera directed toward them as Kara asked, "Liza Nicole de Leon, will you marry me?"

A flood of emotion breached my already emotionally-unstable wall as I watched my best friend at one of her most vulnerable points. I could barely see what I was photographing through tears, but I managed to shoot the entire proposal from that point forward. Liza said, "Yes!" and accepted the ring, and she held Kara before shouting toward me, "You knew the entire time?"

"Of course she did," Kara said and wiped her tears from her cheeks. "She's the closest thing to a sister I've ever had." My breath got caught on the way out, and I choked back tears. I pulled the camera closer to hide my sniffly, crying face.

"Well," Liza said, "I guess that officially makes us sisters, too." She skipped down the stairs to hug me, pulling my camera down and wiping my face with her sleeve. When our breathing stabilized, and I wasn't a complete mess anymore, I took some good images of her colorful ring against the glistening floor. And in that moment, I felt happier than I could ever remember feeling.

Even happier than when I managed to win myself a free house.

nineteen

· · ·

I finished filming some posed shots of the happy couple before Kara and Liza left for a celebratory dinner uptown and an evening to themselves. Victor and I had our own date planned, after all, and I left the Gardens with a new sense of zest. Life was truly lived in the little moments between the big ones, and it was in those little moments that I found myself happiest. I floated down South Street to Tattooed Mom, where, by the time I got to the restaurant, Vic had already snagged us our usual table inside and ordered himself a few drinks.

Once I sat down, Victor handed me a menu and eyed his up and down. Of course, I wanted the tater tots and pierogi, but was I more in the mood for a burger, or maybe a chick'n sandwich? *Is either best for me if I'm trying to fit into a wedding dress in the distant future? But it's date night, and I deserve a treat. Or do I? Yes. I do.*

"Bree," Victor said and snapped me back into reality. "I've been thinking a lot about what you've said about living out of a car, and—you know—we've had a really good time together over the past few weeks, and I don't want you living out of a car like some sort of homeless person for God's sake, so—I, uh—" He stopped to gulp down the contents of his beer and used his finger to loosen the neck of his shirt as if it were making him choke. "I will talk to my parents again and ask if they'll let you move in. You know, until we can get a place of our own. Whether here or in Spokane."

I nearly had to scoop up my bottom jaw from the table. "Wow. What? Really? Are you really thinking about leaving Philly? And do you think your parents would listen to you? I mean, we are getting married. It's not like I'm just some girl you've met online." I stifled a laugh, remembering that we did actually meet on MatchUp, to which I credited part of his parents' criticism of me, and added, "I mean, we *did* meet online, but I'm not just some random hookup, ya know?"

"Oh, I'm aware," he said and smiled. "I wouldn't have proposed to you if you were. And yes. I'm playing with the idea of Washington. I mean, it's not ideal, but that house was worth much more than you'd get for the cash-out option, and it really was nice out there—Oh," he cut himself off, "I almost forgot." He reached into his front jeans pocket, squeezing his hand down and searching for something that must've been toward the bottom. "I found it when I was packing the room up before we left the hotel and forgot it was in my backpack." He gave me an approving nod to take the contents of his hand.

I reached out my palm, and he placed into it a silver earring with a giant, diamond-encased dangling emerald. My eyes bounced from the earring to Victor and back. "Where did you find this?"

"I dunno. I think it was in the bathroom, maybe? On the sink." He smiled and turned his eyes back to the menu, oblivious to the blasts of my heart beating in my ears. "Next to our toothbrushes."

"This isn't my earring," I said as I took my hand back. I retraced the trip in my mind and tried to remember what I did with that earring I found back at the hotel—

"Then who else's would it be?" Vic asked. I looked up from the earring and locked eyes with him.

"This belonged to that girl I bumped into on the elevator," I told him, slightly above a whisper.

"Who—"

"The blonde woman. From the hotel. I bumped into her, and she dropped her earring as she ran into the elevator."

Victor raised his brow at me, then screwed his face as if he were figuring out his next move in a game of chess. "I guess you left it on the—"

"I tried to catch her, but she was gone by the time I made it back downstairs, so I returned it to the front desk in case she came back for it." I felt my blood boil, burning my face and chest, and watched Victor's face drain of all color. "What was she doing in our room?"

Victor's knee bounced so rigorously under the table that the silverware clattered. His jaw pulsed as he ground the teeth on his left side and stared through the floor beside us. "No one else was in the room," he said, swiping his brow with his thumb. With his voice an octave higher than before, he added, "Maybe I found it in the hall and put it on the counter. Or the elevator. Yeah, I remember now; I found it there."

When a person is lying, their body can give themself away. Some cues, like fidgeting and raising of vocal pitch—or the

*babbling of too much information to cover their tracks—could
be potentially chalked up to nerves. Fair enough. But there are
some signs that the body can't control. Certain signs, like the
dilation of pupils, are caused by stress and the brain working
overtime and can easily give a person away.*

And in that moment, Victor's pupils were larger than
Hippo's.

"I need to go to the bathroom." As I stood up, he called my
name and grabbed at my wrist, but I kept walking. I closed
the door behind me and looked at my reflection, unsure of
what I was trying to find. Someone else? Myself? Something
other than the ghost of who I saw. My phone buzzed in my
pocket.

Victor.

I swiped the notification away and looked at the apps on my
phone, trying to make sense of anything. Back, forth, back,
forth. And then it hit me.

MatchUp.

I typed in the web address from my browser and logged in
with my old credentials. After swiping through boxes and
boxes of tutorials on what had changed since I last logged in,
I clicked on the fiery red envelope icon and found my old
messages from old suitors. Since I'd last logged on, I had
countless new messages from new matches, but it only took a
few seconds to find the thread I had with Victor; I opened it
and clicked on his profile for something, anything, to prove
me wrong.

Last online seven hours ago.

No.

I rushed through his photos and saw selfies I'd never seen before. A picture of him in his uniform, a selfie at a club. Then I saw him smiling in his neon green and blue snowsuit at the lodge in Spokane. Then dressed up in the clothes he wore last week when he said he was going to see his friends at the bar.

Had he been cheating on me the whole time? *No, he couldn't have. Not Victor. Not this time.* I thought back and tried to connect the dots—never being available, the scared look when I came back from the hotel, his nervousness when I saw him at Front Street, rejection after painful rejection. *Oh, my God.* He'd been cheating on me ever since—

I swung the bathroom door open and marched back to the table.

"When did you find out about the house?"

"Wha—"

"The prize. When did HHTV call you and tell you I won the house?"

"What are you talking about?"

"You were there. In the breakroom. Kara found out that morning when the crew was setting up to film the surprise, but someone must have called you to let you know to be there. When did you find out?"

"I—I don't know? Like a few days before. Maybe a week?"

"So you knew when you asked me out to dinner." I leaned back on my hip and crossed my arms. "You knew I was going to win a house when you asked me to be your girlfriend again."

"I mean, I did, but that had nothing to do with anything."

"Okay then. Explain this." I flipped my phone over to Victor and showed him his picture in my car. "Looks like you were online earlier today, too."

"What are you doing on MatchUp?"

"What are *you* doing on MatchUp?" I mimicked back. "You know what—don't answer that." I clicked my phone off and walked toward the exit, leaving him wide-eyed and stammering for words in his seat. "Maybe you can find someone to take you home on there."

Victor pushed his chair back and stood, the legs screeching on the floor causing every head in the restaurant to turn back, including mine. He pushed away from the table, perhaps in an attempt to chase me, but the tattoo-clad waitress stopped him and pressed the check against his chest before he could catch up.

❧ ❧ ❧

The commute home was colder and grayer than any I'd taken before. All I wanted was quiet, but even that was punctuated by clanking metal echoing off endless miles of underground tunnels and dripping water from pipes older than any creature alive on the planet. On the train, a parade of homeless faces asking for money and cigarettes, horns blaring for no other reason than to blare, and other riders listening to music on their phones without headphones because, in their stories, they were the main characters, unaware that the people around them were living lives of their own, too. Only when I stood to get off the train did I realize I'd sat in some unidentifiable brown sludge. Of course.

Once home and in the door, I dropped my bag to the side, too tired to hang it on the doorknob. I slid down the doorframe onto the floor into a pile and was promptly collected by Hippo.

There, on the floor and covered in dog kisses, I broke down. Everything, from the emotional hurt Victor inflicted upon me, to my financial woes, to my crappy landlords who wouldn't let me stay in their crappy apartment, to constantly being covered in mud and scum and excrement. I was so stupid to think I was happy. I wasn't. And I worried I never would be.

twenty

. . .

The sun set, and throughout my apartment, there was darkness and cold. Hopeless. Even with the years of memories I held in that space, nothing there felt like home; no peace, just a couple of cardboard boxes and the overhead buzz and whirring of the heater system kicking up warmth to the floors above. No happiness, no life.

Except for Hippo.

After I'd collapsed to my knees onto the floor and accepted her hearty welcome and gift of wet kisses, hugging my arms around her barrel chest and rubbing my tear-streaked face into her fur, Hippo let me hold her on the floor for as long as I needed, which felt like it could and would be for the rest of my life. Together, we melted into a puddle at the door until my eyes were cried out.

When the hollow feeling inside reached and numbed my heart, I stood and sniffed, wiping my nose on the cuff of my jacket sleeve. "Oh, you probably want to go outside, don't you, girl?" I asked, and I picked her leash up from the ground and led her out from the door. The icy winds of the cold front came fast and must have surprised her; even as a dog built more for power and not so much for speed, she darted back inside quicker than she had to get out.

Still stunned and on edge from the wind, I baby-talked to Hippo while rummaging through the boxes in my corner and finally found the bulk-sized tub of peanut butter to share with her by the spoonful. She was beyond appreciative. As Kara was likely still celebrating her engagement with Liza, and as I thought it'd be selfish to bog her down with the details from my evening, I instead sat in the shadows, taking turns with Hip licking off our peanut-buttery spoon. At that moment, it was just me and my dog. And in that moment, I was okay.

I dropped a glob of peanut butter down to her on the floor, and she missed it, as she had had more and more over the past several months. She diligently lapped up the mess from the floor, as she did countless times before, and I reached down to stroke the fur between her ears and under her jaw. "I'll always be here for you, baby," I told her as if she could understand. "Just like you're always here for me." I knelt beside her and kissed the soft pad of fat on the side of her head above her eyes. "You're all I'll ever need, girl."

After capping the jar and dropping it back into the heap of cardboard boxes, I flopped onto my bed, where Hippo hopped up to join me, and, after winning and losing and loving and hating, and after building up and letting down and being had, and after hating myself for it all, I crashed.

The next morning, I awoke feeling slightly better than I had the night before. *Victor is a joke*, I told myself repeatedly, *but then again, I was a fool to think he'd change after all this time.* At least I realized that before we tied the knot.

"Oh my God," I said aloud, "The wedding!"

I fumbled for my phone and checked the time: 7:30. Most of the vendors wouldn't open until later, but I needed to get the money I put down back. Venue, catering, flowers, bakery. I emailed everyone I sent money to with a message stating that the wedding was off and that I requested my deposits back. "Stupid. Stupid!" I shouted at myself. How stupid of me to plan a wedding when I couldn't even afford to eat some nights.

Eight rolled around, and being alone with my thoughts while I waited for email responses would have probably killed me (story of my life), so I habitually refreshed my screen until, one by one, all of the emails found me unwell.

"Dear Ms. Huxley, we are so sorry," they began, immediately followed by, "but as stated in the contract…." First the venue, then the caterers, then the bakery, then the flowers. If I wasn't all cried out from the night before, I would have wept, but I was, so I didn't. I just stared through my laptop screen, numb from it all.

"Par for the course, I guess," I muttered under my breath and collapsed to the bed beside Hippo. There, in that moldy basement apartment, with mere days until I'd be forced out, I'd run out of steam. And ideas.

"What do we do, girl?" Hippo didn't acknowledge me, but it didn't stop me from trying to tease out some sort of answer. "I guess we can scope out pet-friendly apartments on Craigslist. It's not like we have many more options right now." Hip rolled over to her back, exposing her belly for rubs, which I obliged as I gravely opened the browser on my phone.

The search was not unlike trying to find a good book in the clearance bin at the thrift store. No pets allowed, only cats, no pitbulls. Credit check, credit check, credit check. I called the one place I found in my price range that didn't have a breed restriction, but they stopped paying me any mind after I told them about my employment status. "I mean, I'm technically self-employed," I said, hiding the fact that I hadn't yet landed any paying customers for my photography business, but they must've seen through my act. As I hung up the call, my phone pinged with a new notification—a new email. *Odd*, I thought, as I'd already heard back from all of the wedding people. I clicked open the app and choked on my breath.

Good morning, Ms. Huxley,

I would like to formally extend the medical photographer position to you.

"No way!" I shouted so loud that Hippo jumped to her front paws and *boofed* at the air. I squeezed her tight, smoothing the heckles down her back. I scrolled down the email to the salary —more than double what I made at Franklin Family—and with top-of-the-line benefits. Hospital insurance, paid tuition for higher education. Debt reconciliation programs. "Hippo," I whispered. "I did it." Her stance relaxed, and she leaned into my chest for the hug. "We're going to Washington." All we had to do was get from here to there and figure out where to stay for the next three weeks. And then a lightbulb clicked on in my head.

"But first, we're taking a road trip."

"Okay—so, first things first," I said, after the how-are-yous and I'm-okay-how-about-yous, "I broke things off with Victor."

"You *what*?" Kara asked, sounding both shocked but perhaps even a smidgeon happy. "I'm so sorry, Bree. Are you okay? Do you need anything?"

"Honestly, I don't even know right now."

"Like, you were so happy yesterday—what happened?"

Her voice echoed throughout the near-empty basement and reverberated in my head. What happened, I knew. How I *let* it happen, not so much.

"Turns out he was cheating on me the whole time. To make matters worse, I think he only proposed to me because he thought I was about to become a millionaire."

Although I had still cried out all my tears the night before, the words still caused my eyes to sting.

"That piece of—the next time I see him, I'll—"

"He's not worth it," I told Kara. "Don't let him eat up any of your thoughts. I've done that for entirely too long as it is. I hate him, but he's not worth catching charges over. Besides, he's living in Jersey with his parents, so who knows when you'll see him again."

"You're right," Kara said.

Frankly, I pleasantly surprised myself. Maybe three years before, I would have probably found a way to his parents' and slashed his tires, but now, I had something to look forward to.

I rubbed the skin where my ring used to be, still slightly indented from weeks of wear.

"But now for the bigger news."

I stood up and looked for a clean shirt and pants to wear for the day.

"Wait—how can anything be bigger than breaking off your engagement?"o

"I got a job out in Washington," I said, peeling my face away from the phone to pull a shirt over my head for a second. "For a sweet photographer position at a hospital out there. With amazing pay and everything." I paused for a second, trying to brace myself for the news again. "And I accepted it."

"Holy crap, Breanna. That's incredible."

"I know. First, I won the house, now this. It's about time my luck began shifting."

"Luck has nothing to do with it," Kara said. "Well, maybe it had something to do with the house, but you got that job all on your own. Liza helped with the resume, sure, but you're the one who went to school all that time and kept such a clean record at Franklin Family."

"I guess you're right," I said, still skeptical that luck was one hundred percent to thank for the position. "But—on to the next thing. Since I have a few weeks until I can move into the new house out there, I came up with this idea."

"I'm listening," she said with a hint of skepticism in her throat.

"The plan," I told Kara over the phone as I slipped my legs into a pair of jeans, "is to get a burner car, then leave Philly, hitting up several stops along the way—parks, rivers, deserts, whatever—and end in Spokane in time for me to sign the papers for the house. I can sleep in the car along the way, which would easily buy me the time needed until I can sign off on the house, and I'll be able to give Hippo the trip of her lifetime like I wanted."

"It sounds like it'd be the trip of *your* lifetime just as much as it'd be hers," she said from my phone's speaker, "but it does sound like a tremendous undertaking. I mean, the move is big enough, but you don't have a car, and I think that's the biggest part of having a road trip, isn't it?"

"You're absolutely right," I said into my phone as I scrolled the website of a local used-car dealership. "But lucky for me, everyone is trying to sell their cars off for dirt cheap for the holidays. This place I'm looking at right now has a used van for under a grand because it would, quote, 'Make a great stocking stuffer for any first-time driver.'"

"A van sounds like a terrible stocking stuffer."

"Yeah, the van would either have to be really small," I said, reading the details on the vehicle, "or the sock would have to be gigantic. Says it runs smooth, though, so I guess it's worth checking out."

"Go for it," Kara said with a breathy laugh, but her voice sobered up after a sigh. "But honestly, this is a lot to take in.

Whatever you do, don't even think about leaving without coming here to say goodbye, okay?"

"I would never," I told her sincerely, "but if I want to check out this deal, I need to go ASAP. Looks like they have reduced hours for Christmas Eve."

With the call ended, I slipped my phone into my back pocket and took the next bus to the used car dealership. I made up my mind. *This is really happening.*

The weather must have made up its mind, too, and decided that it was done being warm and gorgeous for good, reverting to December's bitter grayness. Downright frigid. My weather app said it was thirty-three degrees out, nearly forty degrees lower than Saturday, and called for a winter storm in the coming days. *One day*, I told myself, *I'll buy that new coat—but not until after I recoup some money from this car purchase.* Maybe if I got my wedding money back. Until then, I was stuck with my dirty, muck-stained parka and brand new-old van.

After two hours at the dealership, I bought myself an absolute clunker of a 2005, rusty red Chevy Astro van for less than a grand (thank you, holiday marketing event). The thing smelled like cigarettes and fifteen Christmas-tree-shaped air fresheners, but it had four wheels and less than a hundred thousand miles on it. The test drive seemed safe enough, so I drove it off the lot home, and once there in one piece, I realized that I'd not only skipped lunch, but that dinnertime was fast approaching.

Looking around my barren apartment, I found that all I had left to eat was a few Clif bars and my trusty jug of peanut butter. *Pathetic.* But then, I had another brilliant idea for the second time that day.

"Wanna go get some pizza, baby?" I asked Hippo. "It'll be my treat."

I told myself I needed to get used to the van's controls anyway as I loaded Hippo into the backseat. Once in the car, which quickly heated much warmer than the apartment ever could, I drove to the pizzeria downtown for some vegan meat lovers pies. I figured it'd be enough to share with Hippo for the next few days, long enough to get my act together as I packed for our road trip. And, since an extra two dollars wasn't going to make or break my housing budget, I tacked on a vanilla whoopie pie, too, knowing full well that I was persistently disappointed by them. "Maybe this one won't suck," I told Hippo as I unwrapped the cellophane from the golden dessert and took a nibble from its pillowy corner. Plot twist: it did suck, but that didn't stop me and Hippo from devouring the entire thing. "I think I can get used to this whole road trip thing, girl."

With our bellies full, we drove back to the apartment, where Hippo ate some kibble to supplement her dinner, and I munched on pizza crust in bed. In the dark, things were beginning to look a lot brighter for us. But then again, I'd never been a good judge of these things.

twenty-one

. . .

For many, Christmas was the best time of year—a day of gift-giving and feasting and quality time with family. As a broke thirty-something from a broken home, the holiday always reminded me of how different I was from everyone else. Upstairs, the sound of my landlords' television shouting holiday carols was slowly replaced by a parade of footsteps and boisterous laughter. That, coupled with the smell of fish and cabbage, let me know that it'd be a long day of staying indoors lest I accidentally make eye contact with someone and be forced into making small talk.

I FaceTimed Kara and Liza in the morning, but they had plans for a family trip to some random cousin's beach house, so they had to get ready for their long journey into New Jersey for the week. Bored and a sliver lonelier than I cared to admit, I texted Mom to wish her and the twins a Merry Christmas, but when the sun set and I hadn't yet received a reply, I figured I wouldn't be getting one.

The rest of the week sped past me. First, I figured out how to remove the far back row of seats of the van to make room for all of my belongings. Next, after taking the seat to the dump, I organized boxes by necessity and packed them into the van accordingly. If I needed, say, a flashlight, I knew where it was and could easily get to it. My clothes and food were closest to the back door, so I could get changed easily and feed Hippo regularly. By the end of the week, I was practically living out of the thing already.

When I awoke on New Year's Eve, it hardly felt like my final day at the apartment.

Then again, nothing felt entirely real or right since winning the Dream Home contest—there was my heartbreak with Mom and the devastation Victor left in his wake. There was even the minor tiff I had with Kara. My whole life for the previous three months felt like they belonged to someone else and that I was just along for the ride.

As I laid on my bare mattress, staring at the ceiling, I tried to think about times when I was happiest. There weren't many, and the hollow pit in my chest made it hard to remember anything other than complete hopelessness. Going to the park with Hippo was a truly happy experience, and I loved that feeling of being in the Magic Gardens with Kara and Liza, but the only times I could remember being happy before that would probably have been back in my photography classes back at college. Admittedly, I felt pride when I got the job offer in Spokane, which was new for me. I couldn't think of many times that I made anyone proud of me. A smile crossed my face, and I let out a *hmph*. Maybe that degree wasn't such a waste after all.

With a stretch of my arms and spine, I opened my backpack and shoved all my remaining belongings—a hairbrush, toothbrush, and toothpaste—into it. Hippo awoke from my frenzy and perked her head up from the bed she'd been napping on.

"You ready for a ride, girl?" Her tail nub began slowly wagging until it built up enough momentum to move her entire butt from side to side. She crouched low on her front legs and held her rear in the air, signaling it was go time. "Okay, okay. We'll go for a ride. Just give me a bit."

I spent the next hour stuffing her travel bag with all her toys and treats and neatly stacking the remainder of our belongings into the boot of my van. It was the first day of the rest of our lives.

With Hippo peacefully snoozing on the floor in a patch of sun, I called Kara on her lunch break about my rash decision. Normally, I hated speakerphone, but since I was not in a crowded restaurant or a bus filled with a dozen people over the legal capacity, I used the hands-free option to free up both hands for scrubbing my apartment down. In true Kara style, she answered the phone before the second ring and greeted me with the same level of enthusiasm as a person greeting their dog after a long day of work. I greeted her with enthusiasm that matched her hypothetical pet.

"Hey, what are you doing today? I have all my crap packed and have to give my keys back to Artem by five."

"Bree—I—hold on."

In the distance, I could hear someone talking to her and a muffled Kara agreeing with them about something or another.

"Sorry, I got called into work, and the doctors said they need me for something real quick, but don't you even *think* about leaving until I see you. Can I come by after work? Spend New Year's together?"

"Sure," I told her and glanced around at all the grease stains from all the dropped peanut butter Hippo had missed over the past year. "I'll be here."

I continued scrubbing the floor and walls when she disconnected the call, creating a luster and sheen previously unknown to that dungeon. Masha came downstairs a moment later with her wicker hamper full of linens to start a load of wash and said she was impressed with all my hard work. She even told me she would miss having me as a tenant. Well, maybe she didn't *actually* say that, but she did say she hoped the next person to live there was as quiet as me, which was almost the same thing. It was the perfect way to end my last day in that squalidity. Almost like I accomplished something.

Once I felt that I had scrubbed every surface as clean as possible—including that recurring patch of blackish mold that haunted me physically and mentally for the past several years—I mindlessly tapped on Creatr. I deleted any evidence that Victor and I had ever known each other. Every picture, every tag, every comment, gone. Once I felt my spirit beginning to heal from the digital cleanse, I posted some pictures of the Magic Gardens and the engagement shots from the day prior. As the likes rolled in, I started poking around the accounts of other photographers and dog lovers, which led me down a rabbit hole of doggy celebrities, then adoptable dogs, then recipes for the best-ever minestrone soup. Allegedly.

Comments began dropping down from the top of my screen.

This is so pretty!

Gorgeous!!!

Do you do weddings, too?

Not yet, I thought, but if the past three months taught me anything, it was that everything was possible.

twenty-two

. . .

If time was a dog breed, 5:30 would have been a Rhodesian Ridgeback: silent on a lion hunt but quick to sneak up from behind and bite me. I had been so in the zone with my comments and replies that I managed to lose track of an entire afternoon. A chime on my phone let me know my DNA results were in, but a second notification from Kara let me know she was outside. I clicked on my email, took Hippo out to use the facilities, and greeted my home's last guest.

"Hey there, sugar bear." Kara cupped her hands around the sides of Hippo's face and smooched the velour between her eyes. With limited eyesight or not, Hippo knew her people, and there was no question that Kara was her people.

"God, this baby loves you," I told Kara as I slipped my phone into my jeans' back pocket. Hippo waggled her rump and licked Kara's hands, completely unaware that by day's end, the two of us would be on the road while her second-favorite human would stay behind.

The three of us followed the sidewalk back to the house and down to the echoey basement unit. With all the furniture sold on the neighborhood marketplace for a few extra dollars to get me cross-country and the rest of my boxes in the car, we sat on the floor. Kara gracefully folded her legs into a pretzel about two feet in front of me while Hippo sprawled on the floor between us, her belly exposed to the ceiling, inviting us to rub it. We did just that, petting and obsessing over the dog. "Remember how sad she looked at the shelter?" Kara asked as she scratched the fuzz of Hip's muzzle.

"Yeah," I said, feeling a spark of heartbreak, picturing Hippo so alone in that cage. "I didn't think it was possible to feel sadder than me, but there she was. We needed each other." We sat silently for a moment, but not so long that it weighed on us. "She's going to miss you. *I'm* going to miss you."

Kara jerked her head up and shot me a squinted look in the eye. "That's right—I can't believe you're really about to go. It doesn't feel real yet."

"I... know. It doesn't. But it feels like the thing to do. I've never really seen any of the world outside of Philadelphia. Aside from the small fraction of Washington I saw." I paused and looked down at my four-legged best friend, blissfully unaware as she was of how much her life would change in the next twenty-four hours. "I guess I want to experience all that I can before Hippo loses all of her eyesight."

"Yeah." Kara's pretend glare softened, and she shifted her focus back to Hip. "I get that. But, like, you know, if you needed a place to stay, you could crash with me, right? Don't feel like you *have* to drive out there because you're out of options. Liza and I are thinking about finding a place together anyway."

"I know you would let me—and I appreciate that—but I couldn't ask that of you," I said woefully. "You two are about to start a new life together. You don't need a third wheel all up in your business. Besides, I think traveling would be exciting. And really, when else would I get the opportunity to do that again? Especially with me starting a new job as soon as I touch down in Spokane." I leaned back on my hands to prop myself up and distance myself from the situation. If I was completely honest with myself, I didn't know the first thing about camping or roughing it, and I had exactly no idea of how Hippo would take to life on the road. She thrived on the occasional walk to the park, but even on the hour-long ride to the shore, she'd whine and pace in the back seat. But she deserved to live her best life, and if that meant dealing with a howling dog in the back of the car for hours on end, be it to get to a mountain range or crystalline lake, then that's what I needed to do.

"The offer still stands," Kara reiterated. "You should at least spend the night tonight after the countdown. You're family to me, Bree. Just remember, an extra body to help with the rent would be pretty nice, so if you want to stay longer, you can," Kara said and clasped her hands together. "Oh! And I forgot to tell you—remember how I said I was gonna talk to the doctors at work about Angela?"

I snapped out of my head and back into my apartment. "Oh…. Oh, yeah! What's the verdict?"

"Well, after I held that meeting, the partners decided to hire an outside auditor to fully investigate the office's finances. Turns out Angela was shaving a huge amount of money from the budget and paying herself on the side. We're talking tens of thousands of dollars."

"Whoa," I bellowed and shifted forward to lean as far as I could into the gossip. "What did the partners do? Did Angela get fired?"

"Fired? Ha! She's fired alright, plus they're pressing charges against her. I doubt she'll ever show her face around the practice again."

"That's so wild, but so great for you! She was the part of that job that made everything insufferable."

"I know, but it gets better." Kara maintained eye contact with me but lowered her head and voice. "Guess who's the new practice manager of Franklin Family?" A smile took over her face, and she couldn't hide her pride any longer.

"No way, Kara—did you—"

"I sure did," Kara perked up and beamed. "The partners and other docs pulled me aside afterward and extended the offer to me. The first thing I'll do tomorrow is clean out Angela's old office and make it my own. Isn't that nuts?"

"Yes. I mean, no. It makes perfect sense, Kara. You're such a hard worker, and you deserve it more than anyone else I can think of." I blinked back a tear, a happy tear, and gave Kara a hug. "Look at you, getting your life together like this."

"Yeah, but it took you to get the ball rolling," Kara said, squeezing me back. "If you didn't leave, we probably all would have continued putting up and shutting up." She leaned back into her spot on the floor, and I sat back into mine. "And seeing you almost move twenty-five hundred miles away made me realize that I needed to make some changes myself if I ever wanted to take my life back." She glanced down at Hippo, who'd fallen asleep on her back with her tongue out, then back to me. "I'm going to miss you while you're gone."

"I'm gonna miss you, too, but it's not forever," I said, unsure of what my next steps or destination would be. "Honestly, I have no idea how long I'll be on the road. Months, years. Maybe I'll get bored, return in a week, and take a plane out to Spokane in a few weeks. Who knows?" I certainly didn't.

"Just remember what I said. It might not be a sprawling homestead in the mountains that you'd like with a husband

and 2.5 kids, but wherever you go, know that you're always welcome."

We hugged again and it hit me. All my life, I worked and strived for the picturesque American Dream, but in reality, I didn't need a husband or kids to feel loved. Hell, did I even want children? I barely knew how to tolerate a dog crying on an hour-long drive to the beach. And kids were sticky. I had Kara, and I had Hippo, and they were all the family I needed. Maybe that guy and his dog on Creatr were right. Home *was* where you were.

"Besides," she continued, "if you and Liza really do turn out to be blood-related, we'd legally become sisters."

"Oh my God! That reminds me," I jolted back and took my phone back out of my pocket to check my email. "My results came in. From the genealogy website."

"That's exciting," Kara sang and peered onto my screen. "What's it say?"

My phone flashed from one screen to the next, expanding and condensing until the words appeared. "You Have New Matches," the page exclaimed. My ribcage could barely contain my heart. When I clicked the link, a list of people with whom I shared my genes—my relatives—popped up in descending order based on shared DNA percentage. The top result was the only one listed as a close relative, and we were indeed at 24.9 percent; according to the site, that person was either a grandparent or a half-sibling, making my heart race faster still.

For a split second, I thought of how my life would change. Meeting a grandparent I never knew, discovering who my father was, maybe meeting him, too. Then, the panic began to creep in. How would meeting someone so important to my life change things? Was I ready to meet that stranger? Would they even want to meet me, a bastard child they never knew existed? How would that affect my plans to travel cross-country with Hippo?

"What are you waiting for?" Kara asked, snapping me out of my spiral. "Click it!" I drew a deep breath, pressed my index finger to the highlighted text, and watched as the next screen loaded. A pink circle with a generic ponytail adorned avatar. A woman. I scrolled down to read her name.

twenty-three

· · ·

It was Grandma.

I lost the grip of my phone and nearly dropped it but stabilized it with both hands. All I wanted was some answers, something—anything—that could help me piece together some sort of family, and I got nothing. Over my shoulder, I could feel Kara sighing, but for the first time since I'd known her, she couldn't find her words. We sat there in the hollow of the basement, staring at my phone as it lit, darkened, and ultimately shut off. Only after Hippo farted so loud that it scared her awake did Kara and I snap out of our hypnosis.

"Bree, I'm so sorry—"

"No, it's okay. I'm fine. Really. I just secretly hoped that Liza and I—"

"I know, I know," Kara whispered, rubbing her hand along my back. "She was too. I guess we should call her—"

"No, no," I cut her off, "we should probably tell her in person."

"Hmm, I guess you're right." We sat in silence for a moment, then Kara tapped my leg with a smile. "You know, it's New Year's Eve. We could always get some dinner before you come over for the night. We can get Liza out of the house, too. Get some empanadas. They always help when I'm down."

"Yeah," I said, pretending to raise my spirits. "Sure."

Kara pulled her phone from her scrubs and called Liza. "Hey, babe. Since Bree is hanging out with us for the countdown anyway, could we meet up with her for dinner tonight? She's thinking about leaving Philly for a bit and has some news for us." She turned to me with her hand over the microphone and nodded toward me, then turned back to her call. "Okay. How about Bar Bombón at, like, seven? Yeah. Yeah. Okay, love you, too. Bye." Kara hung up and slipped her phone into her scrub pocket, then turned back to me. "Alrighty."

I clicked the home button on my phone and looked at the time. Quarter past six. "Well, I guess we should probably head on over," I said as I rolled onto my hands and knees to get up off the floor.

Kara slid up from her seated position like some sort of pilates instructor and readjusted her perfectly unwrinkled work clothes. "Do I look okay?" she asked and held out her arms to show off her scrubs.

"You'd look great wearing a jumpsuit made out of burlap." I poured Hippo her kibble dinner and thought to change out of my t-shirt and jeans, only to remember that all my clothes were already packed into the car. "I guess I'll just wear this."

I locked the apartment behind me and walked down the block with Kara to my van with its four working wheels. With the key in the ignition, I backed out carefully, extra conscious of debris strewn about the road, and pulled off.

❖ ❖ ❖

Bar Bombón sat on the corner beside a single-lane alleyway a mere block away from the posh Rittenhouse Square. During the spring, summer, and early fall, the restaurant opened its floor-to-ceiling windows and spilled out into the street, but in the dead of winter, the outdoor bistro sets stood naked on the sidewalk. The late December sun had already set, and the building glowed amber with strings of warm, round lights, the scent of garlic and chorizo spices filling the air. The always-present traffic on I-95 held us up (I even factored that into our commute!), and we arrived fifteen minutes later than planned. Inside the restaurant, Liza had snagged us a table along the back wall with a bench seat. Kara and I took turns crying during the drive down, but we got our acts together before entering the building.

It only took one peek at Liza for me to crumble into pieces again. She got up from the table to greet us with hugs, and I gripped onto her as if she were a long-lost sister, which I now knew for certain she wasn't.

"Jeez, Bree, it's okay," Liza said as I clung to her, probably simultaneously shocked and perplexed. "I'm here for you."

I pulled a cloth napkin from the table to blot my tears and snorted back the tears that couldn't escape my face. "I know, I just love you so much."

"I," Liza frantically bounced her eyes from me to Kara to me again, "love you, too?"

Kara came around the table and helped us to our seats. "Liza," she said, "we have something to tell you, and you're going to want to sit for it."

When I thought that Liza couldn't look any more confused, she surprised me and knitted her brows nearly into a sweater. "Alright," she wiggled her butt into her seat. "I'm sitting."

"Phew, alright," I said, presenting my hands to the girls. I drew my lungs' deepest breath and slowly let it all out. "Today I got an email from—"

"Hi, my name is Cheryl, and I'll be your server today," piped a pint-sized waitress. "Can I start you guys out with some drinks?"

The three of us sat with our mouths slightly agape for a second, then quickly spouted out our order for a round of water.

"With lemon?"

Yes, with lemon.

Once our waitress flittered back to the kitchen, I realigned my thoughts and pulled out my phone to open my emails. "As I was saying, Kara came over earlier to talk over my plans to travel around with Hippo for a while since today is officially my last day of the lease, and—"

"Wait, you're leaving Philly?" Liza cut in. "When are you coming back? You know you can stay with us, right? Kara, you told her she could stay with us, didn't you?"

"I did."

"She did, but I wanted to get out and explore the world. I haven't seen enough of it. And with Hippo going blind, I wanted to do it sooner rather than later."

"She's going blind? Oh, Bree, I'm so sorry, but I'm glad you're able to take her out for an adventure like this." Liza relaxed her posture and eased back into her chair. "But it's still gonna suck here without you. How long do you think you'll be gone? You can still move in with us after you get back to the city."

"Thanks. I may have to take you guys up on that offer, but I don't know how long I'll be. It could be weeks, could be months. Anyway, I was talking this all out with Kara, and I remembered getting an email." I opened the app back up and clicked the link to my genealogical match. "So I opened it, and—"

"Alright, three waters," the waitress sang, placing our glasses on the table, "*with* lemon." Cheryl gave us all a smile that split her face in two and asked, "Are you ready to order or do youse need some more time?"

"We need more time," we all replied at once.

"Sorry," Kara continued, "could we have three orders of the veggie empanadas and a few more minutes?"

Cheryl nodded and gave us a "Surely!" before retreating to the back again.

Liza turned to me, exasperated, and gently smacked her hands onto the table. "Quickly, before she comes back."

My heart raced. "I know, I don't think I've ever had such speedy service—"

"Focus, Bree," Kara cut in.

"Right, sorry." I stared at the condensation droplets sliding down the side of the glass closest to me. "The results." My phone had gone black, but with a tap and a facial recognition later, I was back on the results screen. I drew a deep breath and flashed the screen to Liza. "I don't think we're related."

Liza's face morphed to express seemingly every emotion at once as if she was speeding through the stages of grief. Kara squeezed her knee, bringing her back to reality, and Liza tore her eyes away from my phone. With tears beginning to line the rims of her lower lids, she whispered, "It's okay, Bree. We're still family."

twenty-four

. . .

After the three of us cried over our woe and appetizers, we snapped a group selfie of us clinking our empanadas together in a toast (I couldn't wait after forgetting to eat all day, so mine had a bite mark) and posted it to our respective social Creatr accounts. *Hashtag foodies, hashtag family.* By the time our veggie Spanish Meatballs and seitan al pastor tacos arrived, which we promptly inhaled, we'd caught up on the insignificant tidbits of our childhoods and traumas we never really explored nor felt the need to explore when we simply assumed we were related. How chubby we used to be, how much we both loved *Sailor Moon* as kids, how we never had any daddy-daughter dances at school. How we both got bullied for being different and how our similarities made us feel more related than ever.

Cheryl rounded back one final time to hand us our debit card receipts to sign for dinner, and after tipping a healthy twenty-five percent, we left for the door. That's when I saw him.

Victor.

He was speaking to the hostess at the restaurant, smiling, almost flirty. She coyly smiled back. The chatter of dinner guests and the blasting drums in my ears prevented me from making out what he was saying, but he looked up and saw me frozen, then motioned to the hostess, nodding as if to tell her I was the person he was talking about. Me. With my balled fists and furrowed brow. He smiled at her and jogged past patrons at the bar to greet me with an unexpected and unwelcome hug.

"Bree, my God, I've been trying to talk to you."

"I bet you have," said Kara, eying Victor up and down. "But now isn't a good time."

"Yeah, I'd say never is the best time," Liza jabbed. I couldn't move, so sticking up for myself was completely out of the question.

Victor pulled back from his unreciprocated embrace and tilted my chin back with the cup of his hand, but I sharply turned away. "Look, I know you're mad at me, and honestly, I'm mad at myself, but we can't just end it like this. I love you too much."

"How did you know I was here?" I finally said, still dazed. "I blocked you on everything."

"You did. Kara, too, but Liza didn't. Not on my burner account, anyway." He tilted his head back toward my sister, who, by that time, was fuming. "Oh, and you're still on my phone as family with location share on."

I thought I was forgetting to delete something, I thought, but it was too late. He'd caught up to me, and now I had to try to weasel my way out. "We were about to go," I told him, thinking of ways to tell him to leave us alone.

"That's great. I can come, too. Or maybe we can break off from them for a moment so we can talk this all out." His eyes were hopeful, the gold flecks in them almost twinkling. "Please?"

"No," Kara cut in. "You had every chance in the world not to mess this up, and you did anyway."

"She can speak for herself, *Kar*," Vic snapped back, emphasizing "Kar" as if calling her that was some sort of an insult. "Please, Bree, I know I screwed up, but I'm asking for just one more chance. I'm begging."

"Victor," I tried to say but could only whisper. I cleared my throat and spoke again, "She's right."

"Bree, no—"

"I'm leaving. Leaving this restaurant, leaving Philly, leaving everything."

"Leaving Philly? When? To where?"

"Tonight. Well, after all the New Year's drunkards have cleared off the road."

I looked down at my feet and tapped my toes against the terra cotta tiled floor. "I'm sorry."

I squeezed between Victor and an empty stool to the front door, Kara and Liza following suit. Victor called from behind, "Yeah. You are."

Prick.

Bar Bombón sat further and further behind us as we walked down the block and past the park to our cars. Kara rode with Liza, surely discussing the events of dinner, and I drove back to the apartment to pick up Hippo. Once there, I made a final sweep of the premises to ensure I forgot nothing, then locked the door behind us. I unhooked the apartment key from my community college lanyard and stuck it through the mail slot of the front door for the landlords, then walked Hip down the sidewalk to the curb. Snow began to drift down from the sky, and the street lamps left a romantic light on the stone-faced row of homes we'd just left.

"I don't think I'll miss this place," I told Hippo. "Like, at all." Hippo huffed and shook her head, which I took as a clear sign that she was ready to move forward with her new life on the road without ever looking back. We turned toward my van and I patted the seat behind the passenger's side for her to jump into, then buckled her in.

Deep within our brains, we have the hypothalamus. This structure is like a command center that wants everything to be copacetic at all times, which means that it acts as the mediator between the brain and the rest of the body. To do this, it enlists the help of the autonomic nervous system; within that system, we have the sympathetic and parasympathetic nervous systems. When we encounter a stressor, the sympathetic system kicks in, stimulating our nerves in what is commonly called a "fight or flight response." Only after the perceived threat is done and gone can the parasympathetic system kick in, allowing our brains to rest and digest what just happened.

After seeing Victor, my brain begged for a moment's peace to calm down and figure out what happened back at the restaurant, but the worsening weather conditions had other plans for me.

The drive to Kara's apartment wasn't a long distance, but it took three times longer than it would have on a normal night. A sludgy layer of road salt mush splashed onto the bottom of my car doors, but the roads were still slick and wet, and the streetlight glow bounced off falling snowflakes, making driving through fog look like a walk in the park. Scared out of my wits, I white-knuckled the steering wheel, my body stiff as a plank of wood, and crawled my way down the tight city blocks. At the stop sign right before Kara's street, my leg seized, and I braked an ounce too hard, sending the van sliding for about six feet and into an intersection. Narrowly missing a dented-up, metallic green Saturn VUE, I loosened my grip and shook my shoulders off, trying in vain to release some anxiety. Only when I saw a pair of headlights shine from a car four or so blocks down the road did I re-grip the wheel and gently pull the van back onto the path.

Once I safely parked at Kara's (but not before tapping into the back bumper of Liza's Outback), I unclipped Hippo from her seat and leashed her for the stretch of sidewalk leading to the front door. She hopped down from her seat but must've misjudged the height of the ground with its foot-tall snowy layer and fell face-first into a bank of snow. The sudden jolt of the lead snapped my arm forward, and, as gracefully as a newborn horse, I fell directly behind her onto the slurry of snow and grime of the cement. Within a second, I cycled through emotions—hurt, annoyance, anger—but landed on heart-clenching sadness. I picked myself up, dusted her off with care, and told her how it was okay, that she was still a good girl. I wiped what mess I could from my butt, knowing it'd stain anyway because I couldn't have nice things, and we knocked on the front door.

"Was that you making all that sound out there just now?" Kara asked in lieu of a courteous greeting. With a broad smile, she said, "I should've known."

"I'm okay, thanks for asking," I told her with mock offense as I shimmied my arms out of my filthy, wet jacket. "The next coat I get will be black; that way, when I inevitably stain it, no one will know."

"Good idea," Liza said from the couch.

I hung up my coat next to their door and tried to steady myself a bit before I had to tell Liza about my car's little encounter with hers in the parking lot. "Oh, and Liza, I... I'm sorry, but I... *may* have knocked into your car with mine, just a *teensy* bit." I pinched my fingers together to show just how *teensy* the damages were as I apologized.

"Oh, don't worry about that. I'm sure it didn't do anything serious," Liza said from the couch, waving my concerns away.

I took a deep, lung-stretching breath, resetting my vagus nerve and finally triggering the parasympathetic response.

Hippo, excited to see her fur-aunt, jumped up beside Liza where she peacefully sat and decided it was the best time to shake off all the droplets of melted snow still stuck to her. "Oh, thanks, Hippo," Liza said as she used a pastel rainbow crocheted throw from the arm of the couch to dry off her face. "I needed a shower anyway."

"God, Hippo, why?" I ran over to her and scooped her off the couch. "I'm sorry, she did that outside—I thought she was dry."

"Seriously, it's no big deal," Liza said, grabbing Hippo's face with both hands. With the cutesiest baby voice, she asked Hippo, "You're just a big ol' lunkhead, aren't you?"

Kara sat beside Hippo and also doted on her. "She doesn't mean to be a big ol' lunkhead, she just is." Hippo flopped into Kara's lap, exposed her belly for some rubs, and smiled with her tongue out on one side when she received them. "Actually, Liza and I were talking about eventually fostering another dog. It's been so quiet here since Ludo was adopted in May." She fiddled with Hippo's ears and gave her a kiss on the bridge of her nose. "But I certainly wouldn't mind you crashing here until then. Bree, you can stay, too."

"Mmhmm, and stay where? In that closet beside the bathroom?"

"It's not a closet, it's a den," Liza said. "It just has a shit-ton of totes stored in there, but we can easily move them all to the living room. It'll fit a twin-sized bed if you don't mind not having a nightstand. Seriously, we have an air mattress if you think you wanna stay here for a while."

The weight of my eyelids and the soreness radiating from my probably-bruised butt whispered in my ear like a cartoon angel to accept their offer, but my stubbornness shut them up. "As tempting as it sounds, I think I'll pass. I want to start driving south before the snow gets too bad."

"Okay, but know the offer stands," Kara added and patted the seat beside her, inviting me to sit down and get cozy.

twenty-five

. . .

I'd never fancied myself a party person. If given the choice, I'd much rather sit alone in a room with a dog than go to a place where I didn't know anyone and talk to people. According to an online personality quiz, it was because I was an INFJ, but according to the doctors at work—well, what used to be work—it was most likely just a part of life on the spectrum. It was probably why Kara and I—and later, Liza and I—got along so well. We were our own peewee tribe of neuro-atypical introverts. A group of *"It's okay to hang out for a little while, but please leave by nine,"* kind of people.

Except on New Year's Eve. By midnight, we were all already asleep on the couch. The four of us awoke to the sound of gunshots and fireworks outside in every direction, which put Hippo in a loud mood. Once I calmed her down with a series of pets and coos, and she realized we were all safe in that space, she showered us all with good luck and New Year's kisses.

"Happy New Year's," we all croaked to each other, then rested our eyes again until I awoke a few hours later to a stiff neck. I squinted an eye to read the time off my phone: 4:38 in the morning. After stretching my arms and straightening my spine, I slid Hippo off my lap and onto the couch, then shook Kara and Liza at the shoulder to wake them.

"Hey, I think I'm gonna head on out," I whispered between them. They both stirred enough to give me a loose hug.

"Okay," Kara said, her voice dry from sleep. "Gimme a call when you get home."

I didn't have the nerve to tell her I wasn't going home. Or anywhere prescribed, for that matter, but I didn't want her to startle that early. For now, she could sleep.

The sun won't be out for a couple more hours, but that means fewer drivers crowding the roads, I reasoned with myself as I collected Hip and locked the door behind me.

Outside, I let Hippo sniff around, eat a clump of snow, and relieve herself before the exciting adventure ahead. When she finished her deeds, I used my sleeve to dust off the layers of accumulated snow from my windshield, then helped Hip into the back seat. Leaning over her blimpy body, I buckled her into her safety harness behind the passenger seat to make it easier to see her in my rear view on the road. "Looks like you've been eating a few too many spoonfuls of peanut butter, beefy girl," I said, stretching my arms past her to click her into place. To my shock, she let out a deep, rumbly growl. I didn't think I'd heard her growl since I adopted her. *Is the harness too tight?* I fumbled with the nylon straps around her chest when I felt someone approaching me from behind. Panicked, I snapped my head back.

Victor.

"What are you doing here?"

"I went to your apartment after I left the restaurant and saw you come over here," he said, with what smelled like an entire bottle of whiskey on his breath.

"You followed me? And then just sat here at your car for," I looked at my phone and did the math in my head, "six whole hours waiting for me to come out?"

"Yeah. I wanted to talk to you, but I wanted to give you some time to cool off first."

"Cool off?" I growled through gritted teeth. "You followed me from my apartment to Kara's, then waited outside in your car for six hours and expected me to be *cooled off*?"

"Yeah, it sounded like a good idea in my head, but in retrospect—"

"Look, Vic, I'm done. Get an Uber or something and go home."

"I don't need an Uber; I just want to talk to you."

"You are in no condition to drive," I said, pointing at his car.

"Fine," he pleaded, his voice hoarse. "I won't drive as long as we can sit somewhere and talk about everything." His upper teeth caught his bottom lip as he sucked in the frigid winter air. When he exhaled, his breath became a cloud that rose until it disappeared into the night sky. "I need you, Bree."

Although no part of me wanted to sit there and say anything else to him, I knew I'd feel guilty if I found out later that Victor had crashed his car on the way home and hurt someone. I looked at Hippo buckled into my backseat, then toward Victor's car down the block, and then to the sky above. For a moment, I held my chin high, let the feather weight snowflakes melt on my face, and debated between my options.

"Victor," I sighed. "I gotta go."

Pushing past him, I walked around the car to the driver's seat. *What he does is what he does*, I thought, and I would no longer allow him to reel me in at my lowest because it was convenient for him. His actions were not my responsibility. Victor pounded on the car door window and pleaded with me to give him another chance, but I started the car instead. It was time I took a chance on me.

I peeled away from the curb and made it to the stop sign at the corner when I saw Victor's lights flick on. He revved his engine and sped toward me, but I whipped onto the main drag of town, sending my phone onto the floor and under my seat, and drove through a yellow light to give myself some distance. When he blew past the red light, my heart rate spiked.

The roads were slick, but my adrenaline surged. I pressed my gas pedal further into the floor, only braking to bank a few extra turns to throw him off. At least I tried. Whenever I thought I lost him in the rearview, his headlights would reappear from the void behind me. My ears began to thump, and, at the last minute, I decided to pull onto the ramp to I-95 and head south. The roads were mostly clear, except for the thin slush lining the highway and Victor fishtailing behind me.

My van gained some distance from him. He slid between the empty lanes of the interstate and skidded out further and further back. Foot steady on the gas, I felt around my floor, desperately searching for my phone, but sat straight when I heard his car revving again and drawing near. Hippo whined and crouched low in her seat.

Victor closed in, and the grill of his car nearly caught the back bumper of mine, but he just as quickly dropped back as if to taunt me. When I thought I could breathe again, his engine roared, and he accelerated toward me again. The bridge beneath us had formed a thin layer of ice, and my tires could hardly grip. Victor's taillights overtook my rearview mirror. Right before he could rear-end me fully, his car jerked to the right, and his front headlight clipped the back of my car, sending mine into a tailspin and then into the median.

And then there was black.

Nothing.

When I awoke, maybe seconds later, my head pounded, and I could hear a desperate, tortured yowl from behind me. "Oh, my God, Hippo!" I screamed.

For being such an emotional crier, I found that my acute stress response consistently turned me into a *fighter* and not a *flighter*. I tried to free myself from my seat, but it was clear my legs were pinned. Instead, I contorted my waist and craned my neck to reach for my baby. Comfort her. Coo her. Tell her how much I loved her. How good a girl she was. From what glimmer of light the street lamps offered, I could see blood in the backseat. Pools of it.

> When the body is depleted of too many red blood cells, the oxygen circulating throughout the body decreases, which can cause shortness of breath; rapid blood loss can also cause dizziness, lethargy, and confusion. In severe cases of bleeding, humans can pass out—or worse—in as little as five minutes. Dogs, being so much smaller and having less blood in their bodies, could experience this sooner.

> But I didn't know; in all the books and articles I read on dogs, reading up on how much blood loss a dog could live through was never something that crossed my mind.

From the back seat, Hippo, very much awake and scared, wailed and wooed as she panted hard, labored breaths.

Years of annual first aid certification pamphlets flipped through my memory. Blood loss. Shock. Tourniquet. With my arms free, I clung to the front passenger headrest. I pulled myself free with a superhuman strength I'd never known or would likely ever know again, ripping my jeans in the process. The urge to live was strong, but the urge to save my best friend was stronger.

My brain streamed with thought faster and with more focus than I thought possible. I tore the hole in my pants larger, shredding a leg off completely and rolling it into a makeshift bandage. I turned the overhead light on and searched for a wound, only to find that Hippo's leg had also been pinned, but hers remained crushed in between the metal and hard plastic framing of the door. She frantically tried to stand from her lying position but couldn't break free enough to gain her footing.

She didn't want me anywhere near her wound. She thrashed and barked in the throes of her autonomic response, but she needed me. I took her leash from the floor and tied it around her snout and neck to muzzle her, then wrapped my scrap of denim around her back leg above her ankle and tied it off tight. She cried in agony. Through the broken glass of the driver's window, Victor emerged.

"Are you okay?"

"Hippo is stuck!" I yelled. "We need to get her out!"

911. I ducked through the passenger door and pawed the floor until I found my phone. Shaking, I punched in my pin, but when the blood on my hands gunked the touch screen, I had to dial the rest in with my knuckles. After an eternity, my phone unlocked, and I called for an ambulance and the police and pleaded for someone—anyone—to help my dog.

Victor ran back to the trunk of his car and reemerged with a navy canvas duffel bag with the words, "Department of Transportation" silkscreened on the sides. "There has to be a first aid kit in here somewhere," he said as he pulled out roadside emergency tools and fished out the travel first aid kit. "Here." He tossed it to me and dug further in, throwing aside jumper cables and bungee cords until he found the toolbox at the bottom. "And don't worry, I was just borrowing all of this stuff—I was planning on giving it back when—"

"Shut up and help me," I cried with the phone to my ear. "Come on—pick up, pick up, pick up."

The operator on the line had a voice for radio, so calm and collected. She asked where we were, if I'd been injured, how it happened. I rattled back the details as coolly as I could—

"I crashed my car,"
"My dog's hurt, she's bleeding,"
"Please help,"
"He just kept chasing me,"
"Victor, my ex-boyfriend,"
"Yes, I'm okay,"
"No, I'm not okay"—until my voice started to crumble from my throat.

I stroked Hippo's face and ears to comfort her, and she let out a pathetic whine. Her breathing began quickening. Sweat dripped from my head, and I swiped it away with my forearm, only to find it wasn't sweat. Blood poured from a gash in my head, saturating my hair, and started dripping onto my face. From the first aid kit, I got out some gauze and wiped what I could, rubbing the fabric over the wound I hadn't even realized I sustained. A searing pain shot through my scalp. It was impossible to forget I had it afterward.

Victor found some bolt clippers from his toolbox and started clipping what he could—fabric, metal, plastic—but was getting nowhere fast. He cursed, and he spat, but nothing helped.

"The responders are almost there," soothed the woman on the phone, and I heard their sirens no sooner than she finished her sentence.

Emergency responders rushed my Astro, looking for people to save. They asked if I was the only person in the car and tried to help me out, but I pleaded with them to help Hippo instead. "I won't leave her," I told them.

"The animal response team is on the way," a woman assured me, guiding me out of the back passenger door to my feet. "We'll make sure she's taken care of, but we need to get you checked out first." A man with a bag full of tubes and equipment stayed behind with Hippo while an EMT checked my pupils against a bright light and cleaned excess blood from my face.

I correctly identified my name, birthdate, and the current date, then wished the EMT a Happy New Year, which made her smile for a second. "Happy New Year to you, too," she said and ran her gloved fingers through my scalp, locating the cut that wouldn't stop bleeding. "This'll need stitches, but it looks worse than it actually is."

"How bad does it look?" I asked and winced when she began to clean the wound. I squeezed my eyes shut and squinted them open to watch my car, but I only saw flashing lights. For a split second, I closed my eyes and saw Victor's headlights flash on in front of Kara's house, and a white-hot heat surged in me. "He did this to me." When I opened my eyes again, I could see that the police had arrived and began walking toward Victor, who had taken ill beside his car.

"Pretty bad," she said, emphasizing each syllable. "I mean, you are drenched in blood, but I think this is the only place you're actively bleeding." I looked down and caught a good look at my jacket and jeans under the bright fluorescent lights of the ambulance. I looked like I came straight out of the prom scene from *Carrie*.

A state trooper came up from the side of the ambulance and introduced himself as a name I couldn't remember. He wore a Kevlar vest over his thick winter coat, badges and walkie-talkies and pouches decorating his chest. His belt held a taser to one side and a gun on the other, but I couldn't be sure which was which. Nothing seemed real anymore. My pulse quickened.

"He's been following me since after dinner last night. He parked outside of my friend's house while I spent New Year's with them and apparently drank until I left." I swallowed back tears but started to choke up anyway. "He followed me onto 95 and clipped the back of the car and—I don't know—I guess I spun out and hit the median? I don't remember. I came to after I was already there."

With his tiny notebook and the pen that seemed almost childish in his oversized hands, the cop took note of my answers and asked, "And could you describe your relationship with this man?"

"Victor? He's my ex. Like, recent ex. But he's been following me around all night."

"I see. And did you have anything to drink at your friend's house?" He raised a brow and caught my eye.

I didn't and agreed to the breathalyzer to prove it. As suspected, there had been no alcohol in my blood, and I breathed a deep breath of relief when he smiled and told me that he never doubted me. "We just have to be as thorough as possible, is all." He reached into the chest pocket of his vest and handed me a card. "Here is all of my contact information. Contact me if you have any other information you feel is pertinent. Otherwise, you can call and request a copy of the report for your records." He looked back toward Victor, who tripped on his own leg and fell during a field sobriety test, and said, "But I think this is a pretty open and shut case."

A fire truck and Animal Response arrived at the scene just before the EMTs strapped me down to the gurney and drove me to the hospital. My first thought was less a thought and more of a bargaining with the universe to keep Hippo safe. My second thought was more of a question: *how am I going to pay for all this? Do I still have health insurance? No, no, the car insurance will pay for this. Right?*

Right?

twenty-six

. . .

Holidays are often the busiest days of the year for healthcare workers. While most folks are home, getting drunk and getting into trouble, hospital staff still have their shifts to work, and, as a bonus, they get to treat all of the folks who got drunk and got into trouble. And then some. Like innocent people who were leaving holiday get-togethers when a drunk driver slammed into them. Statistically speaking, holiday patients were more likely to have poorer outcomes than if they'd been treated on, say, a random Thursday, but the jury was out on exactly what caused that phenomenon. One theory was that the accidents that occurred in that drunken celebratory time left worse injuries than regular days. Another was that staffing was skeletal, with so many employees out on vacations and or requesting off to spend quality time with family. Could've been both. Whatever the case, I was very fortunate that, instead of working in an emergency room, I worked in a private practice that closed for federal holidays.

Unfortunately, however, I was now the reason someone else had to work on New Year's Day.

The university hospital off the interstate triaged me, sending me for a battery of tests and drawing vial after vial of blood. X-ray, CT, MRI. Contrast. After hours of waiting, speaking with technicians, chatting with nurses, and waiting some more, I saw a brown-haired, Brawny-Man-looking physician, who gave me the initial assessment.

"You are a very, very lucky individual," he said, rubbing his five (a.m.) o'clock shadow with his ginormous paw. In a small room beside the diagnostic testing hall, he gave me the full rundown: I'd sustained a mild to moderate concussion and had a gnarly contusion on my head, but luckily, no brain swelling or broken bones, save for the hairline fracture of my left pinky toe and torn soft tissue around my knee, neither of which I would feel until after my initial shock wore off. Not that I remembered him telling me any of that—oh, no—it was all on a printout I received when I checked out later on. Between my swimming head and his forest-brown eyes, all I could remember was that my brain needed rest. "And lots of it," he said. From then on out, if I wanted to move anywhere in the hospital, I went in a wheelchair. Which, to be fair, was probably for the best.

Every wing and hall of the hospital crawled with the sick and injured, people crumpled into seats, wailing into caretakers' shoulders, vomiting profusely into rectangular pink basins. With my tests done and read, the doctor excused himself, making way for a tattoo-clad teddy bear of a nurse who rolled my wheelchair back into a waiting room chair. There, he stuck me with an IV for precautionary fluids and a mild anti-inflammatory to take the edge off my aches.

"Once a bed opens up, we can move you in, but it might be a few hours," he said somberly, apologizing as if it were his fault. It wasn't. It was New Year's morning, and the hospital had probably reached capacity hours before the ball even dropped.

He handed me a pink basin—"Just in case," he said—and promised to check back with me regularly, which he did. Sometime between waiting and his next check-in, I received a surprise visit from the cop who spoke with me in the ambulance. A slight firecracker of a nurse obliged and pulled me aside to a dressing area to talk to him about the accident in private.

"Is Hippo okay?" I asked before answering his question.

"Your dog has been taken to the animal hospital and is being treated by the best animal ER in the state," he said, smiling. I did, too, but with glossier eyes. How fortunate we both were to be so close to the university campus. "As for her exact state, I can't answer. We do, however, have the other party in custody."

Victor. In custody. In all the mayhem of the crash, I never thought about the true repercussions—the legal repercussions —of Victor's behavior.

I never hated anyone more than I did at that moment, but still, for the smallest fraction of a second, part of me wanted to feel bad for him. For all the good times we had together. For how he'd held me when I cried and always made me feel safe in an unsafe world. But looking at him then, the thing that made the world crash around me... as soon as the empathy came, it went, and I felt guilty and disgusted for feeling bad for him. I didn't need him or his good times or his illusion of safety. I needed my dog, and I needed my life back.

"How about my van? And my stuff? Oh my God, my whole life is in that stupid van."

"The vehicles have been towed to a garage, but the van has been totaled. You're lucky to have come out of this thing alive."

Yeah, buddy, I wanted to say. *I know. It's all everyone around here seems to say to me.*

"You can always repurchase whatever's in the car, but I've seen enough accidents to know that you should be thanking your Creator to be here, having this conversation with me today." He pulled out a notepad from his chest pocket, scribbled some words, and then ripped the sheet from the coils. "But, once you're released and feeling up to it, you can get your things from the tow yard. Not the van, though. Sorry to say, there's no driving that thing off the lot."

Huh. Just my luck. Not only did I pack up my entire life and live in a car just to make it fifteen minutes before even that home was taken from me, but now a cop was lecturing me about how close to death I came. *That's the least of my concerns, guy.* Without my minivan, I was homeless. Without Hippo by my side, I was empty.

The cop asked for my recollection again, since Hippo and I were in relatively-better positions, and once I gave him all I knew, he excused himself to another matter. As soon as he turned the corner and was out of sight, I wheeled myself back to the waiting area. I attempted to decipher the chicken scratch on the note he gave me, but I quickly gave up and threw my head back. From behind, I could hear Victor's voice, and my heart raced. *No. Not now.* I frantically searched everywhere to find him, glancing from face to face, finding him laughing that nervous laugh of his from the wall-mounted television in the corner of the room. The screen flashed pictures of my Dream Home, then footage of me smiling, then me tubing down a steep hill. It would appear as if the medical establishment also kept the politically-neutral HHTV on their waiting room televisions, and—just my luck —they were airing the re-run of my taping. Because of course they would. It was how the universe worked, I guessed. Didn't they have some sort of obnoxious kitchenware infomercial they could play to fill the early-morning content desert?

"Hey," a crinkled old man in a white gown across from me said, "that girl looks kinda like you." I looked up at the screen again, and there I was, a toothy smile from one ear to the other, with Victor's arm snuggly wrapped around my waist.

"Yeah," I said, less than enthused. "I guess it does."

Tied to the back of my chair sat a plastic bag full of my bloodied clothes and shoes from the accident. I rummaged through it, found my cell phone from the pants pocket, and called Kara. In her normal Kara way, she answered before the second ring, but her throat sounded groggy instead of her normal chipper voice.

"Morning, sunshine," she croaked.

"Kara, hey, look, I'm in the hospital and—wait, did I wake you? I'm sorry—"

"Hospital? What?" Her voice sharpened as if she'd been awake for hours. "Bree, are you okay?"

"Yes. No—maybe. Victor followed me from your house and crashed into me on the interstate, so now I'm in the ER, and Hippo is at the vet, and Victor's been arrested and—"

"I'm on my way," Kara cut in. Away from the microphone, I could hear her tell Liza to get up and get dressed.

"I'm at the university campus, but I don't even have a room yet—"

"Doesn't matter, already on our way." In the background, I could hear fabric rustling, shoes clopping, and keys jangling. "I'll call you when we get there."

My phone beeped, letting me know I had a call from an unknown number on the other line, and knowing there'd be no convincing Kara to wait until I had a room of my own, I excused myself to take it. On the other line, a woman asked to speak with me.

"Hi, this is Dr. Warren from the emergency veterinary team. It looks like we received your dog from an accident this morning."

"Yes!" I hollered. "Hippo, that's Hippo. Is she okay?"

"Yes, Hippo. She lost a lot of blood, but we're stabilizing her now. We had to sedate her to get a better look at her wounds, and it looks like she sustained severe damage to her back left leg."

"Oh my God," I whispered into my hand, trying not to interrupt the vet.

"She's in good hands here," she comforted, "but we're going to have to go in and see what we can do to help her."

"Yes—anything," I cut in.

"We're not sure what we're going to find in there, but this can be a bit costly, potentially up to a few thousand if we need to amputate."

"Amputate?" I hollered into the phone, startling the woman in the wheelchair beside mine. I sniffed back the tears in my nose and swallowed my pain. Hippo needed me to be strong for her. "I don't care how much, just please help her."

Dr. Warren promised that she and her team would treat Hippo as best as they could and told me to listen out for another call in a few hours to touch base on Hippo's procedure. I thanked her profusely and ended the call with a heavy heart. She'd only been alive for two years, and Hippo had already suffered so much. I lit up the screen on my phone to the picture of her roast beef smile under the time, not quite seven. The sun hadn't risen just yet. When the screen blackened, I tapped it again to light it back up and to see her face, over and over and over.

❀ ❀ ❀

Kara and Liza arrived at the hospital two and a half hours later. "According to the AM radio traffic watch," Liza told me, "an accident on southbound I-95 caused a complete closure for an hour, but has since begun trickling cars through a single lane."

"Sorry 'bout that," I said, pretending to be embarrassed over a faux pas. Truthfully, I was more than a tad embarrassed by the entire situation, but deep down, I know I couldn't have helped it. Still, I felt bad. Bad to gnarl traffic for so long, bad that Kara and Liza came out to see me, bad that Hippo could potentially lose a leg. Thinking about her in so much pain gored me. "I miss my dog."

"Oh my God, Bree—where is she?" Kara asked, quickly blanketing me with a hug. "Is she okay?"

"She's over at the animal hospital. A vet called and said they were rushing her to surgery because of her leg." Kara pulled away, and I looked her in the eye before letting my gaze drop to my knees. "They said they might have to amputate."

"Hippo," whispered Kara to herself. I could see she both wanted to cry and keep a brave face for me. Normally, I think it would have been okay for her to cry, and I would have encouraged it—best to get the tears out than keep them in—but in that moment, I wouldn't be able to prevent myself from falling apart again if I saw her upset. Just fifteen minutes prior, I found myself getting misty-eyed over a Downy commercial (that snuggly bear was so darn cute).

"Ms. Huxley," called my buff nurse, "looks like we have a room opening for you on the floor." Perfect timing. Seeing Kara want to bawl but hiding it for me almost made me start crying in front of the entire waiting room all over again. At least in my own bed, I could cry in peace.

"Is it okay if my friends come back with me?"

"Sure can." The nurse took the handles of my wheelchair, and Liza grabbed my bag of belongings, which I'd been holding in my lap since I kept going through it anyway. When the handles opened, she caught a glimpse of my bloodied clothes and recoiled.

"We'll have to bring you some fresh clothes later on," she said, trying not to get physically sick. The thought made me snicker; Kara and I both grew completely immune to the squeamishness of blood and guts (except for eyes; eyes were gross) in the years we worked in healthcare, and it was easy to forget how many people couldn't stand even a single drop of blood. But it was sweet of Liza to not hurl the bag down the hall in horror. Instead, she pinched it between her finger and thumb and held it at arm's length as she walked until Kara caught on and snapped it up from her. I had to stifle a giggle when she ran to the nearest wall-mounted hand sanitizer station and pumped half a gallon of the stuff into her palm.

"Where are all your clothes, anyway?" Kara asked once the nurse helped me into bed, and I settled in between the blankets.

The room was small, but its window was grand, taking up nearly the entire wall, less the grout, and the trim affixing it to the building. Outside, I had a lovely view of snarled rush hour traffic through the hospital campus's main roadway and dozens of other buildings that appeared to also be made entirely out of glass. Kara and Liza rested their butts on the windowsill counter. They placed my bag on the solitary dusty mauve chair in the corner. "All my stuff is in the car," I told them, "and the car is at a repair shop junkyard somewhere outside the city. The cop I talked to said I can get my crap from the back, but the car's undrivable." I craned my neck to look out the window behind them, to try to find the animal hospital down the street, but the curve of the road cut my view of it. I pointed vaguely toward where I thought it might be and told them, "I think Hippo's right over there."

"I know, we'll get her soon," Kara said, turning her head to try to spot the vet, too. "But first, I think I'll head over to the store sometime, buy you some fresh clothes. Don't want you leaving here in any of this mess," she said and picked up my bag, shaking it in the air for emphasis. "Or worse, a backless hospital gown."

"I think I can pull off backless," I said with a smirk, never looking away from the window.

"Didn't say you couldn't." I looked up at Kara, who gave me a wink. "You'd definitely break necks in it." Even in my darkest hour, she found a way to gas me up.

When Kara and Liza left to go coat and dress shopping for me, I pulled out my phone and called my mom. Yes, I hated her for how she treated Hippo, and yes, I told her never to talk to me again, but she deserved to know that her firstborn was hurt, but more importantly, that I survived.

I called her up, and the phone rang five times.

Certain she wouldn't answer, I cleared my throat to leave a voicemail, but she picked up just before the answering message clicked on.

"Didn't I tell you not to call here anymore?"

"Hey, yeah. I know, but…." Though I clearly understood language and how to work my vocal cords, it still took me some time to figure out how to speak again. "Um, so Victor crashed his car into mine, and I'm at the hospital—"

"Oh, my God—is he okay?" Mom cut in. "Is he there, too?"

"No, what? No, he's in jail right now. And I'm alright, too, thanks for asking."

"Jail? Does his mom know?"

His mom? Since when did Mom care about Victor's mom?

"I don't know. I don't care. He could have killed me."

"You don't care? You don't care. See, Breanna? That's your problem. You only think about yourself."

"Wha—"

Click.

And, like she had countless times before, she hung up on me first, but at least that time, it'd also be the last.

I stared back out the window—to the honking cars and jaywalkers below, to the neon lights bouncing around the panels of glass of the children's hospital across the street, to the truck pulled up onto the sidewalk, unfastening a sticker-plastered falafel cart to the corner, opening shop for the day—and I smiled. Kara and Liza were all the family I needed. As far as humans went, at least. And soon enough, I'd be out and reunited with my closest family, my best friend in the whole world.

twenty-seven

. . .

A parade of residents, attendings, and nurses marched through my room, reading my chart and checking my vitals, and eventually cleared me to go home. I didn't want to be at the hospital, and they were clearly short on rooms, so it ended up working out for everyone. Kara and Liza returned with a marled gray sweater dress from a clearance rack and a brand-new, black, knee-length winter coat (the kind with the faux-fur trim around the hood I'd always coveted) and explained that the jacket would probably keep me warm over the cute, albeit short dress. I told them I was grateful for anything, which I was.

I stepped into the shared restroom and pulled the dress over my head. To my surprise, it fit perfectly. Made my butt look good. Great, even. I couldn't take my eyes off it in the mirror. When I finally stopped admiring myself, I stepped back into my room, where a receptionist with a mobile check-out station waited for me. Oops. "Sorry," I said with a hand over my mouth. "I hope you weren't waiting here long."

With cocked brows and a peeved look on her face, she

smacked a piece of gum in her mouth. "Only a minute or two."

Warm in the face, I accepted my stack of stapled discharge papers, and after the mini panic attack I had when I saw the astronomical bill the hospital included for insurance purposes at the end, I collected my bags and clothes and walked out beside Kara and Liza. The physicians and cop were all correct: even if it was with a hint of a limp, the fact I could leave on my own two feet was nothing short of a miracle. All I could do was hope that Hippo could leave the ER with all four of hers.

"Hospital parking should be free," I said as I watched my footing along the uneven sidewalk.

Kara had parked seven and a half blocks away to avoid the twenty-six-dollar lot fee, although the emergency room receptionist said she'd validate tickets for patients down to five when we checked out. "If they knew they were going to knock twenty bucks off the total, why don't they just advertise that price?" she asked, but I didn't answer in case it was rhetorical, although I thought the answer was probably to deter random people parking in the lot for neighboring businesses and crowding out the patients. But with my newly-diagnosed concussion, I couldn't be sure of that either. Whatever the case, I didn't mind the walk too much. My gait was unsteady, and my legs were still sore, but I felt grateful to use them. That, however, did not mean I wanted to double back down to the animal hospital by foot in the snow.

"I'll pay for the parking at the vet," I finally volunteered after —who knows—a few seconds, maybe a few minutes. All I wanted in the world was to be with my dog, even if it took all day and all night in a waiting room to see her. The money didn't matter.

"It's fine," Liza said, her breath labored from the incline of the sidewalk, "we got it. You just take care of yourself."

The drive to the vet would ultimately have been a quicker walk. The never-ending strip of construction along the boulevard funneled cars down to a single lane on both sides, then a single lane for all to share, as if that wouldn't create chaos and additional road closures from the jerk in a metallic eggplant-colored Hummer who tried to gun it before the flagger could stop him and drove his bumper directly into a Jeep. *At least this traffic isn't my fault*, I thought. Then, I suppose the one I created mere hours before couldn't have been my fault either. Still, that didn't help with the guilt I had about it.

By the time we reached the animal hospital and parked, it was past lunchtime, and my stomach wouldn't shut up about it. The food options at the cafe downstairs were scant, but I needed something in my stomach to prevent me from fainting. I ended up getting a plain bagel with nothing on it, not toasted. Boring, but the quickest option available. It was a far cry from my dinner the night prior, but my body needed any calories I could shove into it.

The bagel, three reception desks, and a bathroom break later, the three of us found ourselves in the correct waiting area for the surgical bay. "Either she's still in surgery, or she's about to finish up," the secretary at the desk told me, "because her electronic chart hasn't been moved from the operating room bay. But it shouldn't be much longer if you want to take a seat." And so, I sat.

And waited.

I picked at my nails and fidgeted with my hair. Kara and Liza rested their heads on each other and dozed off after about fifteen minutes, but I couldn't blame them. I was tired, too. Exhausted. My acute stress response had long drained from me, leaving a sleepy residue of weariness and burnout. *Closing my eyes for a quick second couldn't hurt*, I thought.

"Hi, Ms. Huxley?"

I jolted in my chair. Over me stood a waifish doctor in faded, oft-washed seafoam scrubs and a long, blonde ponytail. "I'm Dr. Warren, one of the Emergency Surgery surgeons on Hippo's case. We spoke on the phone earlier. Good to see you're out of the hospital yourself." Her smile was warm, yet heavy. She took a seat beside me, which felt more comforting than her ominously blotting out the fluorescent lighting behind her with her tall stance.

"Thanks," I said and wiped the side of my face, just in case any drool had decided to escape my mouth. "How's Hippo?"

"She's all done with surgery and recovering in the back."

Tears filled my lids, threatening to spill over. "She made it."

"She did," she said, but her frown stirred a sour worry in my chest. "She had a broken tooth, which we had to remove, and there were some cuts around her face that needed a few stitches, but—" the vet placed her hand on my shoulder and blew out a puff of breath, "her leg needed extensive surgery. She sustained a comminuted, unreduced fracture." Dr. Warren made her hands into c-shapes and shuffled them up and down. "The bone in her hind leg broke in several locations, but instead of remaining flush, they jumbled."

My heart hit my stomach. Her leg. My poor baby's leg. She could barely walk without tripping or bumping into walls as it was. I tensed all of the muscles in my body as if I were back in the car and bracing for impact all over again.

"However, we didn't feel the breaks warranted amputation."

What?

"Her fibula had multiple breaks, but her tibia remained miraculously intact. She has a plate and a few screws throughout her leg and will need to relearn how to use the leg slowly."

Part of me wanted to breathe a sigh of relief, but part of me knew we weren't out of the woods yet. "Hippo can't hardly see as it is. How's this going to affect her getting around on her own?" My heart raced, but that time, I couldn't catch it. In my fragile state, panic began to overtake me again, but I had to count my breath and listen carefully to the doctor. Hippo needed me.

"That's the next issue. Since she had cuts on her face, we did a brief ophthalmic exam while she was still under. She didn't have any corneal abrasions or retinal detachments, which animals sometimes get after an injury like this. Still, she did have significant, long-standing retinal atrophy."

"She took one of those dog DNA kits, and it said she had a PRA-something mutation that could cause blindness," I told her, wiping my eyes with my new jacket.

"I think it would be a good idea to have the ophthalmologist take a look at her after she wakes up to get a better idea of her prognosis there, but as for the rest of her, we expect a full recovery. She'll need physical therapy to help her balance and regain strength in her leg, but most dogs bounce back from surgery pretty quickly. She could need to spend upwards of a week here, but we'll get a better idea of how long when she starts making progress."

"A week," I blurted. Thousands of questions flooded my brain, but the most pressing was how I'd make it for so long without my baby. Especially now when we needed each other more than ever. I swallowed back my tears and worries, sucked in as much air as my lungs could bear, and choked out, "Thank you for everything. Hippo means everything to me. She's my best friend."

The doctor shook her head and stood from her chair. "We'll help her every way we can. You have my word." And with that, she went back to the surgery bay, back to saving the life of someone else's best friend, no doubt.

To take my mind off how potentially serious Hippo's injuries were and how lucky I was that she made it through it all, I wandered around the waiting area, looking at the various posters on the wall. One about feline dental hygiene, another about a cockatiel's muscular and skeletal anatomy. Opposite the long, windowed wall of the hall adjoining the waiting area was a ten-foot-long bulletin board. The lining was composed of several pieces of neon yellow poster board and a border made from a metallic red cardboard trim. The whole thing reminded me of kindergarten.

Throughout the panel, die-cut stickers of cartoon dogs and puppies held up pictures of real dogs and puppies, but I only realized that these were actual animals after taking the time to study that elementary school art project. An almost-hidden piece of paper stapled to the bottom corner printed in a Comic Sans-like font read:

ADOPTABLE ANIMALS. CONTACT ROWEHOME RESCUE FOR MORE INFO.

No wonder there are so many animals still available for adoption, I thought. *These pictures suck. And they spelled "rowhome" wrong.* I doubled back and reviewed all the blurry, uneasily identifiable photos once more. I guess they were all *kind of* dog-like.

"Are you interested in adoption?" asked a voice from behind me.

I jumped and turned to see a hospital coordinator with a clipboard smiling at me. I didn't want to disappoint her with a hard "no," so I played it off by saying, "Not right now; my baby just came out from surgery."

"Oh, I'm so sorry to hear," she replied, partly being polite but mostly sincere. "Well, if you want to come by while she recovers, we're hosting a Rowehome Rescue New Year's adoption event at the outpatient lobby." She handed me a flyer from her clipboard, smiled, and resumed her walk down the long hall.

I looked back at Kara and Liza, both soundly sleeping, Liza with her mouth slightly agape and Kara softly snoring, and decided not to wake them. I followed the treasure map on my flyer down to the main lobby to pet some puppies.

twenty-eight

. . .

The word "concussion" doesn't do the diagnosis justice. It's
a traumatic brain injury. Specifically, one where brain function
is affected. On paper, it sounds much scarier than you see on
TV or might read about in books—unless, of course, those books
are medical texts.

Which I'd read tons of thanks to four years of undergrad
healthcare courses.

And, thanks to years of assisting patients, I knew the rules: no
reading, no computers, no plot twist-heavy movies that
required keeping tabs on characters to ultimately figure out
whodunnit. In short, no activities that involved any real
thinking; the brain was an organ, and just like a stomach
would need rest to heal after an injury, the brain did, too. The
major difference between the two organs, however, was that I
needed my brain to think about healing in order for it to heal,
but thinking too hard would delay its healing.

No two concussions were the same, though. Some were more
severe than others, and some had different symptoms than
others. It wasn't uncommon for the concussed to have issues

with anxiety, sensitivity to noise, ringing in the ears, and difficulty with decision-making. Luckily, I had all those things anyway, just because of who I was as a person. However, thinking back on the bulk of my life decisions up until that point, it was hard to believe that I could outdo myself from a minor brain injury.

It was funny how I always found a way to surprise myself.

I could hear the lobby before I could see it. The room hummed with the chatter of a few people, but mostly, I could hear the excited *yips* and *yaps* of dogs. So many dogs. All the furniture from the lobby must've been moved out or pushed aside to allow for dozens of metal playpens on the floor. Most of the pens had a single dog, panting and smiling, but some had litters of two, three, or four puppies, ready for their new homes. They all looked so much cuter than in their photos.

Across the lobby, I recognized the dyed lavender beehive hairdo and bedazzled turquoise glasses I'd come to know and love during my time at Franklin Family—Ms. Rowe. She was standing next to a pen, carrying two puppies, one in each arm, when she glanced up from her conversation with another older woman and smiled at me, jiggling one of the puppies as if to mimic waves. I tried to make a beeline toward her but had to stop four or five times to pet the dogs.

"Hey, stranger, what brings you around these parts today?" Ms. Rowe asked when I finally reached her, her smile as vibrant and toothy as ever. "Looking for a new family member?"

"Actually, no. Well, maybe." I wanted to spill all my agonizing details about Hippo, about the accident, about Victor, but truthfully, I didn't want to unload on the woman, who barely knew me. All I knew of her—her shingles, her questionable blood sugars—I only knew from her medical chart, so maybe my frame of reference wouldn't make for the best conversation starter. "I was in the area and found out about this event, so I thought I'd come by. What are you doing here?"

"Oh, this is my rescue," she said and pointed to the sign behind her. The misspelling of the word "Rowehome" wasn't a misspelling at all—just her name infused into a logo. *Cute*, I thought. "And I figured New Year's Day is as good a day as any to host an adoption event. Most people are off work and making resolutions to get more active. I figure some people will think of adopting a dog to keep them accountable for daily walks outside."

I saw the angle. Clever. "Down the hall a bit, I saw the poster full of dog pictures with your rescue's name on it," I started, trying to dance around how awful the images were. "Did you —did you take all those pictures yourself?"

"Yes, ma'am," she said with a smile, "though I know photography isn't really my strong suit. You wouldn't believe how hard it is to get a good shot of a dog when all they want to do is run around and not wear the cute flower crown I bought them." She snickered to herself, which, in turn, made me chuckle, too.

"Oh, I believe it," I told her and shook my head. "Back when I first started taking pictures of my dog, I almost gave up on photography altogether. She had her own agenda. But with some coaxing and a lot of treats, I think I cracked the code for taking a quality dog picture." The sentence lingered between us briefly before I cleared my throat and asked, "How would you feel if I helped? With the dog photos, I mean. I went to school for photography and am trying to get back into it." I pulled out my phone to show her pictures I'd taken of Hippo from my Creatr feed. "I love taking pictures of dogs. They always look cute and never talk back."

Ms. Rowe swiped up and down, clicking in and out of pictures and trying to zoom in. "These are beautiful," she said and navigated back to the top of my account page. "And your account looks great, too." She handed my phone back, then handed me one of the puppies she'd been clutching—a white pitbull mix with black spots over her right eye and a wiggly booty—and fished for one of her cards from her jean pockets. "I'd love for you to come by and take pictures of all of these guys. And, if you can make the rescue's feed look as good as yours, perhaps I can throw a couple dollars your way to take over our social media accounts. If you're interested, of course —I'm no good with those things."

"That sounds fantastic," I chirped, exciting the little puppy in my arms, who then covered my neck and ear with little baby kisses. Maybe all those years at Franklin Family weren't all for nothing after all. But then a stormy, looming cloud formed above my head, and I realized that perhaps that, like everything else, was too good to be true. I nuzzled into the puppy in my arms and offered, "The thing is, I'm not sure I can help you out long-term; I probably only have a few more weeks here in the city. Unless you think that I could potentially run everything remotely. Which I would be more than happy to do."

She used her puppy-less hand to pat my forearm and smiled a kind granny smile. "That should be fine, dear. I know you're not out to hurt these dogs."

My heart skipped a beat, but not in a terrifying medical way. "I could never. Also, if you're interested, one of my best friends does web design professionally. I'm sure I can get her to give the site a look over for you sometime. Maybe give it an update. Match it up to the new and improved social media accounts."

"That'd be great," she said and maneuvered the puppy she'd been holding onto her hip like a mother would hold a toddler. "And as long as you can keep my Creatr account running, I don't care if you do it from Mars. But I do have to say it looks like you may have found yourself a new *dog-ter*."

I pulled back and looked at the puppy I'd been holding, her tiny baby nose, her innocent eyes, and felt nothing but love. She squeaked a sweet, sad whine and dove her head back into the crook of my neck. Oh, how she smelled of that sweet new puppy smell.

The number one rule about concussions was to never make any big decisions. The brain was healing from a traumatic injury, and the area of the brain that controls decision making could be temporarily altered, making for impulsive, hasty decisions. No major purchases, no new lines of credit, no new cars or boats or houses. No volunteering your friends to update dog rescue websites or impulsively adopting puppies without really thinking about the logistics of nurturing a dog recovering from a leg amputation.

But at that moment, I couldn't stop myself.

"Is this angel baby still up for adoption?"

"Are you interested? The rest of her litter is already spoken for, including this sweet princess," she said, scritching under her puppy's chin, "but the lovable nugget you're holding still needs a home."

"Yes. No, wait. Maybe. I'm not sure, actually." I hesitated, the haze of concussion clearing enough to let a single ray of sun peak through. "I might not be ready for adoption—yet—but maybe I could foster her for a bit. Like maybe a week or so?"

"That'd be fantastic. Give the baby a bit of love and socialization—she'll need it once all of her brothers and sisters are gone. We have applications over on the table behind me if you're sure you're interested."

"Yeah," I said, not sure of anything in my life at that very moment. "I think I'll do that." With the baby dog in hand, I shuffled my way over to the paperwork table, where I was met by the clipboard lady who winked and handed me a pen.

"Looks like you found your baby a friend," she said, smiling at the puppy.

"Well, just until she finds her forever home."

The receptionist gave me a knowing look. "Of course."

I cocked my brow and finished signing my name. "Right. Well, thank you," I said and handed her my application.

With the puppy in my arms, I padded down the hall and back to the waiting area, where my friends remained sound asleep in their chairs. I tried to quietly slide back into my seat, careful not to wake Kara or Liza, but I clumsily flopped down anyway, clacking the arms of the chairs together and making quite the ruckus. They both woke up, dazed, and immediately cooed over the puppy in my arms.

"Oh, my goodness! Where did you get this baby?" Kara asked, cupping the pup's head in her hands and drawing a deep breath of puppy smell through her nose.

"There was an event down around the way," I said and pointed down the long corridor. "I also just happened to run into my favorite patient from work, and I think I may have a job taking pictures of adoptable dogs for her rescue."

"That's awesome," Liza said, petting the baby. "And you look like you're in a much better mood now."

"I am. The doctor said that Hippo is expected to make a full recovery, and I got a job taking photos. Of dogs! Plus, I found this precious girl there, too."

Kara leaned back from the puppy's face and snapped her head toward me. Her eyes squinted, and between her teeth, she asked, "Did you adopt a new dog?"

"Just fostering," I shot back, speaking so quickly that my words ran together. "You guys said you were thinking about it for a while last night, so I made the decision for you, and also I told the lady that Liza might help look at her website, but she said she was going to help with mine a few days ago anyway, so I was thinking I could donate that service to the rescue instead." I blinked three times and chewed my lip. "For charity." With a fake, closed-tooth smile, I hoped they'd both take it easy on me and my less-than-fully thought-out ideas. Seeing how I was going through so much and all.

Liza composed herself with a deep breath, then opened her eyes. "I don't mind doing her website, but do you really think right now is the best time to foster a dog? You have a healing Hippo who's going to need a lot of attention, and you don't have a place to live. Your van is in an impound lot somewhere, and you can't even sleep in it."

"I wasn't really thinking about—"

"Hold on, hold on," Kara, the voice of reason, piped in. "Let's not panic. Bree, you have two dogs and a totaled car, but you're alive and safe. That's what's important. Liza, we have a car and a roof over our heads, and we *were* talking about bringing in another dog. Maybe we can get Bree's stuff from the junkyard and bring it to our house until she gets settled somewhere," she said and nuzzled the soft ball of fur in her arms. "And test drive this new puppy. We do still have that tiny second room that we're only using for storage anyway; maybe we can fit a small bed in there for Bree to stay for a while like we talked about before."

"I still have some money left from my last paycheck, plus I might have a steady-ish job with the rescue soon to hold me, at least until I get the house and start working in the hospital. As soon as I can get on my feet, I will," I told Liza, almost trying to convince her that I wouldn't be a burden.

"Oh, I was already planning on you staying with us," she said, "I just wanted to make sure you knew what you were getting into."

I sighed a long-held breath of relief and said, "I don't know what I got into, but I'm sure I'm about to find out."

twenty-nine

. . .

Once our new little family got acclimated to each other in the waiting room and the puppy—Mochi, as Ms. Rowe called her —fell asleep in my lap, a vet tech from the back appeared and greeted me.

"I am happy to report that Hippo is awake and doing good," she began with an affirming smile. "But we will probably have to keep and monitor her for about a few days, possibly longer."

"A few days?" My heart ached. Every second away from Hippo felt eternal. "She'll be so scared and lonely all by herself."

"Don't worry. No matter what, we make sure our patients always come first here. We have around-clock staff who will walk her and feed her and give her love; she'll even have time outside of her crate to stretch her legs—" the tech said, catching her mistake after she could take it back. "She'll likely hang around the nursing station under our feet for a while if she gets lonely."

I nodded. "Gotcha."

"She has some pretty serious healing to do, and we're going to want to ensure she stays hydrated. She currently has an IV port for pain meds and antibiotics, but once she proves she can eat and drink on her own, we'll get that taken care of." Her expression slid between confidence and pity. "If you'd like, you can come back and say 'hi' before you leave."

I left Mochi with Kara and Liza and followed the nurse back to the row of cages full of post-surgical pets. There, dazed and sleepy, laid Hippo, with three-quarters of her body shaved and an opaque plastic cone fastened around her neck, lying on her side to reveal a crooked scar peeking out from the top of a neon pink bandage. My heart and stomach fell to my feet. So many emotions—heartbreak, despair, rage, grief—fought for my thoughts, and before I could see—truly see—the unimaginable suffering in front of me, I bawled.

"Hey girl," I said, my voice shaking, and swallowed down the tears in the back of my nose. "How's mommy's best baby?"

Hippo's ears twitched, maybe in recognition of my voice, but she could barely lift her boulder of a head. She opened her eyes, worried-looking, and let out a pathetic whine. I stuck my fingers through the grate of her cage, stroked the top of her front paw, and pressed my face as close to hers as the bars would let me. In a voice shaky from anguish and shame, I whispered, "I'm sorry I let you down, girl. I'm so, so sorry." Wiping away the tears from my cheeks, I asked for her to forgive me, but she'd already fallen back asleep. I could only hope she would, but I'd understand if she never trusted me again.

A nurse tapped my shoulder and told me that it was getting late and that Hippo needed her next round of medicine. She escorted me back out to the waiting area, but it felt too soon. The wounds—Hippo's and my own—were still too fresh. All

I wanted in the world was to crawl into her cage with her and love her, pet her, and protect her. Show her that I'd never let her hurt like that again.

Once we got back to the car, I sat in the backseat, buckled, holding a sleeping Mochi on my lap, and staring out the window. Mute. Kara drove us to a pet store on the way back to her place to get some brand-new puppy supplies for the apartment and settle our slapped-together family into their old space. Baby dogs were such hard work, but I needed the distraction more than I could've imagined. If it wasn't for Mochi, I probably would've spiraled down further than ever before; at least with such a young dog to care for, I had a responsibility to take my mind off how badly I let Hippo down. I needed to be there for her. I couldn't fail her, too. When my makeshift bed—a twin-sized air mattress covered in several old blankets to prevent tiny baby puppy claws from popping it—was fully set up, I dozed off without realizing it. When I woke up, it was nearly dinner time, and I had a snuggly, itty-bitty furball tucked under my left arm, snoring itty-bitty puppy snores, smelling like heaven. *Hippo would love this baby*, I thought.

We didn't end up getting my belongings from the impound lot until the next morning after I showered and had taken the puppy out for her morning walk. Hippo would still need to be in the hospital for at least a few more days, I figured, so I had nothing but time anyway.

When we got to the lot, and the mechanic walked Kara, Liza, and I over to what used to be my Astro, we let out a collective gasp. The van was annihilated. Half of the car appeared missing, and the front was completely smashed into the center console. The fact that Hippo and I made it out with just some soft tissue damage, a mild concussion, and an unreduced fracture between the two of us was nothing short of a miracle.

Most of my stuff had jostled quite a bit in the accident, but for the most part, my things were still in the boxes I'd packed them in. Unfortunately, my relief was short-lived when I heard what sounded like broken glass shifting and settling into the corners of one of the boxes. "I guess I won't be using whatever that is," I said to everyone and no one. If its contents looked anything like the outside of the vehicle, it was a safe bet that most everything would need to be thrown away.

I didn't have much before, but after the accident, I had virtually nothing.

"It was stupid to take a road trip like that," I said, poking my head into the box that held my now broken hot plate. "I wasn't nearly prepared enough."

"Nobody could've prepared for their psycho ex running them off the road," said Kara, who pulled out a trash bag full of clothes, ironically the only thing worth keeping. "I would've never guessed Victor pulling some shit like this. But if it's a silver lining you're looking for, at least you're getting to help this orphaned dog that wouldn't have a family to go home to otherwise."

"Yeah," Liza cut in, "and the Dream Home is fully furnished."

But I wanted my own stuff. It wasn't much, but it was mine. I looked around at my stuff, desperately hoping at least something could be salvaged, but finding almost nothing of the sort. "Thank God for that."

We finished packing up the few unbroken belongings I still had to my name—my duffle bag of camera equipment and that stupid purple wreath—and loaded back into the car when I noticed a missed call and voicemail from Ms. Rowe.

"Hi, Breanna. I hope you don't mind that I pulled your number from your foster application, but I just got word that a dozen dogs coming up from South Carolina to the rescue are ahead of schedule and will be here by tomorrow morning, and I'd love it if you could come by for their photos. If you're feeling up to it. You can bring the little nugget with you, too. I'd love to see her. Gimme a call when you can, okay? Bye-bye."

Welcoming any and all distractions to pass the dragging daylight hours until Hippo came home, I called back and agreed to set up a mini backyard photo studio at Ms. Rowe's house for the next morning. It wouldn't be much for pay, but it wasn't about that. Mainly, I wanted to do something good for these animals, but really, I wanted to get love drunk on dogs.

My head hadn't been right since the accident; my emotional state was already pancaked thin from the stress but had since worn to crumbs worrying about Hippo's health and my concussion. Lately, my brain couldn't keep up with my impulsivity. Foster a puppy? Of course. Come by for a photo session with dogs? I'd be there with bells on. Having Mochi around did help ground me a bit, I had to admit, keeping me in the present and preventing me from thinking in obtrusive spirals. And she was just so darn cute with her *Little Rascals* spot over her eye.

"You okay back there?" Liza asked, probably because my eyes had started glazing as I stared out the window.

"Yeah, just thinking about everything, I guess." I was lucky to have my best friends to help ground me. Until I moved, at least.

We stopped by the hospital to visit Hippo for a few moments but could only see her in between the extra naps her pain medication induced. She'd been a lazy dog before, but nothing like that. After hours of doomscrolling Creatr, the staff finally allowed me to sit with her in a playpen, where I could stroke her ear nubbies and rub her chubby belly. Although all I wanted in the world was to hug her, wrap my arms around her, and squeeze her tight, I held back. With such extensive wounds and scars running along her body, I didn't want to risk hurting her anymore.

After a bit, though, Hippo managed to hop up onto all fours, waggling her entire butt in excitement and covering me in kisses. Tears welled in my eyes (although it seemed everything made me cry anymore), but for the first time in a long time, these were happy tears. Hippo, not caring what sort of tears they were, lapped them up with abandon.

"I miss you so much, baby girl," I told her, cupping her colossal face in my hands. "I just want you home so bad." And I did, even though we didn't technically have a home to go to yet.

As we walked to Hippo's care cage, the nurse told me that she'd probably be best off with a couple more full days of care and rehab before coming back home since her progress had been slow. She'd gotten to her feet with me but hadn't moved around much. "The physical therapist wants to see her walking around on her own without guidance before she goes home," the nurse said as we tucked Hip back in between her blankets for her afternoon dose of IV meds. "She might even be good to go by tomorrow evening if she improves enough."

"Tomorrow?" I asked, unable to contain my excitement. "You hear that girl? You're doing such a good job."

"Let's not get too ahead of ourselves here," said the nurse. "She still needs to get the approval from the doctor, but there's a good chance we can get her discharged for you. Keep your fingers crossed."

By the end of the evening, my hands were so sore from crossing my fingers that I could barely hold my fork for my single-serve cup of ramen dinner. It didn't matter, though. I was too anxious to eat much, anyway.

thirty

. . .

With Mochi in the crook of my elbow, her little chest rising and falling in perfect harmony with mine, I slept like a baby. I hadn't been able to sleep well since the accident, but seeing Hippo standing and smiling must've warmed my heart and eased my mind enough to grant me a solid rest. Perfect timing, too. I had to wake up and get ready for my first day of rescue work.

Work. Temporary, part-time work, but work nonetheless. I couldn't believe it. After all the times I'd been told I couldn't make it in photography, after all the harsh words Mom used to spew at me for "wasting my time and money" on an arts degree, I finally got a job doing what I wanted. Plus, it had the added benefit of helping homeless dogs.

Kara had to go back to the office, and my hospital papers said I couldn't drive until my next concussion checkup, but Liza, who worked from home, agreed to take Mochi and I to the rescue site on the opposite side of the city, saving me a good hour or two of buses and trains with my duffle full of gear. We drove past the hospital that housed me after the accident and past the hospital that still housed Hippo, through a tree-lined street into a cute and quiet neighborhood I never knew existed.

"I think that donut shop you like is around here somewhere," Liza said over her phone's GPS. "Maybe I'll post up there and get some work done while you gallivant around with the dogs."

"Hey, I'll be working, too. It's not my fault that dog gallivanting isn't part of web design." I stroked the silky fur down Mochi's head and neck, soft and downy with youth, and turned to look back at Liza. "But if you do end up going to work over there, can you pick me up a chocolate glazed?"

We arrived at Ms. Rowe's house at 9 a.m. sharp, just as the last dog from the back of a transporter's SUV skipped up the sidewalk and sat patiently by the lavender front door. The three-story duplex looked castle-like, with spires and spindles and bay windows that could easily keep a Rapunzel or two. A covered wooden porch painted in bright yellows and pinks was the giveaway that the place belonged to Ms. Rowe and not some three-hundred-year-old queen.

"This place is awesome," Liza whispered as if she were trying to keep a secret from me, and I wasn't the only other person in the car.

"It really is." The house was the perfect mix of bright colors and polished architecture, much more interesting than the brownstones in Old City or the boring brick row houses everywhere else in town. The house had personality.

Inside, the house came alive. The sound of dog claws skittering around the hardwood floors sounded like music to my ears. Fur flew past in blurs and blobs.

"Breanna, you've made it!" Ms. Rowe cheered as if I were a daughter or a niece and I'd shown up from out of town for a holiday meal. As if she was a mother or aunt who cared.

"Of course! You couldn't pay me to miss this. I've been looking forward to it since you asked."

She led me to her dining room with broad French doors that exposed a cozy, snowy back garden and let me set up my equipment. Dogs circled my feet and begged for pets, which I gladly offered. But they didn't need to beg, really.

One by one, I took the dogs outside, coaxed them with snowballs and rope toys, and took photo after photo of them playing, sitting, posing, and smiling. Shadow, a black Lab mix with one floppy ear and one sticking straight into the air, gave the camera all eyes. Lucy, a white and tan spotted pitbull mix, showed off her cuddly side with a stuffy in the snow. Jackson, a presumed Chow-Corgi mix, had the time of his life when I whipped out a bag of peanut butter treats, and I captured the pictures to prove it.

By one o'clock, we'd only gotten half the brood photographed, but it was time to stop for lunch. Hours had passed since Liza texted me to tell me she'd gone to a library to work, then stopped for lunch at a street cart, but told me not to worry about time. She enjoyed the change of scenery. At Ms. Rowe's, we ordered spinach and seitan tacos from the corner cantina, and Mochi took a pup nap in my lap. She'd spent the entire morning playing in the snow, playing with other dogs, and playing with Ms. Rowe, who admitted she missed her. "I miss all the dogs when they get home," she told me, "but I need to let them go to help more."

"Have there been any leads on a home for Mochi?" I asked, almost hoping there weren't.

"Nothing as of yet. Why? Are you thinking of keeping her?" She raised her brows over her giant Elton John glasses and looked hopeful. Mochi twitched in my lap. Maybe she was dreaming about playing still.

I sighed. "She's a great puppy, and I love her so much already, but honestly, I don't know." I picked up a chip and inspected it, but used it more to fidget with than eat. "My dog Hippo is at the hospital," I admitted and began sipping the air to prevent tears from forming. "We had a bad accident on New Year's, and she's still at the hospital. That's why I came by the adoption event; I just needed something to take my mind off her surgery. She had to get a plate in her leg." I took a sip of water to push back the rising emotion. "They said she'd likely be there for around a week, hence holding this angel for that time, but she'll probably need me more when she gets out."

"Oh my God, Bree—I had no idea." She dropped her taco into its Styrofoam container with the others and wiped her face with a napkin. "Is there anything I can do? I have some connections with physical therapists and resources if you need anything."

I'd barely known that woman beyond being a patient a few days before, and she was extending any sort of relief that I could need to help my dog, whom she'd never met. I never knew people like that existed outside of television shows and movies.

"Thank you, that's really sweet, but I don't know what all she needs yet. This is all so new. But having Mochi has been helpful, for sure. Seriously. I don't know what I'd do if I had to deal with this alone." I thought of Liza and Kara and how I wouldn't have been able to do anything without them. How maybe I was less lonely than I originally thought. I smiled. It was a deep, genuine smile, one that extended from my face to my heart, one that made me feel warmer and fuzzier than I had in weeks. Months. Years.

"Well, the offer still stands. If you need anything, just give me a call."

We boxed up our leftovers and set back to work, where I tirelessly photographed every last dog, including Mochi, and helped a stream of fosters leash and collect their temporary dogs. I texted Liza to say we were wrapping up, and she said she'd meet up with me in an hour or so after she'd finished some project she'd been scalp-deep in.

I packed my gear and leashed Mochi, then bid Ms. Rowe adieu. She wrote me a check from the rescue's account, three hundred dollars (not enough to live off of until the next batch of dogs came from the south, but better than a day of work at Franklin Family), and I told her I'd work on editing the pictures for the website and social accounts as soon as I could.

First, I needed to visit Hippo.

thirty-one

· · ·

Much to my luck, Dottie's Donuts still had open doors and two peanut butter pretzel donuts when Mochi and I arrived. We stepped back onto the sidewalk, salty sweets in hand, and heard the tinkle of the exit bell overhead as the cashier flipped the "Open" sign to "Closed." Snow still lined the streets, but the traffic hadn't quite mucked it up yet, leaving the neighborhood looking like a city wonderland. On either side of us, ornate homes with painted wooden beams of orange and green or yellow and burgundy smiled down at us. Corner units and old houses converted to clothing boutiques and charming bookstores made the city feel more like a small town than a major metropolis. As the sun set, all the homes that hadn't yet removed their Christmas lights lit the porches and sidewalks around them, turning Philly into a quaint Thomas Kinkade painting.

I could easily get used to frequenting this place for photoshoots.

The first donut tamped my hunger, but I ate the second anyway. At the bottom of the brown paper bag, below the sheets of frosty white tissue paper, were scraps of pretzels, perfect for treating Mochi when I called her name. She picked up on the pattern pretty quickly, and by the time we reached the hospital, she knew to keep a trained eye on me.

If it wasn't for that stale pet shop smell and the sound of yammering dogs, the vet clinic would have been indistinguishable from a people's hospital. The worn monochromatic linoleum tiles had seen better days, but so had most of the animals who temporarily called the place home, I supposed.

Hippo still had at least one more day there yet, but I'd been visiting her daily. I handed Mochi over to the receptionist, who was more than happy to play with a baby dog, and a nurse escorted me back to the catacombs of cages filled with hurt dogs on the mend.

Hip was sleeping when I got to her crate. I shoved my fingers as far as I could reach to attempt to stroke her whiskery lips and cooed, "Hey, little girl." She jerked her head up, screeching her cone against the steel walls of her cage, and her butt commenced to wiggle.

The nurse scooped her out from her cage, placed her on the floor, and clipped a leash to her collar. Initially, I worried about her making the short trek to the playroom, but as we walked down the hall, she trotted on her pinned leg as if she never knew any other way to. My chest swelled with joy and hope and a tinge of sorrow.

"She's doing so much better," the nurse said, reading my thoughts. "She might be able to go home sooner than we anticipated."

"Is that right?" I asked Hippo in a baby voice. And the timing couldn't be better. With all my photos taken and nothing but hours upon hours of photo editing and social media curating ahead of me, I couldn't think of anyone else I'd like to cuddle up to and work with.

Except I still had Mochi for a couple more days, minimum.

Hippo needed time and space to heal, not an energetic and playful puppy running up to her and bothering her while she slept. I played with Hippo in the candy-colored, foam-padded play space, distracting myself from thinking about what sort of mess she'd be coming home to—a new, smaller space, flights of stairs, a new puppy. A new puppy! Lord knew if she'd even like the feisty ball of chaotic energy. *But once she comes home,* I told myself, *all will be well again.* We could move out west and live out our happily ever after. We would make it work.

"Hi, Ms. Huxley?" I turned from giving Hippo her softer-than-usual belly rubs and found a stout, older man standing behind me in a long white coat. "I'm Gary, the inpatient surgical manager. Is it okay if I talk to you for a moment in private?"

"Um, sure," I hesitated. "Can Hippo come, too?"

He obliged and ushered me to a quiet(er) corner of the playroom, away from prying ears and eyes.

"So," he said, clicking the top of his ballpoint pen. Like *he* was the one sweating bullets over being pulled aside to talk about his ailing best friend. "It's come to my attention that someone has dropped the ball here." He shuffled a stack of papers and located the one he must've been searching for. "Typically, when an animal comes in for such extensive procedures, we have the owner sign releases and waivers *before* we treat."

I gulped.

"I think I saw in the chart notes that you were hospitalized when Hippo arrived. Is that correct?"

I nodded.

"That's probably how this got missed, then. No problem, though. We just need to have you sign off on her care before we can release her home."

He clipped the top sheet of paper into the clipboard he'd plucked from a countertop beside him and withdrew a pen from his pocket. He guided me through the series of lines and dashed for signatures and initials, then flipped the pages for the billing waivers.

"This is where things get a little…." he paused and pondered for a second, probably thinking of a soft way to explain the situation I'd fallen into. "Hairy."

"Hairy?" There were tons of words that I would have liked him to say or that I wouldn't have minded him saying. *Hairy* made neither of those lists.

"Right. It appears that no one has discussed the financials of this treatment with you. Not in-depth, anyway." He turned the clipboard toward me and proceeded to discuss the treatments, medicines, and costs line after line. Those were costs that I tried to keep track of, but I quickly lost my place. After flipping to the third, fourth, and fifth pages, a grand total: a not-so-modest sum of 12,700 dollars slapped me directly in my face.

After paying for my deductibles and buying a few things to hold me over while I crashed with Kara and Liza, I had less than twelve hundred dollars to my name. My head began to swim, and I realized that I had stopped breathing.

I took a gulp of air and asked the manager, *Gary*, how anyone would be able to afford something like that.

"We could bill you for part of it," he said, "but we'll need at least ten percent up front."

I looked down at Hippo, frantic. "But when is the balance due?"

"By month's end. We do offer a payment plan if you would like to apply."

My credit score sucked. It seemed cruel that I needed to have money to apply for money and crueler still that I needed money to save my dog's life. To save mine. My sadness turned to anger, but I couldn't let that cloud my vision. I needed to figure it out. "What happens if I don't have the money to pay?"

"Unfortunately, we can't release the dog without a partial payment."

"You just keep dogs here indefinitely until their owners can afford to bail them out?"

"I wish we could, but we can only keep them for so long before we have to turn them over to the state."

"To the state?" I asked, much too loudly. Everyone in the playroom looked over at us, then awkwardly went back to their own dogs.

Gary looked around, then quietly proceeded. "Well, typically, we send out messages to the various rescue groups we work with first, but if no one can collect her, she'd more than likely end up at the SPCA. Considering her breed and special needs, it could be hard to get her out to a rescue, though."

I looked down at Hippo, her jowly smile and her tongue out to the side, her distant stare, and I couldn't imagine her going back to a shelter. *She's going blind*, I thought. She'd already had to endure the shelter after some monster kicked her to the street. Abandoned her. There was no way she'd make it more than a few weeks in a shelter before they put her down. She had too many things going against her.

But she never judged me, with my weird habits and my eccentricities. She never complained that I cried too much or that I wasted my time poking around my phone when I could be doing crunches or looking for a new job. She never gave up on me when everyone else did.

I swallowed down the anxiety and pulled my identification from my phone case wallet. "Could I give that credit application a shot?"

The nurse returned to take Hippo back to her crate, and I walked beside her. She scooped Hip back into her crate and closed the grated door behind her after dosing her with her nightly pain meds and antibiotics. The intravenous medications hit her system quickly, and her eyelids grew heavier by the second, her breaths deeper. The drugs may have been expensive, but I would do and pay anything to make her happy. To keep her healthy.

"I'll be back for you, baby. I promise," I whispered to her.

Liza swung the car around the half-circle main entrance to the hospital and collected me and Mochi. From the back seat, she grabbed a box of donuts and a half dozen of chocolate glazed and offered them in exchange for my heartbreak. "I can't eat right now," I told her, but thanked her anyway.

"It's okay," she replied with a sympathetic sigh, "we can always have them for dessert."

By the time I asked Liza to pick me up, I'd already sent her dozens of texts about the total cost, how the stupid agency wouldn't lend me a cent, and how I had to cough up every dollar I had left in my bank account to secure Hippo's fate, so

I think she knew it was best to avoid any mention of it in the car. I needed to disassociate from it all.

The sun completely set while Hippo and I were tucked away from any windows, and the sky draped loose like a sheet of purple velvet. "Looks like it might snow again," Liza said, peering out from above her steering wheel to the sky directly above. "I'm already tired of the stuff."

I thought for a second of exaggerating, saying that I'd be happy if I never saw the stuff again after skidding into a guard rail, but I thought better of it. There was no point in holding a grudge against the weather, especially when it wasn't the snow's fault I crashed. Besides, I sort of thought the snow was pretty if the scenery it laid itself on was pretty enough. So, I simply agreed and asked how her day went.

"Busy, but good. I completely overhauled the rescue's website. It's so much easier to navigate than the old one. Now it just needs some updated photos, and it's done."

"Oh," I said, my voice an octave higher than normal with excitement, "that's fantastic—I'll sort through the photos and give you what I got." I sighed, running my hand down Mochi's back. "Ms. Rowe is going to be so relieved. That site was a mess."

"You're telling me. I had to scrap the entire thing and start from scratch. Whoever played with the code before me jacked everything up. I'm pretty sure they had no idea what they were doing."

"I think that was Ms. Rowe. She probably thought she'd whip something up and got way in over her head." I chuckled. She was a sweet old lady, but she certainly had no real grasp of technology. "She gave me access to her social accounts today, and it was—how can I say this nicely—*horrible*."

We both laughed a genuine laugh and drove up the interstate, quieting to a painful silence as we passed the dented guardrail that I'd smashed days before. Slowly, our conversation picked up again, and we were giggling and joking by the time we made it home for dinner. We had spring rolls and dumpling soup that Kara scored from the corner Chinese restaurant across the street from Franklin Family, with sesame mochi balls for dessert.

The donuts would be kept until the morning. I'd need something scrumptious to mindlessly nosh on while combing through all my pictures.

thirty-two

. . .

My work consumed me as thoroughly as I consumed the morning and leftover donuts. I'd been so absorbed by deleting, zooming in on, and touching up photos that I had let lunchtime pass me by. Better that way, probably. I must've eaten my entire day's worth of recommended calories in donuts, not that it mattered. Victor may have had his concerns over my weight, but I had already dropped nearly two hundred pounds when the police took him away in cuffs. A little extra chocolate glaze wasn't going to hurt.

By two o'clock, the afternoon sun had started peeking through the living room window where I'd set up my makeshift office (a battered rolling chair I pulled from the crawlspace and a patchwork pillow I stole from the couch), causing me to stir in my seat. If I hunched the wrong way, the sun shot waves directly through my corneas; if I sat straight enough, my lumpy pillow desk would be too short for me to see the computer screen. The warm glow of the sun made me sleepy.

I yawned a big yawn and stretched a bigger stretch but was interrupted by my cell phone ringing.

The Philadelphia number looked vaguely familiar, though it hadn't been saved in my phone. Scammers using fake local numbers to con me into answering the phone and trying to grift me out of my social security number made me hesitant. Plus, since I'd been hounded by bill collectors for years upon years, I'd never gotten over that fear of answering and getting bullied for being poor. *At least I know who it isn't*, I thought and picked a leftover piece of pastry from my teeth, smirking. The court already told me a judge had awarded me an emergency restraining order after the accident. His family couldn't make the ten-thousand-dollar bond for his hundred-thousand-dollar bail, but a lawyer I consulted said he'd likely only get a couple years in prison in the end. It didn't seem like enough, but at least I'd have enough time to relocate without him knowing how to find me.

I answered the phone. Lucky I did, too. Gary from the animal hospital greeted me and told me that Hippo had been doing great in her therapy sessions. "She's ready to go home now," he said, sounding much happier to speak with me now that I'd given him the last dime to my name.

I closed my laptop and threw the pillow back toward the couch, missing it, but only by a foot. "Great," I said back. "I'll be there in a half hour."

Liza said she'd worked herself into a spot where she could take a break anyway and drove me down to the vet to collect my eldest daughter, agreeing to hold Mochi while I went in. Sure enough, with the constant congestion along the interstate (caused by an accident I had no part of that time), we made the trip a half hour longer than I had projected. The closer we got, the more I fidgeted. My knee bobbed like a jackhammer, and I'd picked the cuticles of every nail on every finger. I'd combed my fingers through every inch of my scalp twelve times over by the time we reached the parking circle.

I gave Mochi a kiss on the forehead and handed her off to Liza, who commenced snuggling the ripples of skin surrounding her neck and covering her puppy body with tender kisses. The unbearable days without Hippo seemed impossibly long, but, at the same time, a single week with Mochi was speeding past too soon. *God*, I thought, *I'm going to miss that baby dog.*

Down the halls and through the doors, the same path I traveled every day since she'd been held there, I navigated my way down to Hippo. The faces I'd seen and waved to hadn't changed, but the billboard advertising the Rowehome Rescue event morphed into a blank slate of cork, save for a few pieces of loose-leaf paper push-pinned to seemingly random points. To me, that place represented a pivotal time in my life when I almost lost my best friend. To everyone else, it was work as usual. Now, the bleach-scented wings ushered the next chapter of my life, of Hippo's life. Of all our lives.

I checked in with the receptionist, sat in the waiting room, and waited to be called back to see Hippo when a nurse opened the double doors behind the reception desk. Beside her, on a flea-and-heartworm-preventative-printed leash, Hippo flashed a meaty smile and sniffed at the air above her cone. She must've caught my scent, because she stopped in mid-prance, let out a hefty *boof*, and garbled *awoo* to the nurse by her side. "Is that your mommy, girl?" she asked, and Hippo responded with tippy-tappy paws. The clicking of her claw nubs against the tiled floors sounded sweeter than any song I'd ever known.

"Hey, baby," I called to her, causing her to buck back and dart toward me with all her force. Hippo might have had only three working legs, but she still had the strength of a bull elephant. The nurse, who'd not had any trouble with my calm dog on her leash, hoisted to her toes and narrowly caught her balance by flailing her arms at her sides. "Sorry," I bashfully said to the nurse. "I didn't think she would've regained that kind of strength yet."

She handed me the leash, which I slipped my right wrist through, and I rubbed the length of Hip's cheek. "My brave little girl." She leaned in for the pet, and I lowered my whole body to her level, reached my face as deep into her cone as I could fit, and whispered, "I'm so proud of you, girl." From my position on the floor, the technician handed me a white bag of antibiotics and pain medications, and then (after memorizing the extensive aftercare instructions to the best of my ability), I steadied back to my feet, and the two of us trotted our way back to the car. As Liza and Mochi saw us, they looked like they'd been parading around the entryway, inspecting the potted plants and flower boxes for clues of other dogs.

Mochi and Hippo locked eyes. Hippo sniffed the air and moved her mouth as if to whisper a bark. Mochi vibrated as if she was trying so hard to stay rigid and tough, but her wee puppy nerves couldn't help but buzz. Then, in a swift sweep, the two simultaneously hunched their forelegs down flat to the ground, their waggly tushies high in the air. In dog body language, they had signaled to one another that it was time: playtime.

"No no no," I told Hippo like she'd understand what I was saying. "You still have stitches!" The nurse had scheduled her for a follow-up in a week to see if they could be removed, but until then, she needed to be as calm as possible lest she hurt herself again.

In the car, Mochi rode shotgun to Liza, and I stayed in the back with Hippo to keep them separate and relaxed. Despite the backed-up southbound traffic, the northbound lanes leading back home were flowing like water. We managed to make it home in time for Liza to pick Kara up from work and for me to get the dogs acclimated to each other as much as an ailing pooch and feisty puppy could. Satisfied with the level of harmony in the apartment, I flipped my laptop open and edited some more photos for a few moments.

Work, however, pulled me by my arm and dragged me into a state of flow I had no idea I was capable of. Before I knew it, my eyes were painfully dry from lack of blinking. Kara was ushering a vegan meat-lover's pizza through the door. Behind her, Liza brought in a family-sized tub of peanut butter with a tinsel bow affixed to its lid. "I got it as a 'welcome home' gift to Hippo, but I'm sure both dogs would enjoy it."

"Crap!" I yelled. "The dogs!"

I looked at the clock on the bottom corner of my laptop screen, carried the one, and realized I'd been working—and ignoring the dogs—for well over an hour. Jumping up, I darted left and right, looking for them; not in the living room, the hall, or the kitchen. The beating drums of blood rushing to my ears hastened, but just as they began to ring, and my panic fully consumed me, I opened the door to my room. The dogs. They were both on the bed and, to my surprise and relief, they were getting along. Loving each other. Hippo was spooning Mochi at the foot of my mattress, even licking her younger companion's un-docked ears.

"Oh-my-goodness," I panted. The last thing I needed was for Hippo to get admitted again for loosening a screw. The second-to-last thing I needed was to tell the nurse that I didn't listen to her one instruction and *let* Hippo loosen a screw because I allowed her to play too hard. With an active puppy, no less. But it was as if Mochi knew that Hippo needed quiet time to heal, and Hippo knew Mochi needed motherly love. It may have been years since she lost her litter, but my girl never lost her maternal instincts. With my heart full and a bit broken, I drew a deep sigh and asked, "You two want some dinner?" They cocked their heads in unison, both hopping to their feet when I playfully whispered the word, "Dinnertime."

We stuffed our bellies with pizza and fed the dogs their kibble, and then all took an evening walk together around the neighborhood. The dogs walked side by side, stopping to sniff sniffs together. Mochi attentively waited for Hippo to catch up when she started falling behind. At home, Mochi trotted back and forth between Hippo and the wicker basket of dog toys beside the kitchen entryway, making difficult doggy decisions about which toy to pluck out and subsequently place down before Hippo's forefeet to play with. When she found a winner—the orange nylon bone that met Hippo's mood—she then picked out a crinkly blue dragon stuffy for herself and proceeded to gnaw along the spikes of its back and tail.

"They're so good together," Kara said with a whine. "Do we really have to send her back to the rescue?"

"No! Wait, why?" Liza asked, devastated.

"I only agreed to foster her for a week or so while Hippo was hospitalized," I said, sullen. "I have to call Ms. Rowe tomorrow to arrange to give her back."

We all collectively sighed.

"Do you know if she has any prospective adoptive parents yet?" Liza asked, and I could see the cogs moving in her head.

"I don't know for sure. I'll ask Ms. Rowe about it." Part of me selfishly hoped Ms. Rowe would tell me Mochi was still homeless, but then I felt guilty for thinking that.

After that, we all watched the dogs chew their toys in silence, savoring that time we had together while we could.

I thought about sleeping in; I was just too comfortable. Not just in bed, but in life. The dogs, my friends, taking photos. I tried to text to Ms. Rowe before I went to sleep, telling her that I thought about it and wanted to adopt Mochi, but it kept bouncing back as unable to send. A deep anxiety clouded over me. Maybe I waited too long; maybe someone from the event decided to come around and adopt Mochi after sleeping on it, too. The last thing I wanted to do was confirm any of that, so I tried to stay in bed as long as possible and breathe in the moment. But, after putting off my call to Ms. Rowe as long as I could, the dogs hovered over me, whining and sighing, telling me it was time for their morning walkies.

We trotted around the block once for sniffs, twice for Hippo's morning physical therapy regimen, and thrice to burn off a bit of excess puppy energy for Mochi, and returned home, where I tossed my pillow desk to the side and plopped onto the couch, dreading the call. I checked all my emails (surprise, surprise, I had none), made some posts for the rescue's Creatr account, and then opened and closed all of my social media apps to kill time. It wasn't until my last one, my personal Creatr, that I found two new messages waiting for me.

The first was a slurry of messages from some girl I didn't know who claimed to be Victor's girlfriend; wonderful.

> The news said he was cheating on me with you.

She sent along a link to an article. "Local Dream Home winner run off the road by boyfriend." *The* gall *of that journalist writing about me without first contacting me*, I thought. And the gall of that lady. He'd been cheating on *her* with *me*? Whatever. I almost clicked off and deleted the messages, but I decided to continue reading anyway. After insinuating that that was all my fault, Victor's "girlfriend" confirmed what my lawyer said about his bail and possible fine of up to twenty-five grand.

"Good riddance," I typed, then deleted. Being the bigger person would feel rewarding in retrospect, but it certainly wasn't the fun thing to do in the heat of the moment. I thanked her for the update, then hid notifications from her. Message chain deleted.

The second new message awaiting me, also from a woman I didn't know, asked me about my pictures of Hippo and some of the other dogs I'd photographed at the rescue.

> I really liked your photos, and I was wondering if you're available for a photo shoot of my dogs.

> Yes!

I hastily messaged her back. My fingers couldn't keep up with my excitement, and I had to read through my words again to clean up the typos.

> I would love to take some portraits of your dogs.

After conducting a quick search online of, "how much do pet photographers charge" and fanning through a dozen or so results, I sent her the ballpark price range for my portrait services that I just made up. While I was still riding high from the uptick of good news, I closed down the app to call Ms. Rowe.

She answered the phone with her usual sing-songy tone and said she had great news for me. I braced for the worst, thinking she'd tell me that she'd found a home for Mochi and that I'd need to bring her to her new home immediately, but she instead told me about a call from a former client of hers.

"She said she liked the pictures you've been posting online and wondered if you'd want to take some pictures of her dog, Bean. I told her I'd ask you when I talk to you next."

I let out all the breath my lungs held tight and relaxed my shoulders.

"That's the second request I've received today," I told her, "but yeah, I'd love to."

"Great! I'll give her your info and get you two in contact."

"Awesome, thanks," I said and paused. "But I kinda have a question for you, too."

"Is it about that little baby you've been taking care of?"

"It is, actually." I gulped and hesitated, then danced around the subject of giving her back. "Has she had any interest yet? For her adoption, I mean."

"Actually, yes. We just had an application come over for her this morning."

Ms. Rowe's voice sounded further away from the phone as if she were looking at the screen instead of resting her ear on the earpiece.

Then she said, "Ah, here it is."

A wave of pain crashed over me. On the couch to my left, Hippo slept and snored, and in my lap, Mochi had curled into a ball and twitched her tiny feet back and forth in a dream. I thought back to how devastated Liza looked when she realized Mochi could be taken away at any moment and felt a boulder press onto my chest.

"Do—do you—when do I need to bring her back?" I tried to catch my breath and slow the words from leaving my lips, but I couldn't. "Will we be able to see her again? I don't think I can bring her back in before we all have a chance to say goodbye to her."

My heart pounded in synch with my head.

Ms. Rowe drew a long, "Uhhhhhh…," and paused. "Let me get back to you on all that. I think I should make a few calls before I can answer all that."

Over the passing hours, I worried Kara and Liza would be as devastated as me once they got home and realized Mochi found a new home. I almost couldn't bear telling them the truth.

"Guys," I sniffed and rubbed my eyes. "I got some news about Mochi."

Liza saw my heartbreak, sunk into the sofa beside me, and whispered, "No."

Kara's eyes darted between the two of us, and they sighed. "I didn't want to say anything until I got home," Kara said, "but

I emailed Ms. Rowe first thing this morning, and she said Mochi didn't have any applications in yet, so I sent one for her."

"Stop—" Liza stood. "Kara, did you—"

Kara smiled and scooped Mochi off the floor. "I certainly did."

I jumped from the couch and ran to hug Kara. "I hate you so much!" I yelled and cried happy tears into her shoulder. We took turns passing Mochi back and forth, petting and doting and sneaking in baby puppy kisses. No wonder Ms. Rowe sounded confused over the phone.

By evening's end, Kara received all of Mochi's health records and set her up an appointment for the same time and place as Hippo's one-week checkup. To celebrate, I baked a cake from a box mix that I picked up from the grocery store around the corner and made a peanut butter frosting that I let the dogs lick from a spoon. In the dark kitchen, around a small table with its three place settings, Kara lit a rogue birthday candle she'd found rolling around the junk drawer. We sang "Happy Gotcha Day" to Mochi to the tune of "Happy Birthday" and held her up to the cake while I blew out the single candle. We then lit the candle again and sang the same tune, but changed the words to "Welcome Home Day" to Hippo, even though she'd been back for over twenty-four hours by then. It didn't matter—it was the best birthday party I'd ever celebrated, even if it wasn't mine, or even a party for a birthday for that matter.

Kara scooped up Hippo and danced with her around the kitchenette while Liza grabbed hold of Mochi, sat on a wobbly wood kitchen chair, and tickled her bald, chubby belly. Although the apartment was all of five hundred square feet, and none of us could move without bumping into someone or tripping over a dog, I couldn't think of a place I'd rather be. Those walls held so much life and warmth between them. I danced with Kara and forked a piece of cake to feed to Hippo when a chime on my phone ripped me out of the moment. A new email.

I put the fork on the table and opened my inbox, only to find the last person's name on my mind across the screen.

Diana Attenbury.

thirty-three

. . .

"Oh, God," I muttered to myself.

Kara, who hadn't stopped cradling a wide-mouthed, floppy-tongued Hippo and bopping her around the small space between the living room TV and the opening to the kitchen since cutting the cake, paused and snapped her head around toward me. "What—what's wrong?"

"HHTV just emailed me," I said, pivoting the phone toward her to see the screen. "They want to schedule a call to discuss my decision."

I could almost hear the recorded scratch sound effect and all the joy suctioning out of the apartment. Kara slowly knelt to put Hip onto the floor, and Liza brought Mochi closer to her face for a squeeze. No one dared to say a word for an excruciatingly-long thirty seconds. When the quiet couldn't get any louder, Liza, with a pained whimper of a voice, said, "We're gonna miss youse guys."

I inhaled deeply, and my breath sputtered in my lungs like an old engine. "I won't be leaving yet—who knows how much time I'll have here until I can claim the house? Maybe I'll get to hang around for a few more months."

"It won't be long enough," Kara cut in. "Sorry. I didn't mean it to sound that way. I'm just going to miss all this," she said, motioning toward the cake, the dogs, and the kitchen. Her voice fractured. "I'm going to miss you."

I dropped my phone to the table beside me, stood to hug Kara, and swiveled to hug Liza, too. "I know. I don't know what I'll do without you guys."

"We'll always be there for you, Bree," Kara said, squeezing me back. "Even if we are almost three thousand miles away."

"Just say the word, and we'll be at your door," Liza cried into my shoulder. "I mean it, we'll book the next flight and everything."

"I know you would," I told her, my tears soaking her hair. "I know you would."

After a full night of tossing and turning with maybe fifteen minutes of sleep, I got out of bed and saw Kara off to work. Both dogs had their morning stroll, complete with several breaks to stop and sniff the occasional shrub, and I flopped down on the couch to rest a moment. Although I'd felt better than I had in weeks, I did still have my concussion to nurse.

Sitting criss-cross applesauce on the center cushion, and with Hippo and Mochi resting their heads on my thighs from both directions, I opened the web browser on my phone. I clicked on the official Dream Home website, scrolling through the curated photos of the house from its best angles—the foyer, the dining room, the backyard—and imagined myself there. My new life. When I hit the end of the pictures, I opened the cache of images in my phone from when I'd gone for the reveal and relived the surprise and excitement of seeing it all in real life and the happiness I could have sworn I felt with Victor. I kept flipping, photo after photo, until the home pictures ended, and the pictures I'd taken from Kara's engagement replaced them. Buried in that series of pictures, I found a selfie I'd forgotten about: one of the three of us, all with smiles on our tear-streaked faces, and I remembered a time when I was truly happy.

The screen went black when my phone thought I'd looked at it long enough. I thought about unlocking my screen to view it again but thought better of it. Better to get that email done as soon as possible.

In the kitchenette, in the very seat I sat in the evening before when I got her message, I pulled up my email and replied to Mrs. Attenbury, confirming her appointment time. And, since I still needed to come up with the extra cash for travel expenses and food along the way, I sifted through all of my emails and messages, some old and some brand new from the morning, and set up locations, dates, and times to photograph a handful of dogs. Turkey at Independence Hall, Phil at Pennypack Park, and Tofu at the Riverfront. But first, Bean at the botanical garden.

The bright white blanket of snow covering the grounds of the garden twinkled in the sunlight. Aside from the shoveled pathways and the footprints of some small woodland creatures and birds, the snow remained largely untouched. An overnight dusting sprinkled a soft coat of fine powder on the surface of the evergreen shrubs and trees and made for the perfect wintertime photo shoot. I snapped a few landscape shots and sighed when thoughts of my trip to the garden in Washington flooded my memory.

Bean, a possible Rottweiler-Lab mix wearing a green and red plaid bandana, and his human with a matching plaid scarf and knit burgundy pom-pom hat, Maggie, met me at the entrance of the botanical garden after I had my chance to walk the park and scope out the best backdrops for our session together. For two hours, the duo stood, knelt, posed, and played in the snow while I snapped picture after picture after picture. In between takes, we paused to review some of the photos I'd gathered along the way, and before we knew it, our time together had come to an end.

"I'll get these proofs to you by the end of the month," I said, packing my gear and zipping my duffle. Truthfully, I had no idea how long other photographers took to get proofs back to people, and my two-week margin made me worry—was two weeks too long? How long was too long? "But I'll try to get them over to you within the week," I said, trying to cover my tail. "Is that okay?"

"Oh my gosh! I wasn't expecting them until at least Valentine's Day. By the end of the month would be fabulous." She leashed Bean and bent down to scruff the fur on the side of his face. He, in turn, panted a cloud of icy breath and let his tongue flop to the side. "Do you have any cards? I'd love to let some of my friends know about you."

Cards! Crap! I knew there was something I forgot to get. Probably better off, though, I reasoned. I would have had to change the address soon, anyway. "I don't have any cards made up yet, but you can have them reach out to me on my site," I said, scribbling my brand-new, Liza-curated website and my social handles onto a scrap of paper from the bottom of my bag. "Or they can hit me up on Creatr."

After getting Bean's mom's blessing, I posted a picture of the two of them that I took from my phone to check into the location and hopped onto a series of buses and trains back to my two pups. There, I found two pups, two best friends, and messages from two more potential clients awaiting me.

By the end of the week, before I had the time to send out Bean's proofs to his fur-mom, I'd raked in a couple grand in private photography sessions. Liza showed me how to do some basic content design, and together we created a batch of graphics to schedule out over the next few weeks on the Rowehome accounts, granting me the precious time to send out all the best shots to my customers. More emails and messages started coming in, and I scheduled dates for more dogs in between adjusting lights and contrast.

I sat on the sofa with a dog snoozing on each side of my lap and drew a deep breath. Less than a week ago, I couldn't have dreamt of being that happy, that content. Those dogs didn't know my name. They didn't know my age or my height. They didn't know that my favorite food was the soft pretzel with rutabaga fondue from that five-star vegan restaurant in the center of the city or that my favorite color was blue. They knew virtually nothing about me, but they still knew me better than anyone else on the planet. They probably knew me better than I knew myself.

And as I sat on the couch with two of my best friends in the whole world, I could breathe with all of my lungs.

My call with HHTV was set for the afternoon, and because I couldn't risk missing it, I canceled all of my plans up until that time. That gave me ample time to edit, email, and close out client accounts, but I grossly misjudged how long I needed to catch up on all my work. I finished in a few short hours, granting me time to recharge and enjoy precious time with both the dogs. My concussion fog still came and went, but waves came in with less intensity and frequency than they had the week prior, and, overall, I'd felt better mentally than I had in years.

But the slow morning of cuddling the pups sped faster than the work hours. Before I could get both dogs out for a midday walk, my phone rang. The number wasn't any my phone recognized, but I already knew who'd answer from the other end of the line.

thirty-four

. . .

I entered the house, smelling fresh paint. Buttercup walls, wood panel laminate flooring. The place was a dump when we found it, but that made the price right.

It was Ms. Rowe who spotted the house first. She'd seen a real estate agent using a mallet to drive the "For Sale" sign into the patch of lawn between the covered wooden deck and the sidewalk while walking the new Shepherd mix I'd finished photographing moments before.

Liza turned the car around, granting us access to a private walkthrough before the weekend's open house, and we found out the owner wanted to get both homes in the duplex (which they'd rented out for years with seemingly no upkeep) off their hands as soon as possible. And it couldn't have been a better time.

My prize check had arrived seven-to-ten business days after the seemingly endless string of forms and declarations I initialed and e-signed. I deposited my money on a Tuesday, and by that time, half had already been shaved off for taxes. Once it cleared on Wednesday, I systematically took an axe to all of the debts I could think of: all of the spending I'd thrown on credit cards, the bills I "forgot" to pay to the dozens of creditors who relentlessly called my phone (my phone had rung only twice—*twice*—since getting those leeches off my back), and, most satisfyingly, the student loans that hemorrhaged my credit score for the greater part of the last decade. The knots in my shoulders immediately unraveled, and I felt so much freer, even if I was tens of thousands of dollars lighter. Ten out of ten, would recommend. Next, I set aside a few grand for both Aiden and Jaiden for college savings accounts and made sure that Mom couldn't access them. I might not have been able to see them and tell them that I loved them as I wanted to, but I could prevent them from the years of repayment agony, which I hoped counted for something.

And then, just when I was ready to accept the fact that I'd never take Hippo on a journey around the States, the auto insurance company cut me a check for a new car. We'd just come back from our road trip down the East Coast when I got the call to photograph the Shepherd mix Ms. Rowe had rescued from a local shelter's euthanasia list.

Oh, and I helped Kara pay off her school debt, too. It felt only fair since we went to school together, and it felt cruel to let her get swallowed up whole by her loans. She only had a few thousand left, anyway, and it was the least I could do for all her help after the crash. She refused at first but later agreed to let me loan it to her to avoid the never-ending compounding interest on the thing, but I never asked for that money back. Never would. The last thing either of us needed was money coming between our friendship. But with such a debt lifted from her budget, homeownership suddenly became within closer reach.

"I think I want to do this," I whispered to Liza in what was probably once a dining room.

She looked around at the billowing cobwebs in the corners and peeling wallpaper across the foyer. Her lips twisted into a devious smirk. "Let's do it."

I lowballed my offer for the home to the bottom, and Liza, after FaceTiming Kara throughout the house, made hers for the home on the top. The place needed love, which we all had in abundance, and hard work, which would be a walk in the park compared to everything else we'd been through. By winter's end, we got our answers, and by spring's end, we had our keys.

Kara was hard at work painting her and Liza's bedroom upstairs, and Liza toiled in the kitchen, sanding cabinets and breaking a sweat. I made for the den on the first level—my new studio, to deposit my boxes of photography equipment, one by one, side-stepping and dancing around Hippo and Mochi, who found a length of rope to play tug-o-war over in the foyer.

A knock at the door aroused the two dogs, which I *hush-hush-hushed* and announced, "I got it!" to the air. I opened the door to a delivery woman and a package, signature required, and closed the door with my hip. "I think this is it!"

I took the box to a stack of taller boxes in the dining room and opened it with a screwdriver from Liza's workspace. She craned her neck out from around the kitchen island to catch a glimpse as I removed my prize from the cardboard: a SMEG Dolce&Gabbana mixer.

"Wow," Liza said and dusted her hands on her pants.

"I know," I said, holding it in the air to view it from all angles. "This thing is like a work of art."

"I think I have the perfect spot for it," Liza called and took the mixer from me, placing it on the faux-quartz countertop of the cabinets under the open-shelf dish display, already stocked with the boldly-colored ceramic bakeware I thrifted the day prior. "It matches perfectly."

Later that day, after we'd packed up our paints and our sanders and after we'd moved our final box into our new space, Hippo and Mochi sat on either side of me. Kara, Liza, and I shared our first meal together at our new house: white bean salad and minestrone served with a loaf of artisan bread.

"This all turned out amazing, Bree," Kara said with a hand over her lips, chewing a mouthful of bread.

"It really is good," agreed Liza, sopping up her soup with her bread.

"Right? And to think, everything here cost, like, four dollars." Praise be for the almost-expired food racks of the produce and bakery sections. "You know, I think I could get used to this."

"Same," said Liza.

"Cheers to that," said Kara, holding up her glass. We all clinked our waters together and toasted our new life together. It was all I'd ever wanted.

After dinner, Kara cleared the plates and washed them while Liza dried and placed them back to their new homes, and I took the dogs out to the backyard. The days got longer, the sun stayed out later, but as the sky pinked at dusk, the first fireflies of the season flashed Morse codes of neon green and lemon yellow in the air.

I pulled out my camera and snagged a shot of the dogs romping and fireflies glowing that would later land on the cover of *Philly Pets* and earn me a permanent position as their resident photographer. The calls for pet portraiture kept my schedule pretty full, but I'd still clear out a day of work whenever needed to shoot for Rowehome and all its adoptables.

Hippo played as if she'd never had surgery, and I thought Mochi must have played some sort of role in that. I was sure of it. With a younger dog running around her, she had to keep on her toes, but that wasn't to say Mochi had been a pest. Not at all. In fact, she'd been quite caring and sweet to Hippo. As if she knew she couldn't see. She always dropped toys and bones onto Hippo's front paws so she didn't have to root far to find them, and she always waited for her big sister to walk to her before leaving a room. She was such a sweet baby.

Mochi had settled in quite well. When she sensed that Hippo needed a break, she'd run up to me and paw my arm, signaling that it was my job to keep her occupied. We'd tug at toys and walk down to the donut shop, where the cashiers and cooks all knew her by name, or down to Loco Pez for some seitan tacos, or sometimes we'd just walk down to Ms. Rowe's house, where we would get to play with other pups and Mochi's grandma would spoil her with treaties and dog biscuits.

In the backyard, though, Mochi and Hippo always zoomed together. While the dogs formed a mosh pit around the yard's perimeters, Kara peeked her head out the back door and shouted to me, "Hey, a package just arrived for you!" *Odd*, I thought. We'd just moved in, and I hadn't yet ordered anything except the mixer. I sat in the grass and ripped up the brown paper tape from the seam of the cardboard box. I found a small gift receipt from the shipper.

Happy homecoming!
XOXO, Rowehome Rescue

"Aw, it's from Ms. Rowe," I said to Kara and ripped the package open. A plastic-wrapped tube hid beneath crumpled-up brown paper, and after unwrapping and unfurling it, I saw we'd been gifted a welcome mat for the house.

HOME IS WHERE THE DOG IS.

I read the words aloud. A trail of rainbow paw prints lined the top left and bottom right corners. "I love it."

"It'll look great on the porch," Kara said and helped me up from the ground.

Out front, I plopped the mat to the wooden floor of the porch and adjusted it with my foot to align it properly with the door. With my hands, I adjusted my purple toile wreath, fluffing up the ribbon that held the colorful little bones and paw prints in place. "It's perfect."

That wreath, that mat, that life. Everything. For the first time ever, I was home.

acknowledgments

Whoo, boy. Where do I even begin?

I guess first and foremost, with everyone who helped me logistically? Massive thank you to Emylie Zollo and the Green Crow team for seeing the potential of this book and helping it become a reality. Equally, an incredibly huge thank you to Tina Ann Forker for her developmental edits, clarifications, and moral support the entire way—this book simply would not exist without you. Thank you to Adrienne Kisner for her editing expertise. And, perhaps most importantly, thank you to Tofu; you are the best writing assistant in the entire world.

They say it takes a village to raise a child, and while I know that writing a novel is obviously not a child (it is objectively more difficult than rearing children), I could not have birthed my book baby without the help of everyone from the Drexel Creative Writing program circa 2023. Nomi Eve and Ann Garvin, for all of your guidance, support, and inspiration; Andy Snover for helping me get through some ugly first drafts; Nikki Stinson, Julia Warner, Nicholette Guy, Rylee Cella, Ashley Bhasin, Aekta Bhatt, Kyra Cruz, Regina Guarino, Adam Zahn and so many others who helped along the way.

Thank yous are due to Kelly Rowe and Lindsey Warren for all the group chats and memes that kept me going through the writing and publishing journey—you two have been some of my biggest cheerleaders, and I want you to know that I am yours. Same for my siblings, Shawn Hill, Josh Hill, Erin

Wildman, and Kevin O'Connor… though he should probably be toward the bottom of this list. Thank you to everyone else that I forgot to mention by name (that's on me and I'm sorry about that) who have helped me along this writing journey, no matter how small the contribution. Ditto for that guy who runs the falafel cart behind Penn Presbyterian for making the best falafel I've ever had in my life.

Oh! And thank you to my husband, George Petner, for washing the dishes so I could finish writing out scenes, and to my sons Killian O'Connor and Joey Reagan for generally tolerating me as a mother.

Last but certainly not least, a thank you to Phil, for being the inspiration behind Hippo; you may have had a head made of solid concrete and weighed as much as a refrigerator, but you were the cuddliest little baby in the entire world, and I love you. You were a good girl.

Keli O'Connor

REHOMING BREANNA HUXLEY

Published by Green Crow Publishing, LLC
www.greencrowpublishing.com

ISBN: 978-1-967309-03-0 (ebook)
ISBN: 978-1-967309-04-7 (paperback)

First Edition: September 9, 2025

0 9 8 7 6 5 4 3 2 1